# BUTTERFLY LOVERS

# BUTTERFLY LOVERS

## CHARLES FORAN

HarperCollins*Publishers*Ltd

http://www.harpercollins.com

First edition

Canadian Cataloguing in Publication Data

Foran, Charles, 1960-
Butterfly lovers

ISBN 0-00-224390-3

I. Title.

PS8561.O635B8  1996     C813'.54     C96-930717-9
PR9199.3.F67B8  1996

96 97 98 99 ❖ HC 10 9 8 7 6 5 4 3 2 1

Printed and bound in the United States

Stories have no point if they don't absorb our terror.
—Don DeLillo


Suppose there was an iron room with no windows or
doors, a room it would be virtually impossible to
break out of. And suppose you had some people inside
that room who were sound asleep. Before long they would
all suffocate. In other words, they would slip peacefully
from a deep slumber into oblivion, spared the anguish
of being conscious of their impending doom. Now let's
say that *you* came along and stirred up a big racket that
awakened some of the lighter sleepers. In that case,
they would go to a certain death fully conscious of
what was going to happen to them. Would you say that
you had done those people a favour?
—Lu Xun

for Liu Junhui, "Julius"

IF ASKED BY MY DAUGHTER FOR THE STORY OF HER MOTHER and me, this is what I'll tell her:

Once upon a time there was a man who was doing okay. His name was David. He was married to a woman called Carole, and they lived with her dog Potemkin in a large room that had a high ceiling and tall windows affording views of a neighbour-hood in a city, a city on an island. They were happy together. David had his work, which he believed in, and his wife, who he believed in more. Carole had her work, which she, too, believed in, and her husband, who she trusted was a decent guy. Potemkin was there as well: yapping and drooling and peeing on the carpet. It was a family. In a room. Doing okay.

One day there was a knock on the door. David and Carole had never had visitors before; their happy life had never been disrupted. He answered the summons. Who is it? he called. A messenger, replied a voice. What is your message? he asked. I am here to tell you and your wife that you're prisoners in this room. Prisoners? replied a startled David. Have you ever tried to open the door? wondered the voice. He confessed that he hadn't. The messenger suggested he turn the knob. Behind him, Carole said, It's a trick! Behind him, the dog barked.

He tried the door. The knob stuck. See? called the voice. Suddenly, David felt sad. Suddenly, he needed out. Out to what? Carole asked him. He wasn't sure. She said he had a problem about certainty. That he was the kind of man who would be forever indecisive, for lack of confidence, and eternally timid, for lack of self-esteem. She said that people like him were better off not opening doors. They were better off believing what they believed and living where they lived.

Though her words were probably true, they still made him angry. He wanted not to think of himself as she did. He wanted not to believe his personality was so narrow and closed. Of course, the locked door made these thoughts pointless. But then the messenger spoke up. I can open it for you, it said. You can leave. Right now? asked David. Right now, the voice confirmed. In fact, try again. David stared at the door. Knowing that his courage would soon fail, he reached for it. Carole's words froze his hand in mid-air. Have you thought this through? she asked. What's to think about? he replied. Your problem, she said. My problem will be my problem, he answered. And me and Potemkin, she added. What will we be? The dog could yap, drool and pee in the room until doomsday for all David cared. But Carole was his companion. She was his only love. Let's do this together, he said. It'll be easier that way.

The voice gave them some advice. Before you turn the knob, it said, take a look at each other. A hard look. An honest look. David and Carole listened to the counsel, but shrugged it off. After all, they'd been together for years. They knew each other's face as well as their own mirror image. The voice, they figured, simply couldn't understand such intimacy.

David opened the door. They stepped through.

And had a baby. A beautiful baby girl. Her hair was wheaten. Her skin was honey. And her name? Her name was candy in her parents' mouths. Her name, Natalie, was you.

"You finished yet?" Ivan asks me one afternoon in Remys.

"My coffee?"

He nods.

"Almost," I answer. "Why, are we in a hurry?"

"Hardly."

"Some place to be?"

"God forbid."

I swallow the dregs anyway, to satisfy him.

"You're just dying to get out of here, aren't you?" he accuses. "Let me rephrase that. I'm dying. You're just getting out of here."

"A nod is as good as a wink to a blind horse," I say.

"The life of an old fag is the cock of it."

"Hat, Ivan," I correct.

"Fag, David."

"Whew," I say, lighting a cigarette. "Aren't we murderous today."

"Aren't we fucking off to China for a year in three weeks. Aren't we torching the family home, not bothering to file an insurance claim, and walking away with only watering eyes and a cough. Forgetting there is someone else still in there."

"Who?" I ask, one of these dreadful, sleep-eclipsing parental images flashing through my mind.

"Me!"

"Oh."

"You're relieved?"

"Kind of. I mean, of course not," I say.

"My lungs will fill up soon enough," adds Ivan, sparring with the smoke from my cigarette. "Must you collapse one beforehand?"

The cigarette is snubbed out. With impatience, I admit: he is putting me through the ringer. "This used to be the liveliest café in Mile End," I complain. "Everyone smoked and drank. *You* smoked and drank. There was—"

"Don't change the subject."

"Which is . . . ?" I ask wearily.

"Such dreary company, I know. Twenty-one short days, and you can put all this in the past. Forget it even happened."

"I'm looking at you," I say.

"The fuck you are."

"Trying, then."

"You're going away."

"Right now," I clarify. "I'm looking at you right now."

"Are you almost finished?"

"Hardly."

Ivan has a theory about people. He believes that we end up strangers because we don't really look at each other. That we make what is familiar—i.e., the faces of those we know best—foreign; that we treat a natural bond of shared features like a threat to our own selfhood; that we flee from the only other creatures in the universe that could possibly find attractive, and legible, our twisted, strained expressions. The problem isn't in nature. Nor is it the mystery of the human psyche. Our darkest secrets are highway billboards. Our stickiest impulses are prime-time TV. The problem, claims Ivan, are lousy survival instincts. We think we need a stronger lock on the door, where in fact there is no call for security. We assume the walls should be reinforced, when we'd be better off knocking them down. As for reshingling the roof, don't bother. The ceiling will collapse nonetheless. It's going to crash down on all our heads.

He is definitely wary of ceilings these days. He is definitely waiting for one to come down on top of him. I understand. I would also maintain that I am looking at him: that we are not—and never could be—strangers. For fifteen years I've thought of Ivan Fodorov as my best friend. For fifteen years we've hung out together. We both like books. We both like coffee. We're even members of an exclusive club, though it is about to close its doors permanently. The Laurel and Hardy quality to our appearance is awkward, I grant, but can't be helped. Like me, Ivan is thirty-four; unlike me, he is tall and lanky, handsome in the brooding manner of male models. Fashion has always mattered to him. The black clothes and Oliver Twist gloves, the grey-rimmed glasses and earring in the left lobe. He is still a head turner down on Ste. Catherine East, still vain and affected. He is also becoming more and more his parents. Ivan has his mother's smile and his father's frown. Within him is both Titania Fodorov's innate generosity about human nature and Gregor's equally indelible stinginess. The bequeathment, in other words, is complex: no surprise, his personality is complicated, and interesting.

Not a bad observation, eh? Only it isn't one I'm even supposed to make. After all, Ivan and I are Groucho Marxists. The club—or better, our chapter of it, since although we are aware of no other members, we assume the society is global—has strict requirements in this regard. One must be either a fundamentally uninteresting person, which is tough, or else be someone who is simply no longer interested in anything, which is easy. What we are most inclined to be uninterested in, of course, is Marxism. That is fine. What many former Marxists end up becoming are pompous bores. That is not interesting, and therefore also fine. Suppose, though, that one is a Groucho Marxist who is merely confused, with no faith but plenty of longing, no answers but tons of questions? That is not fine. Worse, it is pretty interesting.

"So why am I going to China for a year?" I ask.

"You mean you don't know?"

"My own heart is a riddle to me," I say to please him, again.

"You're going there to make up for wasted time. To finally be obliged to shut up and put up. To escape your own grinding thoughts. To find new excuses to be desperate."

"So far, so good."

He admits a grin. "You're going to a place *that* big to prove to yourself that you aren't *this* small," continues Ivan, enclosing the room with a sweep of his long arms.

"Amen," I say.

No question, Remys is my home away from home. No question, either, it is a tiny, closed place. The café may lack an apostrophe in its name—a Quebec language quirk, like me—but it could never be accused of lacking personality. Whether or not that personality is large, never mind benign, is another matter. Two rooms are linked by a doorway and a serving window. In the room where Ivan and I sit in our customary alcove are tables and chairs, a bar; through the doorway awaits a pool table and video games, a fooz-ball machine that appears to levitate during matches. The floor is of tile, more or less necessary in Montreal, unless customers remove their boots at the door, the ceiling is of vintage tent plates, now cancerous from years of cigarette smoke, and the walls are whitewashed.

Remys is located in Mile End, the northwest edge of the city's Plateau region. The neighbourhood may be home to a ragout of Portuguese and Italian families, secular Jews and medieval Hasidim, renovation-mad francophone yuppies living upstairs from generational welfare clans, not to mention the growing incursions of Vietnamese and East Indians and an impressively extended Guatemalan brood a few doors from my place; all these people may live in Mile End, but few of them frequent the café. Remy Fidani's clientele is predominantly grant-happy student, dole-fed radical, Canada Council-crumbed artist. Smokers of Marlboros and Gauloises, consumers of café au laits and Bradors from the bottle, readers of *Le Devoir* and the weeklies, journals unavailable except in shops with names like "Dis-Ease" and books special-ordered from one of the university stores, never collected, and then stolen from the shelves once staff have given up trying to place the title in the proper hands. The Remys clientele includes lots of black-clothed men with goatee beards and ponytails—the latest fashion—who are disappointed with the era, and lots of frizzy-haired, unmade-up women who are disappointed with the men. It includes guys like Ivan, and faces I recognize from McGill and protests and meetings and, no doubt, from years of watching them watching me.

"One more reason," says Ivan. "You think you're going to China to do some good. To be of help to those people. You think that maybe, just maybe, you can make a— "

"Wrong," I interrupt.

"Oh?"

"I'm going only for myself. Because I need to. It has nothing to do with being good or helping anyone. It's not about that."

"Then you might not cause much harm after all," he says. "Though I wouldn't count on it."

I ask him to explain. But he just offers his weariest sigh, meant to speak volumes about our capacity for self-deception and, needless to say, inattentiveness. Normally, Ivan's smugness wouldn't bother me. He is a decent man, incarcerated—as I am—in a self-made prison of ironic detachment from virtually everyone and everything and an unironic need to be attached to those very same people and things. Aloofness and cynicism, a hysterical disdain for the achievements of others, are, I know well, the classic counter-attacks of the insecure. Today, though, I am looking for some backing. Not that I lack confidence about the year abroad. Quite the opposite: though I made the decision quickly, and my thinking flirted between reasoned arguments and unconscious urges to just get the hell out, I am more sure about this decision than any I've made in years. What I lack confidence at, I suspect, is *being* confident. I don't come by it naturally.

I ponder this. For a while, apparently, because Ivan, hypersensitive to my public silences—I will explain shortly—taps me on the arm.

"You okay?" he asks.

Leaning over, I scratch a keyhole in the window frost with my nails. Through the aperture I watch snow blow across the sidewalk. Humans cant headlong into the breeze, hands protecting their throats, only their eyes exposed. Exhaust fumes from cars are alchemized into vapour; mouths and noses expel plumes of smoke. The sky is cinerous. Flakes do not fall from the haze; they suddenly materialize in the light, occluding the air like a swarm of bees. Next I glance down at my watch, a mistake. It is three-thirty in the afternoon.

"It was dark out when I woke up this morning," says Ivan. "I thought of pretending I wasn't awake, and trying to sleep through till tomorrow."

"I thought of a story I studied in high school," I counter. "Want to hear it?"

"Do I have a choice?"

"You can go out there instead," I say, indicating the window.

"Please tell me your story, David."

I reach automatically for my cigarettes. "A husband and his wife live on a farm somewhere on the prairies. It's winter, and the man has to walk several miles to visit his father. The moon was twice-ringed the night before, forecasting bad weather, but he still goes. While he's gone, his wife paints their bedroom door. She is also visited by a handsome neighbour who she's secretly attracted to. Pretty soon there's a blizzard outside. The husband is trapped away from the house. The neighbour is trapped inside it. Eventually, the man and woman end up in bed together."

"Sex," he says. "What a relief."

"They figure it's safe. The husband wouldn't dare walk home in such weather. They can screw all night, and he'll never be the wiser. Besides, both of them are lonely: life is difficult, unsensual. . . ." I pause over that word, a curious choice. Itchy, I run my fingers down my forearm, the nails leaving skid marks on the skin. I also put a cigarette in my mouth, fire a match, and only then notice his truculent gaze. The match is extinguished. The cigarette, which I want— even need—to smoke, joins its companion in the ashtray. "During the night, the woman dreams that her husband comes into the room and stands over her, so close she can almost touch him. Waking up, she decides that the other guy, snoring away in the bed, is actually the lesser man. She regrets her infidelity, and vows to be a devoted wife from then on. But the next day they find her husband's corpse in the snow. What's strange is that the body is on the *far* side of the farm;

the guy walked right past his own house, probably blinded by the storm. Only the wife notices the paint on his hand."

"Ah."

"You get it?"

"I get it."

"He *had* come into the bedroom," I explain anyway, "found her with another man, and returned to the storm to die."

Ivan blows air from his cheeks. "Typical," he says. "A repressive fable for a repressed culture."

"Sorry?"

"The woman gives in to her passion. Result? Shame and everlasting guilt. The man is confronted with the false code of male honour. Result? He chooses to off himself, rather than challenge the convention."

"But the story is a tragedy."

"Pure farce."

"It's about fate."

"Try fools."

I betray my anger.

"Don't mind me," he adds disingenuously. "I always thought Othello was a macho shit. Homophobic, too, most likely."

He asks me to pay for his coffee and to leave Chantal, the sexy but unsmiling waitress, a tip. I oblige. Since being hired a month ago, Chantal has not tendered a customer or co-worker or Remy himself even the most tepid of smiles. Granted, her retro-punk apparel and facial trimmings—an ear lined with silver studs, eyes caked in mascara—are tailor-made for the sneer. But her face is otherwise perfectly designed for smiling. It is resolutely oval: horseshoe jaw and plum mouth, harvest-moon eyes beneath crescent-moon brows. Swarthy Mediterranean looks, possibly Italian. A rounding-to-full smile, revealing rows of pearly whites, would bedazzle, make her that much more attractive. I lust after her, naturally, as I lust after most of the café regulars. Should that sound totally pathetic, let me add that in 1987 I lured into bed Masha Cloutier, a Remys waitress of long-standing who relocated shortly afterwards to Quebec City, no reason given. November 1987, to be exact: twenty-five months ago. Hardly a boast. Hardly a memory, in fact; we were both potted; I only remember burning her toast at breakfast the next morning.

Still, Ivan and I have made a pact: we will get Chantal to smile before Christmas. That leaves just eight days, and puts extra pressure on my joke.

"How many anglophones does it take to make love?" I ask her in French.

"Your change," she answers.

"Four," I say.

She stares at me. Her eyes are lit by intelligence but not warmth. For sure, distrust. Maybe rage.

I elbow Ivan nervously.

"Why four anglos?" he asks without the enthusiasm he promised.

"Two in the bed and two under it to shake the posts."

Nothing.

"David wants you to smile."

Though Chantal doesn't smile, she does perk up. Several customers have commented on it; the new waitress has time for one patron only—Ivan Fodorov. Ivan assumes she is a lesbian, and is being ironic. Others figure her for a bisexual adventurer. I am too dismayed to have a theory.

"His joke wasn't very funny," he says to her.

"What joke?" she replies.

I slink away. On the wall near the door is the latest Remy Fidani masterpiece. No mere servant to the creative elite,

Remy is himself an artist of immodest distinction. His medium is charcoal and his subject is transmogrification. A half-dozen of his sketches hang in the main room. Each features a human body in a kneeling or squatting position. Atop the form rests the head of an animal. Cats sporting whiskers like musical notation, dogs flopping pancake ears, pumpkin-eyed horses, a pig with nostrils the size of mushrooms: Remy roams the wild kingdom for models. The new drawing provides a clever variation. Weighing down a sleek feline body is a human head. The neck is narrow but the skull is grotesquely huge. The face, though ballooned, bears a likeness to Michelle D, one of his most faithful customers.

On the sidewalk, the air attacks. Ivan plays scarecrow; I slap my gloved hands together, the sound like someone beating a carpet with a stick.

"Back tonight?" he asks.

"Can't. Chinese lesson."

"The good little foreign visitor, eh? Mangling his two hundred words of vocabulary. Fucking up verb tenses. Getting gender wrong. Everyone laughing at him, calling him a fool just to hear him parrot the word, the same stupid smile plastered to his face."

I look at him.

"I'm bitter," he shrugs.

"No kidding."

He steps closer. At six-five, Ivan is almost a foot taller than I am. In conversation, he can use his height to either create intimacy by leaning in, or else to intimidate by glowering over the person. The choice betrays his mood. "You're leaving me here to die," he says through his teeth.

"You'll wait until I return."

"You'll never be back."

"Of course I'll—"

"As far as I'm concerned."

"Nonsense," I say quietly.

"Desperation," he answers.

I shouldn't keep him any longer—both our faces are seared red by the cold—but I can't help myself. "Do you think the guy in the story stayed in the bedroom long enough to study his wife's face a final time?" I ask.

"I'm freezing!"

"Do you?"

"Your tale has a fatal flaw," says Ivan. "It had to be pitch dark in the room. He couldn't have seen his own hands, let alone her face."

"The moon must have come out."

"During a blizzard?"

"I think of Natalie's face all the time," I continue, ignoring this quite valid objection. "I know it's not the same. She's just a child. But I carry—"

A gust staggers us both. At once, the fillings in my lower jaw start to ache.

"I carry this image of her in my mind, the way other parents carry photos in their wallets. She was maybe two, and had fallen asleep with the light on. It was after we, I mean, after Carole had asked me to—"

"The fall, yes, yes. Be quick."

"I was down in Longueuil for dinner, and went to kiss her good night. She lay on her side in the crib, a blanket tucked right up to her neck. I must have stared for a minute before noticing how she'd arranged her stuffed animals. The girl had erected a wall around herself using bears and cats and a rabbit. Carole told me she'd been up a lot with bad dreams. So she'd built a fortress to keep her safe inside, and to keep bad things outside."

"And?"

"She was two years old!"

"What really bothered you?"

He knows already. Suddenly, I don't want to talk about it. "The inference that she was already damaged by life, I guess. Already harmed."

"And?"

"Fuck off."

He waits.

"That I was outside of her, too," I mumble. "I was one of those who was causing the damage, doing the harm."

"That you *felt* outside."

"Same thing."

"I don't think so."

I want to argue the point. I want the conversation to end. Knowing this, no doubt, Ivan precludes further waffling by marching up Bernard Street in the opposite direction.


I want to argue: I want the conversation to end. I want to assert my views: I want to maintain a dignified silence. I want to sleep with a woman tonight: the thought of even flirting with a grown-up female, let alone proposing sex with her, sends pearls of sweat rolling down my spine. I want to never again be hurt the way I was: I want to wallow in the old miseries for a few minutes before bed each evening, to encourage a night of the old dreams. I want to resume being Carole's husband: I want her to find a guy who has the look and smell of success. I want, more than anything else, to be for my daughter whatever archetypal fathers ought to be: pipe-smoking and slipper-wearing, employed in the upper echelons of industry. I want the girl *not* to have a dad like me.

It is truly Sir Franklin out this afternoon and, rather than freeze to death or cannibalize any fellow explorers, I hasten home. I live exactly two blocks from Remys, but still manage to lose myself in a reverie. The painted-door story, so evocative of the charms of the Canadian winter, rattles around in my skull. By the time I reach the corner of Jeanne Mance Street, Mile End has dissolved into a prairie and I am a farmer trapped in a squall. Snow obliterates the landscape, dissolving the distinction between horizontal and vertical, earth and sky. The cold stings, but what terrifies most is the near blindness: not seeing beyond my feet, hearing just whistles and pipings. A line of fence-posts, three-quarters interred, provides the only guidance. I sink into drifts and stumble through plough ruts, wipe my crusted beard. My breathing stays even for spells, then suddenly draws up short, as if out of fright. No farm is visible ahead. My point of departure vanished moments after I set off. On all sides is blowing snow and blurred light, a raw, biting whiteness.

The question, when it finally occurs to me at my corner, is the more pleasing for having no obvious answer. What part am I playing in the story: the wronged husband purposefully seeking oblivion—the conventional casting—or the bachelor on his way to his neighbour's bed? Even that I feel capable of the latter role is cheering. David LeClair, seducer! The island of Montreal giggles at the thought.

## 2

AN AMAZING FACT: I DON'T OWN AN ANSWERING MACHINE, and yet on entering my apartment I routinely cross to my rotary-dial phone and stare at it, as if the receiver might suddenly rise up on its hind legs and rhyme off the names of all who've called. More amazing still: I routinely mention to Ivan and Carole and even my mother that I'm thinking of finally getting a machine, and that I'm sure they'll be relieved to know that I'll soon be in step with the age, and not once has any of them, even while buzzed on beer or wine or—in Adele's case—cognac, said: *Thank God, David. We are so relieved. Now you'll understand how hard we try to keep in touch, how much we care!*

Closing the front door, I head for the phone. It rests on its belly, inert, conspiratorial. Raising the receiver, I misdial a number, blow air into my hands, dial again. As ever, the message at the other end rankles.

"Adele Guy here. You are being screened, so speak cautiously. If you provide a number, make sure it is correct. If you leave a message, make sure it lasts under a minute, and is purposeful."

Mother never picks up. A precaution, she tells everyone: like any intellectual worth her ideas, she has enemies at the university and in the media, within the government and its appendages. But, like any socialist worth being purged, her number is also listed. She seeks screened contact. She invites purposeful response. I spent the first eighteen years of my life with this woman. In the days before answering machines, she made me reply and ritually deny her presence in the arm-chair beside the phone, her gaze—and the smoke from her Gitane—reducing me to tears as I scribbled down the infor-mation. I got chastised for my lack of composure. Her tone was bitter, as if my nervousness confirmed some sour truth about children, one personally injurious to her. Mother never asked about the tears and I, too confused by my wild emo-tions, never tried to explain them to her. I suspect I thought she would eventually get it. I suspect I assumed she was *attempting* to get it. And you know what? To this day, to this hour even—4:45 on December 17, 1989—I suspect I am still assuming that Adele is still attempting to unravel the mystery of her young son's phone manner.

Which is pathetic. And why I don't often dwell in the con-demned house of my childhood memories. And promise not to conjure too many more quaint recollections.

She is there, I'm sure, scolding the receiver with her stare. No way I'll beg her to answer. Opening my message with a the-atrical sigh is acceptable, though, as is speaking in English, out of spite.

"Wednesday afternoon, Adele. I leave Quebec in three weeks. Any chance of seeing you before then? Christmas might be nice. I promise not to buy you a gift. Return this call, please, or write me a note. . . . Oh yes, I need your help to get a credit card. The bank won't give me one, but might if you'll co-sign. Tenured professor, published author, and so on. Notice I didn't call you 'Mother'? That was to butter you up. Hope it worked. Hope my minute isn't—"

Three beeps, and the line goes dead. I recradle the phone a little too hard. My ears burn. My heart punches at my chest.

Mirror, mirror on the wall? No one fair to report at all. A face too round, even in youth, too soft and eager. I've always been chubby and have always wanted to lose thirty pounds, less for my waistline than for my features. As it is, neither a bang across the forehead nor a scruffy beard can divert attention from the chipmunk cheeks and puffy lips, a beak nose realigned years ago in a baseball mishap, apparently, though I don't remember playing the sport as a kid. People say I look Irish. That is because of the carrot hair that curls in damp weather. My eyes, though, are Ganges brown, hardly pure Celt. Variously described by men and women alike as gentle, even attractive—the word "bedroom" has never come up, mind you—those muddy pupils and red-shocked whites constitute my best feature, along with an explosive but avuncular belly laugh, an effect aided by a gut that Jell-O jiggles when prodded by a droll comment or a smiling child. Aryan-eyed Adele maintains that I'm the image of her own father, a franco-Ontarian who beat up his wife, took work as a scab, and spoke English in the shops of St. Henri to mock his neighbours and shame his family. He enlisted in the Canadian Army in 1943—still another contentious act—and died on a Normandy beach when she was a teenager. A hero to some, she says with a shrug.

I think I look pretty much like a thousand other guys walking around Montreal or Toronto, London or Paris. You know us, I bet: white-skinned thirty-somethings whose barrel chests and sausage legs once possessed a certain masculine power, a certain bullish grace, but who haven't gotten with the physical-fitness craze, or else can't fight the family genes, and so are now moulting in reverse: from thick to fat, taut to sagging, swagger to shuffle. Guys whose cheeks keep puffing until the face has merely lines, despite beards maintained expressly to create the illusion of angles, and whose necks insist on widening out, as if we are doing weights. Whose asses, once firm apples, are now plum puddings, and whose stomachs people assume we no longer try to suck in, even though we are still trying—like hell, as a matter of fact.

And apparel? Casual, you might note. Impoverished, you might well add. Adele once again claims I've both her father's physique and his poor fashion sense. For sure, clothes don't do well on me. Shirts, okay: button-twisting tight across the chest and floppy in the arms, but otherwise a fit. Pants, though, are hopeless. The aforementioned ass, ham-hock thighs, and the inexplicably bulging calves of a Swiss alpinist. Dress pants bag at the crotch and behind; jeans, no matter how form-fitting, just don't.

Funny: Mother's comparisons have always been with her father, not mine. But then Jacob LeClair doesn't inhabit the house I avoid visiting. Dad's abode was torn down when I was a boy. He got burned-out, bombed, sent packing. He was exposed, proven bankrupt, consigned to the junk heap of history. Not to be replaced by a similar dwelling, either. Just levelled.

Zuo Chang needs a moment to compose himself. My Mandarin teacher removes his jacket and sweater, his tuque and earband, his scarves and mittens; he slips out of his boots and pulls off and folds an outer pair of socks; he scrubs the icicles from his brows and scrapes at the frozen tears on his cheeks, all while wearing the same non-expression on his handsome face. Easily read, the non-expression relates shock and dismay, a heroic but faltering determination to survive this nightmare. Welcome to Canada, Zuo, a meaner host than I would say.

"Hi," I begin instead.

He nods.

"Can't talk yet?"

He nods again.

"I'll get the tea."

Our routine is set. While Zuo Chang derobes and smooths his hair before a hallway mirror, I fix a pot of jasmine tea. Then, seated across from each other at a coffee table in the living room, we sip from ceramic cups. Zuo—Chinese men call friends by their family name only, apparently—likes his tea hot, and takes fast, noisy slurps, pinching the rim of the mug between his fingers. I prefer to hold mine between my palms and test, out of foolish habit, my tolerance for searing heat. Only after an initial cup has been emptied is it time for the lesson. Zuo Chang uses the pause to examine his surroundings; I use the pause to finish my tea as quickly as possible, heedless of a scalded throat.

I'm aware of how my apartment appears to others. I'm aware of how it appears to me. Self-awareness, I've lately decided, is a terrible burden for one convinced his current circumstances are not a reflection of his true fate or promise. It's like being an immigrant. You speak a language with wit and charm, are an educated, sophisticated adult, a skilled worker with ideas and enthusiasm, and yet, simply by virtue of a shift in personal tectonic plates, you're transformed into a tribesman or highlander or backwoods yahoo: a victim of a system, of the century, of all that shitty history we over here so craftily—okay, there was some luck involved—avoided. You become a government file in a pile that climbs to the ceiling, a head shot snapped against a backdrop of cement grey. You're not who you once were, and you don't know who you'll eventually be. Who you are at the moment, at least, is simple enough. You're nobody, and you know it.

Maybe I'm being oversensitive; maybe Zuo's cursory examinations of my home are without judgement. Two doubts nag. First of all, the place *is* a kip. I pay $270, unheated, for a three-room flat, and even in Montreal that is suspiciously cheap. Neighbours upstairs like Jacques Brel records and having sex on the kitchen table; my neighbour downstairs, Lena Buber, suffers from flatulence and enjoys chatting with her dead husband while taking a bath. My bowels are steady and I see no reason to one-hand it in the kitchen, but I do argue with the radio often enough, and I do, when lying on the couch late at night, no better able to sleep here than in the bedroom overlooking the street, exchange nocturnal greetings with the pigeons bundled up on the windowsill. *Coo coo* the neighours might hear. Angel music, even to one with a tin ear.

What else about the place? Wrong side of Esplanade for sunlight, excellent for cold shade and depressing shadow. Pipes running down the outsides of walls, paint peeling into Rorschach tests. Hardwood floors, full of sighs and complaints, and two doors—one to the front staircase, another onto the back balcony—with mezuzahs on the inside frames. A water-closet and a bathtub on legs. Ornate wainscoting and fake pillars in the bedroom. No stereo, a television I fished out of someone's garbage for use as a lamp stand, and bookshelves. Six bookshelves in all, each containing five shelves that average twenty-six titles per row, less if the spines are of cloth. Otherwise, despite having lived here for nearly three years, I haven't done much fixing up. Furniture by Sally Ann. Decorations by Zellers.

The second doubt concerns Zuo Chang. He is not like my usual guests. Actually, I don't *have* usual guests, but even if I did, he would still be exceptional among them. I understand him a little, I think. I understand that Zuo is a refined person, trim and compact, with gentle, aristocratic features that harden swiftly when he is angry, his eyes narrowing until they disappear beneath brows and skin. I understand that he stops regularly to consult the hallway mirror, and brushes hair back from his forehead with a flourish. That he uses cologne and is fussy about his fingernails. That he is intelligent and gifted, a cut above most teaching hacks: an artist, to be exact, probably respected back home—perhaps famous. Finally, I understand that he casts a cold eye over my apartment, and struggles not to feel demeaned at having to teach in such a setting, on such a level, with someone like me.

He's stuck, of course: one of those human-interest stories that litter the pages of liberal newspapers and are waved around press conferences by conservatives-and-far-worse as examples of the gathering immigrant tide, the pigmented, public-funds-draining future. But at least Zuo Chang has had the advantage of being not so much Chinese—hardly a bonus, if one studies our national history—as a Tiananmen Square refugee. The images are still fresh. The outrage still galls. Other millennium-ending international news stories, such as the fall of the Berlin Wall and the wobbling Soviet Union, only serve to confirm the obduracy of China, the viciousness of the old men in Beijing: to affirm the reputation of Canadians for doing the right thing, setting a good example, then patting ourselves on our broad northern backs.

Zuo came to Montreal in April to deliver lectures on traditional painting at one of the francophone universities. His six-week trip received the blessing of both the college in Beijing where he taught French, and his national government. He had a wife and child, went the reasoning; China was relaxing; he would likely return. Startling events in his nation's capital that spring caused him to pause. Other Chinese in Montreal advised a wait-and-see policy. Zuo Chang waited, with growing unease, as the student protest dragged on, and then saw, on TV, with growing dismay, as the authorities responded to the relaxing process: tanks and armoured personnel carriers on Tiananmen Square, battles along the major thoroughfares, soldiers firing into crowds. The Goddess of Democracy toppled. "Order" restored. The following evening, Zuo got through to his college. His family were fine, but a colleague had been wounded, two students were dead, and twenty more remained unaccounted for. *Stay there for now*, his wife had told him. *Everything here is awful.*

Again, he was advised by others: apply for asylum, accept benevolence and sympathy, wait some more. By September Zuo had the necessary papers, accommodation in the apartment of a UQAM professor, and was sending out job applications and art portfolios. Schools in town were suddenly swamped with the résumés of highly qualified Mandarin instructors; galleries began returning, unexamined, submissions thick with paintings of waterfalls and bamboo stalks, sheets of calligraphy that looked hasty but were, apparently, artistic and expressive. He wound up giving private language lessons for twelve dollars an hour and one calligraphy class a week at the Stanley Street "Y." It wasn't much, and left no cash to send home. But his time was his own, Montreal was a clean, uncrowded city—overrun by pigeons and squirrels, not people—and the autumn was glorious, the air sweet and the sunlight pure, Mount Royal a painted fan.

"Look at this," I say, taking a letter from an envelope. "It arrived yesterday."

Zuo glances at the paper. "I don't read English," he says.

I translate into French.

*December 4, 1989*
Dear Mr. David,

I am pleased to confirm offer for you to teach at our foreign languages college, in Department of English. You are asked to be in Beijing by January twenty-one, and to teach classes in translation for department chief Feng Ziyang. The college will give you room in Foreign Experts Building and one thousand yuan salary each month.

Please call me soon with date you wish to fly from Canada. A ticket will be put in mail.

Sincere greetings!
Zhou Hong


Zuo humphs. "She always gets Western names backwards," he says in French. "I tell her again and again the family name comes second."

"Tell who?"

"Zhou Hong."

"Zhou Hong is a woman?"

"She is my wife."

He says the word in Chinese. He also does not smile or relax his features. Though I think I recognize the term, I still request a translation. Zuo provides one, and I settle back in the couch in astonishment. I sent my résumé to a half-dozen Beijing schools in August, on the advice of a young man I met once, for twenty minutes, in Remys. He was just home from China, having broken his contract with a university in the capital. Most of the foreign staff at his school had fled before the massacre, he explained; the few that hung on got out in the days following June 4th. Almost none had plans to resume their duties in the fall. Consequently, jobs would be going begging in Beijing. If ordinary people didn't apply quickly, the guy predicted, the colleges would be forced to hire born agains from America. Christian organizations were amassing armies of foot soldiers in Hong Kong, and were bombarding the city's educational institutions with applications. Once in, the fundamentalists would go to work: proselytizing in public parks and baptizing in toilets, selling a wacko American Dream. The Chinese, reckoned the man—in his only benign comment about the race—were wise to the game, but, if no one else came along, would still have to give these people the jobs. I could turn my cover letter into a confession of political extremism or sexual dysfunction, social miscreance or physical decay; I could come off as a manic-depressive or basket case, even a likely suicide, and still get a contract so long as I made no mention of either God or AIDS.

I mailed the letters. Shortly afterwards, I spotted a notice in a health-food store advertising private Mandarin lessons. My teacher turned out to be on staff at one of the colleges I had applied to, and he offered to write a letter of support. Zuo Chang said only that he had connections inside the school's Foreign Affairs Office, where hiring was done. His wife's name, let alone her occupation, was not mentioned.

"That note you wrote for me in September," I ask. "Who was it to?"

"Zhou Hong."

"Who is your wife?"

"Correct."

"Then I really do need to thank you."

"No need," says Zuo, shooing my gratitude away, like it is a pesky wasp.

"But you probably got me the job."

"You are a friend," he replies in Chinese. "I help you whenever I can."

"I'll help you, too, if I'm able."

"Of course."

I laugh nervously. He doesn't. Zuo Chang is dead serious. He always is.

"Do you know what the definition of a friend is in China?" he asks, reverting to French.

"Someone who cares about you?"

"Someone who can do something for you."

The thought gives me pause. Zuo and I often lapse into silences during lessons, and I still haven't figured out if they are comfortable ones. Refilling the tea mugs, I light a cigarette. A month ago I reduced my hours at Collège Plateau, where I, unique among the part-time staff, teach introductory courses in both French and English, and began to study Mandarin with a scholarly intensity unmatched since my undergraduate years. Each day I memorize twenty-five ideograms and fifty Pinyin words. I also advance a chapter in the exercise book and play over and over the cassette designed to get me hearing—and speaking—the four tones that distinguish concepts sharing identical spellings and near-identical pronunciations. Written Chinese requires a long apprenticeship. The oral language is much simpler, but also infuriatingly subtle. Though I have a good memory, my ear is bad, the fault, I suspect, of a musically malnourished childhood. People from outside Montreal are often astounded by this: how could someone who is bilingual, speech unaccented in both official languages, and who dreams a free-form linguistic jam, have trouble acquiring a third or fourth tongue? My answer—that I didn't have to "acquire" English or French:

that they were inside me at birth, like the colour of my eyes and tint of my hair—is never satisfactory.

My cigarette coils smoke up into Zuo's face. He sits back in his seat.

"Does it bother you?" I ask in Mandarin.

"Tell me the word."

I pronounce the verb. He makes me repeat it until he is satisfied.

"You don't smoke, Zuo?"

"Intellectuals rarely do."

"Really?"

"Workers and peasants only. At least, the men. And some older professors at the college, those persecuted during the Cultural Revolution"—he provides the term in French—"they are addicted, and still smoke cheap local cigarettes. Feng Ziyang is an addict, though he also likes to receive gifts of Marlboros."

"Feng . . . ?"

He points to the letter on the table. "Your department chief," he says. "He is forty-six, and a victim of Chairman Mao. I am thirty-eight, and less harmed. None of my friends smoke. It is unhealthy."

I crush a perfectly good cigarette, again.

"Zhou Hong is an unusual person," he suddenly declares. "No one else is like her. She makes sure of it."

"Sorry?"

"Her mistakes on the job, like with your name, are typical. Small, stupid things, the kind that count. She cares little for—" I lose the word. "And gives too much of herself. People criticize her. They abuse her kindness."

From my own experience, I know that when a teacher races too far ahead of his students, he finds himself alone on the track. He also finds a sea of blank faces watching him run. Curiously, Zuo Chang never seems to notice my puzzlement. I ask him to slow down. From his expression, it's obvious he is unaware that he has been speaking in Chinese.

"She is passionate about music," he continues in French. "Especially Western composers of the nineteenth century. Dvořák and Mendelssohn, Chopin's nocturnes and all of Schubert. But she was trained in the English language, not music. And even her English skills are unimportant: she is an administrator. Her interests are impractical. Unrelated to achieving success in her profession."

I know better than to comment. Normally cool and controlled, Zuo is agitated tonight. Dapples of sweat dot his forehead. His eyes bleed fatigue.

"She will not survive long in China," he adds, his own words clearly disturbing him. "She lacks the necessary skills."

This time, the silence is definitely uneasy. I flip through my exercise book. When I look up, I find him examining the grain patterns on the surface.

"They want me to teach translation," I say in French, abandoning the lesson. "I'm not really qualified."

"You have published translations?"

"A few. Mostly in journals."

"Then you are a translator," he says. "Able to teach your craft to others."

"But I've never studied my 'craft.' I've never even thought about it. The languages are mixed up inside my head. I don't need to translate anything."

Zuo Chang smiles, his composure regained. "You are a translator because people have commissioned you to translate valuable material for them. Others have recommended you by their actions. You work hard and are devoted. In presentation, you *are* a professor of translation, and therefore command the automatic respect of others."

"But I know I'm not a professor of—"

"What you know privately is irrelevant."

"And Zhou Hong must have read my résumé. She knows I'm not really qualified."

"She knows you have a graduate degree and have worked in your field," he says. "She is safe from criticism. You have presented your credentials to the college, and been assigned duties based on them. You are safe as well."

"I won't be criticized?"

"Not to your face."

I want to laugh. But is Zuo mocking the system, the concept of face, or me? "And you're safe, too?" I ask. "You recommended me in good faith?"

"Good what?"

"On the understanding that I was a professional."

"Yes," he answers unhappily, "I am safe, too."

He assigns me ten pages of the exercise book and agrees to another tutorial on the weekend. At the door I wait until he's bundled up before slipping him an envelope.

"You said that you don't have to translate from French to English," he says, pocketing the money. "Or vice versa, I imagine. This is a foreign concept to me. Which language is yours?"

"Mine?"

"Your race. Your being."

"I don't think I know," I reply.

He frowns. "In Beijing you will be more welcome as an English speaker. Especially if your accent is American."

"It is, I guess."

"Good. American English is dominant. All forms of English

are respected. You would be wise to present yourself as an anglophone."

"Another false impression?"

"An impression," answers Zuo. "If it is well made, whether or not it is false makes no difference."

"But you teach French?"

"French is only the fourth or fifth most important foreign language in China. As a student, I had no choice; it was assigned to me. Now I am being practical. In Toronto or New York I would be another silent, stupid immigrant. At least in Quebec I can read newspapers and watch television. I can use language to convince people to treat me with respect. I have to be content. You do not."

"I want the respect," I say, the old earnestness returning, "but not if it means dominance."

"The two are the same."

How categorically he states it! As if the remark is fact, not opinion; as if it is accepted wisdom, not a harsh vision of society.

"Maybe I'll only speak French in Beijing."

"That would be impractical."

"Maybe I *want* to be impractical."

"A mistake of emotion," adds Zuo at the door. "And of passion. A weakness."

He is rebuking me. I feel the sting, and promise myself to bear it in mind.

## 3

THE SEIZURE—MY FIRST IN A MONTH—CATCHES ME OFF guard. I'm cleaning up after Zuo Chang has left when my vision clouds. Emerging from the fog is the usual vista: a precipice opening onto a narrow, bottomless chasm, like in Road Runner cartoons, and a roving inner eye that keeps charging the cliff, veering out over the edge, then pulling back. The exhaustion rises and is followed, tellingly, by a feeling of emptiness. It is like trying to keep alert behind the wheel of a car; it is like waking yourself up to avoid an unfinished nightmare. To fight the fit, I must bite my lip. To not fight it, all I need do is wait until the camera lens, ever more daredevil and manic, skitters too close to the drop-off, extends too far out, and I plunge.

At least I have only my misery as company tonight. Public attacks, even if they go undetected, are still humiliating. Ivan once described what happens. I can be at a table of people, in the middle of a conversation, when suddenly I sag back in my chair. Expression drains from my face. My eyes tend to widen, but also gradually dim, like a receding headlight. Once I spilled coffee on my hand and did not flinch. Another time I treated the sugar dispenser as a gavel. The blackouts last from one to two minutes and appear to others, he was quick to add, as mere brooding, a withdrawal to sulk over some perceived insult or private pain. Nothing out of the ordinary for a Remys regular.

A good friend, Ivan. I don't believe him.

When I was eighteen, I was diagnosed with epilepsy. Psychomotor: petit mal. No writhing on the floor, no foaming, no real danger to myself. Simply a condition, a misfiring of synapses that, triggered by fatigue or stress or, in my case, a mix of adult anxiety and teenage rage, could produce brief lapses of consciousness. Petit mal was easily treated with the drug Dilantin, three hundred milligrams a day. I took Dilantin for twelve years. Seizure-free years, too: periods of independence and scholarly success, marriage and parenthood. Then I stopped. I stopped wanting to ingest pharmaceuticals the way kids ingest candies. I stopped wanting to hide the pills when we had guests and lie on applications. I stopped wanting, moreover, to feel like I was keeping a lid on an aspect of my own being, a puritan lacerating his flesh in punishment for natural desire. When someone—Carole, probably—pointed out that epilepsy *wasn't* an aspect of my being, that it was an abnormality to be corrected, I was puzzled. Long before I was diagnosed, I knew I had something buzzing in my brain. It never occurred to me to treat that thing as a defect. A child's response to the world, I suppose: how can I be weird or wrong when everyone around me is utterly and fascinatingly weird, and totally and menacingly wrong? Since I've given up the drug I suspect I've started to believe this again. Not believe, actually: simply sense it, observe it, feel it to be true. Self-serving crap, others—my ex-wife, first and foremost—would surely say.

I lie on the couch. Close my eyes and cross my arms, dig nails into skin. A minute passes. Counting my own thumping heartbeats isn't calming, but listening to the sill pigeons is. *Coo coo* they murmur from outside the window at my feet. Are they freezing? Probably. Does the heat escaping from the frame provide adequate warmth? Hardly. Shouldn't I do something? I did once, on a night like this, cracking the window a few inches to let more heat out. The birds flew off in a panicked flutter, not to return for days.

The spinning slows, the vacancy is gradually filled. I fight the seizure, and win. This time.

Dinner is canned beans on toast, a slice of store-bought pie, a cigarette by the front window. Though I can't imagine she would venture out, I watch for Lena. My eighty-three-year-old neighbour leaves her apartment once a week to buy food from the grocer at the corner of Esplanade and St. Viateur. The shop is a hundred metres from our building, a ten-minute walk for Lena in summer, twenty minutes when there is snow. She has fallen on ice before, twisted her ankle—I did her shopping for a month last January, cashing her pension cheque at the store—and frequently returns home with coughs so raw they wake me up a floor above her. Still, declaring the sidewalks too treacherous, Lena Buber lugs her cart down the centre of the street to the corner, where she fills two grocery bags with tins of sardines and bags of onions and cans of condensed milk. Then she hauls her cargo at glacial pace back up Esplanade without shame or company. I insist, in winter at least, on helping, even if all I do is walk alongside, ready to grab her when she slips. For this, she calls me her "Boy Scout" and repeats, like a mantra, her parable of model youths dragging old ladies across the streets of Bucharest, not to show respect for the elderly but to curry favour with officials, hasten their rise in society. The comparison is so ludicrous I take no offence.

Even Lena knows better than to buy supplies tonight. I don't, and encase myself in various synthetic products, legs stiff as plastic tubes, headgear a cross of IRA volunteer and Arab princess. I still nearly tumble down the staircase and still find walking into the wind akin to being on the wrong end of a sandblaster. My destination is thirty metres due north. By the halfway mark I am tearing. By the intersection my cheeks are raw and I can't see straight. The light is red. I cross.

"*Calice!*" I mutter, prying open the door to the shop. Once within the frame, the wind shoves me inside, then slams the door shut. For a moment I stand stunned in the light. Focusing, I look over at the counter. A face grins back at me. I squint to confirm the identity.

"Making the rent, Firoz?" I ask.

"Barely, my friend."

"Times will change."

"For the better?"

I shrug.

"Welcome to my home," he says.

Firoz Velji owns and operates one of two small groceries—called *dépanneurs* in Quebec—at the corner of Esplanade and Bernard, one of four shops within a single square block, one of a dozen stores providing the same service to the same Mile End residents. Not that Firoz needs to worry about a *dépanneur* a street away; his immediate competition, Lee Hue-Sook, is plenty. Sook and her staff—a taciturn husband who speaks only Korean, two college-aged sons fluent in American English, and a trilingual daughter pouring over a calculus text behind the counter most evenings—run an efficient operation. She has the freshest fruits and vegetables, the most varieties of cold meats and cheeses, morning deliveries of baguettes and nan bread. She keeps her prices competitive, doesn't stock junk, and perfumes the air of her bright, spotless premises with the bouquets of flowers she arranges during slow periods. I do most of my shopping there, in secret, first checking across the intersection to make sure that Firoz or worse, his wife Zera, isn't watching.

I'm not proud of the subterfuge. Firoz is a friend, and needs the business. But his shop is a disaster: rotting vegetables and stale bread, cereal boxes under skeins of dust. Customers can barely get inside the door, thanks to a jutting counter he built himself, and anyone of above-average height—Firoz is five-three, and was thinking Indian—has to crouch when paying, for fear of a cigarette display that overhangs the cash register. Aisles are blocked by stacks of no-name soft drinks that no one buys and cartons of Mexican toilet paper that he paid for in cash from a guy driving a rented van. The beer fridges are at the back, an arduous trek, and Firoz or Vera have to personally guide novices to the milk and butter displays.

The Veljis got by in this state once, relying on a devoted clientele, many of whom they knew by name. "I sell to people, not to a demographic," Firoz told me, proud, I think, of the ideal implicit in the sentiment. These customers didn't mind the fluorescent lights and cracked tile floor, the irregular hours—Firoz isn't a morning person—and unannounced days off, the curry camphor that permeates the shop. These customers knew the family lived upstairs, two adults and five children in four rooms, and that the oldest son, Hanif, had been given the storage area at the back as a bribe not to leave home, not to cease helping out during meals or when his father was indisposed. These customers hadn't been put off by the boy's stereo, the television installed behind the counter to make sixteen-hour days endurable, even Zera's moods.

But many of them are gone now. They've moved on, or else gotten proper jobs and higher life-style standards. The corner has grown too respectable, not to mention competitive, for a store like the Veljis'. As a result, the business has sunk into even more bald poverty and deeper disarray. I always buy my beer and cigarettes from Firoz. Not much else, though. I can't afford to.

"What's the score?" I ask, taking my usual place on a stool beside the counter.

"The Rangers lead."

"Second period?"

"Just started."

I buy a bottle of beer, my regular purchase, and a pack of Craven M. The beer stays in its brown paper bag; the plastic on the cigarettes is torn off. Firoz makes change on a ten-dollar bill. The change is all silver coins; his prices are appalling.

"Cold?" he asks.

"Miserable."

"Does a cigarette warm you up?"

"A bonfire couldn't warm me up tonight."

"In such weather," observes Firoz, "many people would rather go hungry than venture out to shop. But not you, eh? David, my most faithful customer."

Firoz Velji is forty, slight and bow-legged, with a permanently shy smile and beagle eyes. His hair faded to grey long ago, his cheeks droop, and he has the slow-motion mannerisms typical, I've noticed, of many Indian men. A shopkeeper since he came to Canada in 1976, he is the son of a prosperous merchant who died in poverty, Firoz has repeatedly told me, after the government "nationalized" the family business in Dar es Salaam. He is making a point: though the Veljis were victims of a half-baked African socialist experiment, Firoz remains solidly Left, solidly committed. He assumes this is a bond between us, which it is. But having commerce in the family genes clearly doesn't guarantee acumen. In his case, the impediment is temperament. Adolescent shoplifters who ransack the store are asked by Firoz in a climbing voice to leave. Salesmen pitching cold calls are invited to display their junk near the front door. Wholesalers who short-changed the Veljis the week before are welcomed back, handed complimentary no-name soft drinks. Even the shoplifters reappear, doling out change stolen—no doubt—from their parents' pant pockets and purses to buy single cigarettes and candy bars whose generous expiry dates have long passed.

He is too nice, in other words. Too kindly. I am moved by Firoz's gentleness, his faith in people, his ideals. Even his timidity and, one suspects, deep sentimentality hardly speak ill of him as a human being. Of course, virtually everyone *does* speak ill of him, calling him weak and ineffectual, but not me.

I am studying the man, though.

A woman enters the shop, asks for *Le Devoir*, which the Valjis don't carry, then inquires about the hockey game. Next, a teenager wearing only a jean jacket tries to buy a six-pack. When Firoz, almost blushing, wonders if the boy has proof of age, he gets sold a story: the beer is for the kid's father, who is already drunk, and who broke his leg two years ago trying to negotiate the icy stairs from their third-floor walk-up. Firoz looks at me and I shrug. The tale is so piteous it rings true. I hold the door open for the boy.

"You've never been to India, right?" I ask, still mulling over my conversation with Zuo Chang.

"Never."

"But you're Indian?"

"No question."

"How does that work?"

"My parents were Indian," he answers, "my wife is Indian, and my children are Indian, too. Also Canadian."

"And you?"

"More or less. Depending on ingredients," adds Firoz, smiling to himself.

I wait.

"It is like Zera's curries. Sometimes she finds all Indian ingredients, and so the food is very much like back home. Which is not exactly home, either," he says, his eyes twinkling. "Other days she cannot locate this or that thing, and so must improvise. Then, the curry becomes mixed, becomes like *here*, one might say. Always delicious, though. Always good food."

"Got it," I lie.

"Those who worry about ingredients will worry, my friend. Want only purity, one hundred per cent approved. Never accept compromise and reality. Never be satisfied."

"With their dinners," I say tentatively.

"All meals," he clarifies.

I swig from the beer. The bottle is still pressed to my lips when I sense her behind me. The abrupt presence of a scent— a mix of nutmeg and lemon—is what gives her away. Zera Velji loves to sneak up from the door at the back of the shop. Catching us off guard, overhearing an incriminating comment, brings a rare smile to her face.

"Trying to get us arrested, David?"

"Hi, Zera."

"Policeman walks in and sees you drinking alcohol on premises," she says, repositioning her braid over her shoulder. "What happens? Our shop is closed down and Firoz goes to prison."

"Wow," I say, dropping the brown bag into the wastebasket beside the door.

"Maybe *you* go to prison instead, Zera," offers Firoz.

"You would like that, wouldn't you."

"They have special prison sari. Blue and grey. Very sexy, I am sure."

"You are sure?"

"I am joking."

"What is funny about—?"

She stops herself. The effort is almost physical: Zera withdraws a step and lowers her head. The gesture is mesmerizing. Though I am intimidated by Zera Velji, I find her an elegant woman. Her skin is copper, her hair is coal. Her features are small but her mouth is full, despite lips too often pursed. Zera has expressive hands that underline not what she is saying but thinking. When nervous, she washes them in the air; when angry, she grasps one in the other and squeezes, as if in self-punishment. When happy, she reaches out and rests her hand on Firoz's forearm, an intimate gesture. Once, she absently touched my arm the same way. That split second of contact sent a shiver up my spine and filled my head with images: a round belly, folds of soft brown flesh.

A traditionalist, Zera refuses to cut her hair or wear pants. She shifts her braid over her sari again and, nodding at the wisdom of some inner counsel, looks back up.

"At least I spent money tonight," I try. "Beer and some cigarettes."

"Anyone else come in?"

"Only a boy," says Firoz.

"Firoz sold him a six-pack," I provide.

"Firoz!"

"Just kidding," I hastily add. Too late, of course: his face is lit with guilt.

She has a snipe ready. Firoz and I brace ourselves. Noticing this, she backs off. "Watch your hockey," she says with false pique. "I am going to bed."

Her husband nearly weeps in gratitude. "Leave me room, woman," he says. "I don't want to move you over in the dark."

She departs without a good night.

"A small consolation," says Firoz, impressed by his own wit. "A warm bed on a cold winter night. Small consolation, but enough for a man like me."

The Canadians win the game, and I ask Firoz to store the Craven M's behind the counter. I also keep stashes at Remys and in my desk at the language school, officially to discipline myself into smoking less, unofficially because I'm the guy who hides his glove in the apartment of a woman he hopes to see again. At the door, I apologize for my mischievousness with the beer.

"No apology necessary," he says. "You are my friend."

"Friends can still do stupid things, Firoz."

"No apology," he repeats.

Sleep eludes me that night. I hear Lena coughing. I hear love-making upstairs. The sex sounds rougher than usual, more clumsy, as if the man and woman are new to each other—a lonely wife, a predatory neighbour. Outside, the moon is obscure. Outside, fence-posts are interred.

Outside, trucks have been trundling down the street all evening, blasting horns to warn car owners to move their vehicles or else have them towed. Behemoths with funnels like Saskatchewan combines are now inhaling the snow mounds and showering them into dump trucks for disposal into an opening on the St. Lawrence Seaway. These battalions thunder through the dark, their bulk splitting asphalt and rattling staircases, blowing open improperly sealed doors. How fellow Montrealers slumber through these invasions of the city is beyond me. I always wake up with a start, and fade back to sleep only after sustained mental conjurings of Natalie in her playroom with her dad, in her backyard with her mom and dad. That doesn't work tonight; I keep seeing the girl alone in her crib, a wall of stuffed animals as pathetic defence against nightmares and monsters and parents who won't stay together, even for her sake.

Once things have quieted upstairs, I stand at the front window in my briefs and T-shirt and smoke—on behalf of the lovers—a post-coital cigarette. Across the street, on a parallel balcony, is a man bundled in a coat and hat, also dragging on a cancer stick. Visible beneath his coat are pyjama bottoms and slippers. Visible on his face is the usual dumb defiance and creeping humiliation. It is four in the morning and, according to the midnight news, minus twenty-five out. Nevertheless, there he stands, hunched over like a soldier too exhausted to properly duck enemy fire. I don't know the guy, but I like him already. I also know, so to speak, his story. For years, he and his companion both smoked. Then she quit. Tolerance of his weakness became her cross, her trump card. She bore it bravely, played it shrewdly, for a while. But then it became obvious that the man had no intention of being reformed. He had no interest in being shown the way: no desire to see the light. Clearly, he was a reprobate. She didn't stop loving him—she wasn't *that* superficial—but she didn't respect him as she once had, either. How could she, when he showed so little respect for himself? Qualities lost are hard to regain. Impossible, really. To the balcony he was banished, first when she was home, then all the time: the smell infested the furniture and poisoned the plants. As a matter of course, she will be asking him to leave. As a matter of course, he will be going, knowing as he does that he can never—no matter how much he'd like to—leave himself in the way she requires.

## 4

CHRISTMAS EVE, AND REMY IS DETERMINED TO CLOSE EARLY. Customers are peeved. Actually, I'm peeved and, beyond caring how it looks, canvass the room to rally support for an extension. Remy Fidani leans cross-armed on the counter, following me with his smirky gaze. He is dressed in his customary turtleneck and high-waisted trousers that emphasize the curve of his buttocks, the size of his bulge. His skin is olive, his black hair is thinning. His bald spot, we speculate, is secretly shined. A family man—his beleaguered wife and brood of boys make token appearances in the café, only to be whisked back outside before she can utter a complaint or they can break a glass—Remy is equally a wolf among the chicken coop of his staff, a crew composed of attractive young women who plan to soon be singing on a stage or publishing in softcover. Rumours link him with at least one waitress per season; sightings of kitchen gropings and splayed legs in the storage room add a note of abandon to the daily hum of burping coffee machines and pool cues smacking balls.

Sure enough, the people I query have places to be: *réveillons* and dinners, tree-trimmings with loved ones.

"Sorry, David," says Remy.

"And you're closed all day tomorrow?"

Ivan takes my arm. "Forgive him," he tells the café owner. "He has a small problem."

"No fucking life?"

"No food in my apartment," I correct.

"I close at ten, sharp. Beg me no more, please. My skin creeps."

"Crawls."

"He'll beg you no more," promises Ivan. He escorts me back to our table.

"I have a life," I complain. "It's just, you know. . . ."

"Fucked?"

"*Le mot juste*," I sigh.

"Remy has a family, remember. The wife he knocked up in high school and the kids he keeps siring to fill a pew at church. They have to be attended to. Plus, there is the current mistress to enjoy a Merry Christmas meal with. He has a busy night ahead."

"Chantal could lock up."

"Chantal?" replies Ivan sharply. "She is his turkey. He is her stuffing."

"What?"

Though he shrugs, his eyes glow anger. I gape at the counter. Pigeon-chested Remy with the punk waitress? Unthinkable. But, as if on cue, he slides up behind her at the coffee machine, where she is steaming a cylinder of milk, and commences to wipe a nozzle, up and down, up and down. Remy whispers in her ear. If his words are sweet nothings, they must taste sour: she neither smiles nor laughs. Her body language, too, is sugarless—stiff, her slender shoulders almost pinned back. His glasses refract light. Her bracelets tinkle.

"No way," I try.

"Every way," answers Ivan, playing with a spoon. "Every time, too. Hitting on the most vulnerable. Just like a proper asshole."

So saying, he tosses the spoon, now shaped into a diver, across the table to me. Mangling utensils is supposed to be my nervous tic. Remy once banned me from the café for a week for bending his spoons. I pleaded sexual frustration, had the sentence reduced to twenty-four hours. I came in tonight intending to do damage; though we ordered only beers, I asked Chantal for sets of cutlery, which she supplied without, naturally, comment or facial expression. To show how black my mood was, my goal was the knife. Spoons, I figured, were kids' play. Forks required caution, but little craftiness or strength. Knives, though, truly tested a man. I promised myself I'd reduce one to a wishbone, or else suffer a month-long banishment trying.

I want to talk with Ivan about this mood. Christmas Eve isn't the most appropriate occasion, but then he, too, is single, and we can always claim that the holiday has become a tawdry farce, its true values buried under an avalanche of ploys to keep the masses shopping. Even now I am at a loss to know what to do with my rage. I call it mine because no one, as far as I can tell, has hypnotized or demonized or clockwork-oranged me into becoming consumed from time to time by a feral, unfocused anger, along with a sister impulse to lash out. Saying this isn't easy. Like most people, I'd prefer to pin blame for all unhappy aspects of my personality on the usual suspects. But it simply doesn't feel drummed into my brain by family/church/society; it feels, I'm sorry to admit, like nature. Not first nature, maybe, but second or, at bottom, third.

Ivan and I used to joke about it. "Guy stuff" we called the rage, or at least the playing out of its madness: wars and pillage, conquest and overthrow, murder and rape. For years we never connected our personal experience of this contingency with the persistent public failure of governments and groups—mostly, if not exclusively, male in make-up—to successfully apply a system we argued would improve human society. For years we never made the connection between the fact that our motivation to think and act in certain ways was often, if not always, based on criteria that were, to put it nicely, capricious and unsystematic, with the fact that, again and again, attempts at realizing the ideals of socialism kept falling victim to what appeared to be capricious, unsystematic behaviour on the part of the realizers. Guy stuff was only one example of the sort of complication that keeps ideological purity so elusive—what Friedrich Engels calls "false consciousness"—but it was the one that mocked most openly our own beliefs. Remember that, unlike for older generations of Reds, whose ideals were grounded in domestic concerns like better wages and a national health plan, we got off on second-hand news, the allure of elsewhere. Uncle Ho fighting imperialist America. Che radicalizing in a jaunty beret. Chairman Mao swimming the Yangtze. Chairman Mao waving his Little Red Book. Propaganda meets radical chic. Left politics meets cultural kitsch. We loved it up. We pretended it was ours. We also pretended we weren't who we were, living where we did. Acting as we were probably destined to act, too. Like children with toy guns pretending to liberate a Burger King, then staying on for fries and a shake.

But that's not what I want to ask Ivan. It was ages ago; we've made self-criticisms; we're Groucho Marxists. The here and now of the matter is that tonight I'm blindly furious, and seek advice on what to do. Not how to dissipate the rage—he will be so alarmed!—but rather how to channel it: to be, while not a killer or rapist, then someone dynamic and edgy, worth keeping an eye on.

Only it is Ivan who is fuming. About Remy, apparently, and the waitress Chantal. He goes on for so long about this, and uses such harsh language, that it finally dawns on me to inquire about Denis.

"The name rings a bell. . . ." he answers.

The name belongs to the man Ivan has been living with for the last six months. Though I've met him several times, in noisy bars and at one dinner party, I can't say I've ever really spoken with Denis. Not at length, at any rate: not about anything meaningful. Nor has he feigned more than a polite interest in me. Ivan has always kept his love-life private, especially since the death of his long-time companion, Jacques Turcotte. Ivan's recent lovers, in turn, have kept his friends—the straight ones, at least—at a distance.

"Easy come, easy go," says Ivan.

"What happened?"

"The usual crap."

I repeat the question. In an unusual gesture, Ivan runs a hand down over his face, closing it into a fist below his chin, as if to tighten loose skin. Then he reaches across the table for my spoon. He wears a trim black suit and a narrow silver tie. His hair seems darker than usual, apparently with the aid of gel; his eyes, while bright, are half their normal size. Unless I am mistaken, he is wearing eyeliner, along with blush on his cheeks.

Before giving over the spoon, I glance at an upside-down reflection of myself in its basin: an ugly, graceless man, healthy as a horse.

"Denis promised to help me die," he says. "Then he changed his mind and fucked off with the video machine, all our linen and Max."

"The cat?"

"Poof."

"He took Max?"

"Don't act so shocked."

"But—?"

"Not quite the same thing, David."

"Same as what?" I ask.

He bulges his eyes. The connection slowly reaches my consciousness; I slowly start to sweat, to—I suspect—rouge a little myself.

"I'm sure I'll get visitation rights on weekends," he adds. "Our lawyers will work it out."

"I'm sorry about Denis."

"It's fine."

"How could it be fine?"

"It's not fine then," he corrects. "In fact, it's fucking disgusting. Like what Carole did to you. Like what Remy is doing to Chantal."

I must be glowing like a stoplight. "Back up a second," I say. "What Carole did to me?"

"Left you, I mean," shrugs Ivan. The second spoon is fast becoming a pretzel.

"But you defended her at the time. You said she had to do it. You even said, you prick, that in the long run it would prove to be the best thing for everyone!"

"She did have to do it. In the long run it will prove to be the best thing for everyone. But she was also living with you because it was practical, and then leaving you, also because it was practical. She never said that, she probably never thought that way, but that's how she acted. In the end, Carole was unable not to be who she truly is, even if that proved pragmatic and aloof. It's the same with Denis, only his true being is weak. Remy is a user, and is cruel. He's the worst."

I light a cigarette.

"Fucking disgusting habit," he says with perhaps unnecessary venom.

Not wanting to agitate him further, but also fed up with the abuse, I gently stub the cigarette in the ashtray. It breaks anyway.

"Serves you right," he observes.

Remy announces that the café will be closing in ten minutes, no extensions, no excuses.

"Almost finished?" I ask.

"Amen," answers Ivan. He nooses his neck in a body-length black scarf. "Time to *réveillonner* with Gregor and Titania. Pretty similar to *réveiller*, don't you think? *Sonne le réveil*—Ivan is coming out for Christmas."

What a curious language lesson. Ivan's French is almost as good as mine, and his Russian is vastly superior. He is, in fact, a talented linguist, and should be working as a professional translator, not a waiter in a restaurant on Mountain Street. His parents, who still save their real celebrations for the Orthodox Russian Christmas in early January, live in the same Outremont apartment where he grew up. The building is a five-minute walk from the café, and less than a kilometre from his place down near Jeanne Mance Park. He visits them—

"Coming out?" I repeat aloud.

"Wake up, Mama! Wake up, Papa!"

He nearly shouts the words. Immediately, he glances around to see if anyone has noticed. Then he picks up the pretzel spoon and tries to undo his work.

We've talked this over a hundred times. Always, our conclusion has been the same: don't tell them. The Fodorovs are in their late sixties, and devout, Old World, homophobic. They are also content to be ignorant of the truth if the truth is beyond their comprehension or, more importantly, their acceptance. Lie about girlfriends. Lie about bachelorhood.

I ask.

"Smooth the way for further revelations."

"On Christmas Eve?"

"They'll get over it," he says with a grimace. "I won't."

His plan is disastrous. Worse, it is self-destructive. I know it, he knows it. He knows that I know it. So now everybody knows everything. And you know what? It won't stop a thing from happening. I believe that is called tragedy. I believe some think of it as fate.

At least my rage has abated. Nothing like a strong intimation of death to calm the nerves.

We approach the counter, where Chantal stands alone. "It's now or never," I whisper. "Try something."

"Watch."

She rings up the total.

"Trade you a kiss for a big tip?" Ivan asks her in French.

The waitress brightens. Her eyes widen, her mouth curves. Up close, she seems less hard and more nervous. She also looks younger—a kid, really. On most of her fingers are rings; stacked halfway to her left elbow are bracelets. A tiny gold cross rests snugly in the hollow of her neck, the chain almost invisible against her tawny skin.

"I've brought mistletoe," says Ivan, displaying a cluster of plastic berries. Every year Remy lines the front windows of the café with Christmas lights and fake mistletoe. Every year he "forgets" to even plug the lights in.

"You only," she says to Ivan.

"What about David?"

"What about him?"

My grin holds.

"Those my berries, Ivan?" asks Remy. He draws up close behind his employee, his crotch, no doubt, pressed against her buttocks.

"I don't know, Remy. Are they really this small?"

The café owner glares at him.

"Ivan wants a Christmas kiss," I interject.

"Go on, Chantal," says Remy. "Give the guy a peck. He won't do a French on you, I promise."

She leans across the counter, as much, probably, to put some distance between her boss and her backside as to kiss Ivan. Her lips are pursed, though, and her irises show mischief. Ivan bends forward, expecting *un bec*, possibly a nibble. What he gets is a lathering: Chantal runs her tongue along his lips and then rams it into his mouth. Remy claps his hands in delight. Patrons clang spoons against glasses.

"Twelve dollars and fifty cents, plus a big tip," she says coolly.

"Yes, ma'am," answers Ivan. He gives her a twenty, and expects no change.

"I'm tingling all over," he admits.

"So am I," I add.

She *almost* smiles.

"Good night, boys and girls," announces Remy, pointing to the clock on the wall. Noticing him round the counter to clear our table, I hustle Ivan through the door. Still, we don't miss the bluster.

"My fucking spoons!" our patron complains.


Snow is falling. Weather reports were declaring it too cold for precipitation, but an hour ago a stereotypical Yuletide shower commenced adding another layer of white to the city's winter tan. We head up Bernard towards Park Avenue. A fake tree, planted in the window of a dry-cleaner, winks red and green. A Portuguese bakery displays an edible crèche, also lit. Choir carols drift down from an apartment above the shops.

"Are you sure this is a good idea?" I finally ask.

"I'm sure it's a terrible idea," answers Ivan. "I'm sure it's self-destructive and even self-pitying. I'm sure of two things, David: the decision to tell my parents *will* prove disastrous, and I *won't* live to regret it."

"Gay, eh . . . ?" I begin.

His answer, the ritual completion of a favourite patriotic pun, is a long time coming. "Fucking-A," he says without fun in his voice.

At the corner, I have to change subjects. The banality of my concern shames me. "The bank machine ate my card this afternoon, and I'm penniless," I say. "Could you loan me sixty dollars?"

"Ate your card?"

"I put it in the slot, punched in my code, and waited. After a minute the screen told me to contact my branch. Then the visor went back down."

"Must have been something you said."

"Have you got yours?"

The automatic teller at the bank on Park is in a glass room bright from overhead lights and slippery with melted snow. A camera watches us from on high. Ivan withdraws the cash.

"Me and plastic don't get along," I say back outside. "My bank is refusing to give me a credit card, too."

"Even with Adele co-signing?"

"I haven't had a chance to ask her. Tomorrow, I'll get Mother to commit."

Ivan, for some reason, inquires about my apartment.

"I'm trying to sublet it for the year," I answer. "Know of anyone who needs a place?"

"I might."

"Have him or her call me."

"Any time?"

"I'm easy to get hold of," I reply.

It's a joke between us, but also the truth. I am known in certain circles for my crank views on the culture of answering machines. The fact is, though, I am far easier to reach than almost all my friends, including Ivan, who own machines and leave taped messages for callers, usually in at least two languages, that range from the whimsical to the serious, the cheerful to the morose. People are astonished by my pick-up rate. People are bemused. They are also pitying; the guy is always home; he has no life! My explanation is simple. I'm home, I figure, as often as the next person. When the phone rings, I pick it up. I say "*Oui*/hello?" and then wait for the caller to speak. I am never annoyed at being called, never interrupted in the middle of something incredibly important—granted, a bustling sex life might change my view on this—and never vain enough or paranoid enough to have to know who the caller is, and what he or she might wish to say, before deciding if he or she is worthy of my attention. It doesn't matter if I am solicited: I politely decline. It doesn't matter if I am barked at about debts or duties: I promise to do better. It doesn't much matter if I am called names, wished ill health, a swift demise: I wish them the same back. The point is that I'm content with the contact. Often enough, I'm pleased.

Does this, too, make me pathetic? If so, then for once blame the era rather than the individual. Sorry I'm not neurotic. Sorry I'm not stressed out.

I am hungry, though, and after saying good night to Ivan I walk down Park towards a Greek restaurant on St. Viateur. It is closed, but across the street is a bagel shop open all day and night, every day and night of the year. A wood-burning stove stoked by logs jammed at the side of its mouth, like toothpicks, keeps the room warm and fragrant. The sole employee, a man in a smeared white apron, raises his head from the counter.

"Excellent with turkey, eh?" he says, filling a paper bag with bagels.

I wish him a Merry Christmas.

Balconies along my own street are already swollen with snow. Indicative of how wintry December has been, they don't usually reach this level until February; it is akin to a bread rising into its dome shape in five, instead of thirty, minutes. As always, the balconies stir memories. A memory, more precisely: a tableau. I know I promised not to indulge. I know I said, or implied, that it served no purpose. But this memory is different. It doesn't *feel* twenty-five years old.

Adele always refused to clean off the front balcony of our apartment on Clark Street. Her stated reasons were lame, and it probably came down to the simple fact that all the neighbouring mothers got on their boots and got out their brooms—reason enough for her not to. If I, a boy of eight or nine, hadn't forced the screen door open every morning to create a fan of packed snow, the balcony would have been sealed off until spring. I had my reasons. By early January the drumlin was as high as the railing, and I had diligently hollowed it out with a garden trowel to create a cavern I could lie in. The danger of the cavern was frostbite. The beauty of it was privacy; no one, including Mother craning at the window, could see down into the hole. She called the mound an open casket, which I didn't really understand. I felt safe in there. At night especially, beneath a nebulous sky and a veil of wedding white, I would lie for an hour, not moving, not exactly thinking. Nor even remembering, except for fragmented images, like being swung in someone's arms and tucked into bed, and orphaned smells: aftershave and hair tonic, dress shirts that reeked of cigarette smoke. Mostly I was just silent and still. Floating in water, feeling content, embraced.

In the drumlin, I saw what escaped me otherwise. I saw how my mother sat by the phone most evenings, a Gitane pinched between her fingers and a third cognac on the end table, glancing at a book and claiming not to be waiting for calls, sighing in fake exasperation when one finally came in, forcing me to take a message. I saw how, when she was tired or frustrated or simply drunk, she cast an eye over her only child that was chillingly clinical. I saw how teachers at school thought of me as a poor boy, a sad boy. How, for some reason, I fancied myself to be Wee Willie Winkie, running through the town. Never actually stirring, I would race from street to street in Mile End, calling through the windows, rapping on the locks. Are the children in their beds? It's past eight o'clock.

What else happened? Something epoch making. Something enduring. I'm looking back on the drumlin now, a quarter-century later, and deciding that, yes, it started in there, during those winter nights, with me all alone, kind of.

## 5

I WAKE TO THE SONG OF THE SILL PIGEONS. IT IS MORE A *purrt purrt* this morning, as if a night of merry-making has left the birds raspy and winded. How I got from the bed to the couch isn't clear. Who drank the bottles of beer lined up on the coffee table is also a puzzle, though the throbbing in my head and fungus covering my tongue provide solid clues. In the bathroom, where I swallow aspirin and brush my teeth, careful not to exchange more than a hostile glance with my mirror-self, I hear through the communal vent the sound of sloshing water, and of Lena Buber muttering to her husband Yehiel in Yiddish. I had planned to knock on her door and Boy Scout my way into paying her what will be, I suspect, her only Christmas visit. But I am already behind schedule. Brunch with Adele is in twenty minutes, and afterwards I have to take the subway straight out to Longueuil. Carole had distinctly not mentioned my staying for dinner; I will be back in Mile End by late afternoon. Lena's bath, and visitation, should be over by then.

The walk to my mother's apartment takes ten minutes, but actually requires, for most, a lifetime or longer to complete. Mile End is scruffy, working class and immigrant. Outremont is elegant, professional, and largely pure-wool French. Mile End is full of laundromats and dollar stores and parkettes without trees or grass. Outremont boasts cafés and chocolateers and public spaces befitting the estates of monarchs. Mile End has a garbage problem, a break-in problem, a wrong-kind-of-people problem. Outremont frets over cracks in the tennis courts and soaring property taxes and what is to be done about dog owners who don't scoop up after their pooches. Mile End is where most of us live and die. Outremont is where certain people are born. Oh sure, you can get there other ways, through a great job or an astute marriage, or else you can hunker down along the deteriorating rims of the neighbourhood, where passing buses rattle bed frames and neighbours get arrested in the small hours, or you can be a Walt Whitman-bearded, black-coated Hasid—a nation, if not a historic time zone, unto themselves—but in general you simply *don't* get to Outremont, because that is the accent and body shape and worldview that fate has dealt you, and for most human beings class is dismissible only in school.

I am thinking about how Adele got here as I ring her bell. She lives off the lobby of a small brick building, meaning I can both see the door to her apartment through the glass and hear my rings reverberate through the ground floor. After a fourth sounding a neighbour pokes his head out and buzzes me into the lobby. He knows I am Adele Guy's son, and knows, as I do, that Mother keeps an extra key along the top of the door frame. I let myself in. For a moment, I nourish a happy thought: she has had a heart attack, and lies sprawled on her bed. I am not being morbid. Illness offers a solid alibi for leaving a door unanswered. Death is even more airtight. Absence, however, as in inviting-your-son-to-Christmas-brunch-and-then-accepting-an-invitation-elsewhere, is way too outrageous—a jury would never buy it.

The apartment contains no dead body. It does stink of cigarettes, a hopeful sign—she could just be picking up last-minute supplies—until I check the butts in the ashtray beside her chair. They are overnight cold. Jutting up from the tray in her bedroom, like a fighter jet nosed into sand, is a half-smoked carcass, its head faintly warm. That is a bad sign: she was dressing in a hurry, meaning that she was once again late, and so rushed off without premeditation or intent. All this detective work renders my own hands unsteady, and I scavenge, finding a pack of Gitanes in the magazine basket next to the toilet. The smoke works like a soothing word from a parent in the ear of a distraught child. I am calmed. I am contented. Light canting into the living room casts the motley furniture and disarray of books and papers in undeservedly gentle hues: the browns and golds of devout scholarship, the radiant whites of austere lifestyle. How Adele got to Outremont, I suppose, is easily enough explained: she cast Mile End, and me, off. Once the link with Jacob LeClair faded—I looked less and less like my father from about the age of eight onwards, apparently—it was replaced by one with the neighbourhood. Imagine that: a child doomed in his mother's eyes because of where they lived. As if I wore a map of Clark Street on my face. As if I carried that place around within me and was responsible for its state.

The sequence of events is key. In 1974, at age eighteen, I announced to Adele that I was moving out, in order to join some CEGEP friends in a flat on St. Urbain Street. She had no objections: it was, as she sweetly put it, about time. Of course it was about time: I had been picking up the vibes at home for more than a year and, once I had swallowed the hurt, had been looking for an arrangement. Within a week of my departure she'd bought the place in Outremont. My first evening in her new home—on, appropriately enough, the night before Christmas—she declared that her two-decade-long exile in the desert was now ended. Adele provided dates: May 1956, the month that Khrushchev denounced Stalin, shattering the already cracked Communist Party of Canada, and staggering one of its most ardent members only weeks before the birth of her child, and July 1974, the month she moved onto Querbes Street and met a new neighbour, a television producer named Pierre, who quickly became her friend and lover, a counsellor in matters of career and personal well-being. All Adele Guy's years of betrayal, of personal unhappiness and intellectual entropy, were abruptly over. The sooner forgotten the better, Pierre advised.

Except that Mother wanted to recall her exile. For her, those years were exemplars of drift, both private and public, of a period that an individual or a society had to survive in order to emerge the wiser, the better prepared. Her own career suddenly flourished. Tenure at the university, blocked by spiteful colleagues for a decade, was granted. Her book came out. Her articles began to appear not in academic journals or newsletters but on the opinions pages of daily newspapers. She was invited onto TV programs and soon became a fixture, her persona a perfect talking head: the arm-waving, chain-smoking intellectual, totalizing in her views, scathing in her critiques, learned—she had lived through so much!—committed to Quebec.

What had Adele Guy lived through? She explained this to me as well. Three transformations, she decided. First, there was the teenager who campaigned for Communist member of parliament Fred Rose and worked with Raymond Boyer after the party's disastrous split, who helped organize the Hochelaga garment union and scuffled with police during a march to protest the order of execution against the Rosenbergs in the U.S. That girl became the young woman responsible for the letters to *La Presse* and *Le Devoir* in 1956 publicly shrugging off Stalin's crimes, while in private she raged. The letters that same woman wrote to the same newspapers in October, decrying the Soviet invasion of Hungary, constituted a final, all-too-public humiliation, and she retired from politics to finish her Ph.D. and raise her son. The years she devoted to these tasks made up the "drift" and merited only a summary sentence. The third transformation involved Pierre and the Outremont apartment and the emergence of the "real" Adele Guy, the former Stalinist and becoming-a-former Maoist, the defender of Castro and Allende. The nationalist who loathed nationalisms; the believer in mass movements who joined no movements. The iconoclast whose ideas were, by her own admission—she was, and still is, almost aggressively honest—orthodox and conventional. Oh yes, the former mother with, as far as I could tell, a former son who she finally got around to inviting to dinner in her new home six months after they went their separate ways.

How I adored her. Her fire and passion, her confidence and drive. How she never wavered, never doubted, and so could shout her opinions and sing her creeds. As a young man I wanted only the confidence for myself, but wound up with only the creeds. Worse, I wound up with the glib, trendy ones: the Little Red Book and Black Panther salute, Paris '68 and FLQ gibberish. In recent years, those had become Adele's points of reference, too, and she was less credible for them, but at least underpinning her 1970s politics was the urgent, at-home work that had shaped her as a young adult. She was authentic, in so far as she remained a person driven, for better or for worse, by ideals. I started off with the glitz, the red-splotched posters and closed fists, the sexiness and self-satisfaction, and *then* tried to obtain the convictions. Not by experience, either—no winters building schools in Nicaragua for me—but scholarship. Inauthentic? That would be unfair. But certainly untested and abstract, safe. And here's the kicker: I pursued graduate studies in Marxist history—

61

"Faith and Betrayal in the Spartakist Movement"—set as a goal a professorship mingled with activism, and even married a like-minded woman, all, I now suspect, in order to get Adele to like me more, to not file me among her disappointments.

If that truth won't drive a man to smoke two cigarettes at once, I don't know what will.

In fact, I light up the rest of the pack. Using her lighter, I fire eleven Gitanes, drag once on each, and then deposit the sticks in various ashtrays and sink edges around the apartment. Within a few minutes the place is in a London fog. Hysterically pleased with myself, I wander from room to room waving my arms to circulate the smog and taking deep breaths, the better to putrify my clothes and poison my breath: to piss Mother off when she returns and appal Carole when I get to her house, and perhaps induce her to recall the night I returned from the café looking for love, and she rebuffed me because of the smoke smell in my hair and beard—as strong, she had put it, as the scent of another woman.

My coat back on, my mouth foul and my legs unsteady— okay, I'm hung-over—I pause before the answering machine. The red light is lit, meaning she is hoping for messages. This activity stands in contrast with the state of Adele's other gadgets: a clock radio that has never told time or produced more than FM static, an unplugged TV, and a large box atop her desk that claims to contain a computer but is filled, I presume, with books. Of course, those technologies do not relate directly to her lifelong struggle with her own nature. The answering machine does.

I press the two-way memo button.

"Adele, it's me. In your apartment, beside your chair, smoking your cigarettes. Thanks for the Christmas brunch. The sausages were fine, but I thought the eggs were a little runny. No matter, it was the company that counted. Thanks for going to all that. . . ."

I can feel the sarcasm draining from my voice and the disappointment flooding in. The curt diction, the quavers at sentence endings: she will detect it at once and be exonerated by my weakness. I switch to French, in search of mettle.

"I needed to talk to you. Not about the credit card, though that's important enough. About when I was a kid. When I'd lie inside those snow drumlins on the front balcony. What I was thinking about out there; what was going on inside my head. You never asked back then, and you won't now. So I'll just go ahead and—"

Three beeps, and I'm out. Suddenly woozy, I assail the kitchen. The refrigerator is empty except for a slushy lettuce and the freezer is a frozen-foods display—meat pies and TV dinners, a leftover of indeterminate nature—but I open and close the main door repeatedly, in case I've missed something. A loaf of bread atop the counter appears mould-free, and I toast two slices. Though Adele has no butter, her cupboard contains three jars of marmalade. I fold the bread slices into quarters and stuff the pieces into my mouth.

The machine now blinks. Mother will spy the signal from the doorway and, anxious as a war bride checking the mail, hurry over to the table with her hat and gloves still on, her boots pooling water on the hardwood.

I revert to brisk English. "I forgot one thing. I was probably having fits on the balcony. Have I ever mentioned that I have psychomotor epilepsy? I guess it's never come up. I guess I've never detected much interest from you in either my body or my mind. For that matter, have we ever discussed the breakdown of my marriage or the fact that Natalie, too, is being raised by one parent? I guess that hasn't come up, either. Oh yes, and Jacob. My father, I mean. Have we ever really talked about him? Like, say, what happened to the guy? Where he went, who he went with? I think you loved him, Adele. I think he's the only person you've ever loved. Including, I mean excluding, Pierre and—"

Saved by the beeps? I suspect so. Ever the Wee Willie Winkie, I make a quick tour of the smoke rooms, extinguishing the cigarettes into ashtrays and sinks. It is hard not to be disgusted with oneself in these circumstances. To start off cool and ironic, to end up plaintive and needy. Of course, I could erase the message, leave only the cigarette scars and smoggy windows. I could doctor the evidence so she would have to be impressed by my calculating revenge. But I am a child of Watergate, I guess. Let the record show.

The subway blasts through a tunnel under the St. Lawrence Seaway, swaying from side to side, smelling faintly of oil. I have a car to myself and sit with my eyes closed, hands folded across my stomach. Leaving the island of Montreal has become an oddly unsettling experience. Granted, I've never been much of a traveller—a month in Europe as an undergraduate, a few train trips to Toronto to use the archives at York University—and have always lived in Mile End. Still, a twenty-minute ride to a southshore suburb hardly seems reason enough to feel displaced. To counter the sensation, I ponder a detail of Chinese grammar. In the oral language, verbs have a single tense: the present. Speakers are obliged to make clear if they are talking about a past act or a future intent; the use of precise sequences, called time words, is vital. Zuo Chang once illustrated with a strange example. "In Beijing," he said, "I live with Zhou Hong. In Montreal, I live with Suzanne." Confused, I asked if the verb "to live with," as in *cohabitate*, was identical to the verb "to stay with," as in *to share an apartment*. Zuo didn't understand my question. He continued: "Before, my wife is Zhou Hong. Now, I am without a wife." Again, I had a query: What was the difference between "having" a wife, as in *to be married*, and being "with" your wife, as in *together*? This time, he ignored me. "In the future," he summarized, "I have a wife again." "You mean when Zhou Hong comes to Canada?" I immediately asked. "No," he immediately answered. "You mean she *isn't* coming to Canada?" I wondered. To this question, he frowned. "It's your grammar that is wrong," he explained. "Not what you say—how you say it."

Funny how adults find ways to shade even rules of language with self-serving ambiguity. Whether the impulse is satiric or obfuscating or plain dishonest, the result is the same: you can't trust what is being named. Can't trust the words. As for the speaker, your trust in him or her will have to be instinctive, against better judgement, in spite of the evidence. Children, in contrast, approach language with a wonder that must make God feel young again. Natalie's first months of speech, as far as I was concerned, were analogous to the seven days of Creation. It started when she was about eighteen months old. Every morning, at five-thirty sharp, she would open her eyes, rise up in her crib, and commence naming things. By sunrise, the girl had exhausted objects within her vision, and would call for transportation. To Carole's amazement, I, otherwise a hibernating bear to rouse, would bound out of bed to act as her coolie. Riding high on my shoulder, her right arm extended and her finger pointed, like a variation on a William Blake engraving, Natalie would indicate object after object and affix them identities, meanings. Her vocabulary wasn't extensive. But what she did with those resources! I tried to help, supplying missing words that would come to roost in her memory after a few repetitions. This went on for a month, at least, and if the early risings left me exhausted, I didn't care.

Do you know what it is like to slip into a child's room at night to kiss her on the cheek, and watch her smile in her sleep, because her daddy is all powerful and protecting? What that knowledge does to *your* understanding of the world? What it is like to serve a hungry or ill-tempered girl her dinner of chicken and rice or pasta with meat sauce and—watching her empty the bowl, the colour returning to her cheeks and the quickness to her movements—have swell within you a primal, utterly unapologetic pride: my daughter is eating! Is healthy and vibrant! And how, later that same evening, as you further annoy your wife by insisting on cooking a frozen meat pie for yourself, despite her offers to fix an omelette, you realize that, be she fifteen or fifty, your daughter will still seek the comfort of chicken and rice or pasta with meat sauce, because those were the foods that soothed her? What those intimations tell you about your own destiny? In our narcissism, we tend to confer upon the awakening to one's sexuality the status of most shattering discovery. Let me disagree. Awakening to the reality of being a parent—who we once were and how we were shaded, who we are now and why we are responsible—blows that squishy little epiphany out of the water. Not because being a parent makes us better or fuller or more attuned to natural forces. What parenting does is not attune us to feces and urine and fury and fear, to hunger and thirst and sadness and ecstasy, to connection and disconnection, attachment and separation: to all that we control and can influence, and to all that much more over which we are powerless, and must submit; what parenting does, rather, is confront us with natural forces, and shows us our proper place in the schema, and says, There, do the best you can. Compared to this lifetime in the jungle, your first proper orgasm is a morning at a shopping mall petting zoo.

The subway slows to a stop at a bright underground station. End of the line. Beginning of the mainland. Absurdly, on the platform I check to see if anyone is here to greet me. You know the scene: Dad steps off the train, sinks to a knee just in time to catch in his arms the beaming pigtailed daughter. Then he rises, trophy in arms, to greet the equally radiant wife.

"A tie, David?"

"You don't like it?"

"I remember it," says Carole. "Didn't you have this before we got married?"

"Sorry I asked."

"You look fine."

"And you," I inquire, on both knees in the front hallway, "what do you think of Daddy's tie?"

The girl crooks her head in mock puzzlement. Natalie's blue eyes are penny-round; her smile, when it is unclouded, is wide as a painted clown's. Receiving an unclouded smile, rather than one of her repertoire of tentative or half-hearted expressions, helps me unthaw.

She tugs on the tie. "Silly!" she says, making for the basement stairs.

"Can't I have a kiss?"

"No!"

I follow her to the top of the landing. Words escape my mouth before I can properly complicate them. "Hey," I ask. "Don't you love me?"

The stairwell is dark, and I flick the switch. A figure at the bottom darts from the light with a giggle. "Don't you?" I repeat.

I feel Carole at my back, and hear her sister, Lise, at the stove in the kitchen. I won't turn around. Instead, I will wait, hands gripping the door frame, my body language casual—I hope—and relaxed.

"Yes!" says Natalie from below.

I turn.

"Of course she loves you, David," says Carole. She looks into my eyes.

"Smells good, Lise," I answer evenly.

Actually, the food smells so delicious, and I have eaten so little in the past twenty-four hours, that the odours are making me dizzy. As usual, my mind has been racing since I arrived. No question, Carole's house is a proper home in a proper neighbourhood. No question, it is the home I couldn't, and still can't, provide for Natalie. What convinces me of this isn't the park at the corner with the new jungle gym or the local library stocked with kids' videos, or the playmates in surrounding bungalows or Carole's fenced-in backyard. What convinces me that my ex-wife has created a positive environment for our daughter is the simple fact that their situation triggers no memories of my own youth. Everything that doesn't conjure Adele and Clark Street represents an affirming image of family.

I hear my name called.

"Smells good, Lise," I say again, smoothing my beard with my hand.

"Thanks. But I wondered how you were."

"Fine. Okay. Not bad."

"Are we supposed to choose?"

"David is off-island," Carole tells her sister. "He gets discombobulated."

"Fish out of water," I agree.

Only I use a different expression in French: *ne pas savoir sur quel pied danser*, which translates badly—"not sure which foot to dance with." These days, I speak French with the women in my life. Natalie is as yet innocent of English, though she wouldn't be, had she spent the last three years in polyphonic Mile End instead of monophonic Longueuil. Spent, I mean, the last three years with me and her mother, in the neighbourhood where she was born. As it is, she won't receive any English at school until Grade Four, way too late. Carole and I used to switch freely between the languages, along the usual Montreal party lines: English for business or, in our case, politics, and French for love or, in our case, arguments. No characteristic of the city's personality delights me more than this linguistic schizophrenia. No formal representation of its duality can match the thrilling, unique disorder of the two tongues in daily collusion and, on occasion, collision. People who complain about the roar, or who wish one language to be once more ascendent, like the good/bad old days, appear not to understand the first principle of any dynamic personality: its fragility. Nor do they get the point about messes, in cities and humans alike. That what complicates also enriches; what makes us volatile also makes us compelling.

At least, so I hope.

Now, Carole and I communicate almost exclusively in French, in part, I suppose, because of our girl. I don't mind this. Not enough to complain, at any rate.

The sisters stand side by side at the stove. Though they are separated by two years, Carole and Lise could pass for twins. Same sensible faces framed by sensible sandy hair, same freckled skin and wry smiles, same blue eyes no longer wrinkle-free at the corners. I married the older one. If asked, though, I would be the first to admit that Carole Lapointe, an outspoken, hard-smoking doctoral candidate at McGill, chose me from among a gallery of interchangeable bearded men on the graduate union Social Action Committee, and invited me into her bed, and suggested cohabitation, and eventually brought up the matter of marriage, on the condition that we both agreed the institution was not to be taken seriously. At the time, I couldn't believe my luck. Nor can I believe it now. Seriously. Even after all that has happened, a gentle word from my former companion or a hug from my daughter is enough to convince me that I once was lucky.

Lise Lapointe, still unmarried, is the director of a retirement home out near Olympic Stadium. Her sister began her career as a substance-abuse counsellor at a centre run from a downtown hospital, but now heads the human resources division of a holdings company—owners of shopping centres and convenience stores—with its head offices in Longueuil. Carole's current lover, a man named Jean-François, works in another section of the office. Judging from the scent of one chair in the den, the guy bathes in cologne. Judging from the tie often dangling from the bathroom door, he has good fashion sense.

Natalie calls from the basement. I am relieved to have an excuse not to talk with Lise, but don't want it to appear too obvious. Foolishly, I offer greetings from Adele.

"How was brunch?" asks Carole.

"Okay."

"What did she cook?"

"Sausage and eggs—nothing too homey."

"Adele's style," she agrees. Carole has always liked Adele Guy. To this day, she invites her down to the house from time to time. Mother always accepts the invitations, always stays late, and often, Carole confesses, has a few liquor-sharpened words for me once Natalie is in bed. Professor Guy also smokes a pack of Gitanes per visit, the stench infesting the sofa and curtains for weeks afterwards. Lately Carole has begun to fabricate excuses to be in Outremont on Saturdays. That way she and Natalie can meet Adele in a bistro on Bernard, where the fumes will dissipate before reaching the child's lungs.

"As parsimonious as ever," I say. I have no intention of telling them what happened.

"Your mother is an important thinker," announces Lise, a fan.

"Kind of an unthoughtful one, though."

"As far as you're concerned. . . ."

"An irrelevant perspective," I concur.

"You can't help it if you—"

"You sure *smell* like Adele Guy's son," interrupts Carole. "Did you roll in an ashtray this morning?"

"It's a new cologne," I reply. "Like it?"

Lise crosses the room and gives me her iciest once-over. "Not as much as your eyes," she says.

"Okay," I answer, at a loss.

Natalie calls again.

"I should go downstairs."

"And how's Ivan?" asks Carole's sister.

I pause before this other minefield. "Ivan has his problems," I say.

"Anything serious?"

"Denis left."

"You mean he died."

"No, Jacques died. Denis just took the video and the cat and went away."

"I didn't even know about Denis," says Lise. This quality in Lise Lapointe is baffling; though she has never hesitated to show her impatience with, and disapproval of, her sister's (ex) husband, she has also steadfastly maintained what seems a genuine interest in the details of my life, and the lives of certain of my friends.

"He took Max?" asks Carole.

"It's the age we live in," I reply.

She, too, stares at me until, appropriately remorseful, I drop my gaze.

"I've always liked Ivan," says Lise.

"A lot of women do."

"I didn't mean it that way, David."

"Neither did I. A lot of women like Ivan. A lot of men, too. He's a popular guy."

I turn towards the doorway.

"I'm sorry I can't ask you to stay for dinner," says Carole suddenly. "It's just—"

"I have plans."

"You do?"

"Please, Carole. . . ." I say in English.

"I mean, good. I hope—"

The sound of my feet on the stairs drowns out the rest of her sentence.

I have two reasons for not being fond of my ex-wife's basement. First, I was raised in a second-floor apartment, and have since managed, no matter how precarious my finances, to keep my bed above the frost line. Too many friends are basement dwellers, and their attitudes, if not their lives, always wind up the worse for the experience of constantly gazing up at the world, like the inhabitants of dungeons in children's stories, and still seeing only baby carriages and bicycle wheels, defecating dogs and puffy ankles. Being generally unfit for habitation, suburban basements tend to be even more subterranean. Consequently, when they are used to store virtually every artifact—dressers and chairs, lamps and rugs, a couch still bearing the marks of Potemkin's dementia—of an earlier life, a life lived with an unloved ex-husband in a formerly loved part of the city, under, in retrospect, unhappy circumstances; when an ordinary cellar is transformed into a memory palace, and that mansion is intentionally left to ruin—then, there is extra cause to dislike it.

Once my eyes adjust to the gloom, I negotiate my discarded past to a spot near the furnace, where Natalie sits on a rug before a dollhouse large enough for her to sleep in. Her back is to me, and the furnace hum cloaks my approach. My daughter wears a red ribbon in her goldenrod hair. Her dress is also red, and she has on white stockings and black shoes with Santa Claus decals on the toes. The outfit is a little precious, but then so is Natalie. I say that with only the gentlest parental irony; she is four, beautiful and bright, and everyone, me included, keeps telling her so. I wouldn't mind kissing her ears—I used to nibble on her lobes until she peed from laughing—but she might be startled. Same with enfolding her from behind: my hands are ice, and would convey the wrong message. So, kneeling on the floor, I kiss the top of her head and inhale the shampoo scent of her hair. Closing my eyes, relaxing my shoulders. Until she says something. Until she starts to squirm.

The dollhouse is actually a stable and the figures the girl holds are players in the nativity scene. I remember the monstrosity well; built by Carole's father, for decades it adorned the front lawn of the Lapointe home in Laval. Then Jean and Lucy Lapointe relocated to a condominium in Fort Lauderdale and, in a fit of remorse—and practicality—over their desertion, doled out most of their worldly possessions to their kids. For reasons unknown, except possibly that she was pregnant, the fervent atheist Carole got the crèche. In Mile End, we stored it in the furnace room behind the apartment; in Longueuil, the stable has joined our furniture in basement obscurity.

"Playing house?"

"Mom won't let me bring it upstairs."

"Why not?"

"She says the house is ugly."

"It is," I agree.

"But a baby is being born there!"

"You know about the baby?"

"Grandma told me," she explains.

Except for a memory bubble that rounds out her annual trip to Florida, Natalie has no real sense of her maternal grandparents. For her, grandmother means one person only—Adele. She seems truly fond of my mother, an affection I can't fathom, even in a child.

"Want me to tell you the story of the baby?" I ask.

"No."

"I'll make it fun."

"Let's play something else," she says, rising to her feet.

"Sleeping Beauty?" I ask. Natalie loves to act out her favourite legend. Taking the part of—who else—Beauty, she curls up on the rug in a century sleep until I, the miscast Prince, sink to one knee and give her the required kiss. Her waking, a marvel of overacting and self-delight, is not to be missed. "What a handsome prince you are!" she always compliments.

"Not that," she decides today. "Mom and Dad. You be Dad."

"I am Dad," I foolishly point out.

"In the story, silly."

She leads me across the floor to the furniture, much of which is arranged, I now notice, as a mock living room. More precisely, it is arranged as our old living room: the coffee table with the water stains, the chair we bought for twenty dollars and meant to have recovered, the famous couch. Beneath my feet is the fake Persian carpet, worn smooth as marble, that someone abandoned in the alley one summer. Atop an end table teeters the lamp we picked up at a garage sale our final spring together, its shade made of multicoloured glass rectangles. Even this wasn't good enough for upstairs, apparently. Not the lamp, nor the half-dozen framed posters from the Musée des Beaux Arts and the Met in New York, nor the 1922 portrait of the Lac St-Jean Lapointe clan, sturdy merchant folk in Eton collars and bustled dresses, that her parents gave us as a wedding gift. Carole found none of these belongings worthy of her suburban shack? Stunned, I stand with my hands at my sides, awaiting instructions. Natalie orders me to the couch.

"Smoke outside, please," she says.

"What?"

"And stop trying to save the world!"

My eyes widen.

"Are you playing Mommy?" I ask.

"Don't you think our baby is the most beautiful baby in the universe?" she says, cradling the child in her arms. "Don't you think so?"

"Of course."

"He'll be beautiful. Let's call her. . . . Mmm, what should we call our baby?"

"Jacob?" I try.

"If she's a boy. But suppose he's a girl?"

"Natalie?"

"Good. Natalie is a beautiful name for a beautiful baby girl. Let's call him Natalie."

"Her, you mean. If it's a girl."

"He's a girl, Daddy. You know that."

"I know that," I agree, abandoning the pronoun lesson. Time is in danger of collapsing around me. The musk of dog, the sensation of the couch fabric, the presence across the rug of a doll-sized version of Carole, even my own weird sense of diminishment, as if I, too, am now three feet tall, a child awed by the dimensions of adult things: it is all adding up to an unwelcome plunge into the chilly waters of memory, both those running above the surface and underground. I pull back by turning petty.

"What else does Mommy sometimes say?" I ask.

Her feet dangle over the front of the chair. She taps her toes together. "You never liked Poke-him, did you, Daddy?"

"Of course I did, dear," I reply, the words ash in my mouth.

"You were mean to him."

"He kept chewing holes in the couch."

"He was a puppy."

"He was never properly trained. He belonged on a farm, not in an apartment."

"You killed Poke-him."

"I did not—"

"He was a nice doggy!"

From one of the many unhealed wounds along the back of the couch, courtesy of the much-mythologized Potemkin, I absently tear out tufts of stuffing. Natalie scolds me.

"Sorry," I say.

"Just like you," she sighs.

"What does Jean-François talk about with Mommy?" I ask, swallowing my shame.

"He never knew Poke-him."

"What does he talk about now?"

She ponders this. "'Have you seen my tie, Carole? I'm late.'" I nod.

"He doesn't sleep down here," she adds. "He sleeps in Mommy's room."

A thought, both terrible and wonderful, crosses my mind. "Do you think I sleep down here, Natalie?" I ask.

My daughter's face goes blank, her response to difficult, troubling concepts. Her eyes become not walls, as with adults, but clear, bottomless pools.

"At night," I venture, "do you sometimes imagine I'm sleeping on this couch?"

"Sometimes," she answers in a small voice.

"Don't be afraid to think that. Don't worry that it's wrong. In fact, it's true."

"It is?"

"I'm down here."

"In my imagination?"

"If you need me, I'm here," I say. "Don't ever be concerned that you've got no dad."

Even I cringe at the comment. Immediately, I wonder if I can manoeuvre Natalie into agreeing to keep the conversation secret. But she abruptly slides off the chair and plants a kiss on my cheek. "Okay," she says.

The girl bounds up the stairs.

Five minutes go by, maybe ten. The sensation is paralysing: that if I stir, the exhilaration will dissipate; that if I don't stir, the sense of loss will never abate. Finally, a voice calls down to me. I claim to be on my way.

"What were you doing?" asks Carole in the kitchen.

"Playing house."

"But Natalie came up fifteen minutes ago."

I shrug.

"I should really get rid of that thing," she says. "Waiting until my dad dies to throw it out is cowardly."

"Show some respect," I say.

"You wanted to leave the crèche in the back alley the same day they sent it to us!"

"You can't treat people that way."

She gives me a look of concern.

"I think I need a smoke," I concede.

Carole indicates the sliding doors onto the back patio. Large swaths of the glass are opaque with frost. Where the outside is visible, it shows snow flying upwards from the ground. "Do it fast" is her advice.

I fetch my boots in the hallway, but not my jacket. Make them watch me suffer. Make them feel bad. Whatever are their feelings, I do suffer: after barely a minute, I am horse-whipped by wind and doubled over with cold. A crowd has gathered to watch the flogging. Besides Carole and Lise and Natalie with her lips pressed to the glass, there is also a man in grey pants and a sweater. I nearly swallow the cigarette. For a moment, I flash back to the apartment on Clark Street, and to the men I would occasionally chance upon in the living room in the evening or the kitchen in the morning: unshaven adults with downcast eyes and Pall Mall auras who ruffled my hair and swallowed cups of black coffee and then left. Without fail, they left; almost without fail, they didn't return. The man inside Carole's kitchen doesn't remind me of those visitors. He is no taller than I am, and is, I declare with absolute honesty, of equal paunch and, if anything, more sag. Nor are his features exactly chiselled. Try puttied, and never quite dried. Worse, his face is friendly and open, even puppy-doggish. My confusion is great, my physical distress greater.

I flag Carole to open the door.

Instantly, a hand is extended. "A pleasure to meet you," says the man.

I wince internally; the accent is Parisian. "Sorry about my hand," I answer.

"Excuse me?"

"My hand must be like ice. From the cold. From being thrown out of my own house."

"Jean-François doesn't speak much English, David," says Carole. "And what's this about your—?"

"Was I speaking English?"

"You always do," offers Lise with still another withering look. "Even when you talk in French."

"I speak little English bad," says Jean-François in that language. He has a decent smile: good teeth, white but not blinding, definitely uncapped. His firm handshake is also pleasing. The cologne is frank enough, though, and no doubt the sweater is of cashmere, the shoes Italian. None of this makes sense.

"David is off-island," says Carole, forgiving me my slip. "He doesn't function well. Do you?"

"Huh?"

"Natalie, go show Jean-François what Santa brought you for Christmas."

She takes the visitor's hand and, beaming, escorts him into the living room. I need to sit.

Lise excuses herself.

"Tea?" Carole asks me.

"Coffee," I reply. "Food, too, if you have any."

She pours two cups of coffee, takes a plate of fruitcake down from atop the refrigerator, and joins me at the kitchen table. I know what is coming next; what I will be obliged to listen to; what I have secretly come to hear.

"What's with Lise?" I ask first.

Her frown mirrors that of her daughter. She glances at the doorway to the living room and drops her voice. "Lise isn't very happy. Her life is, you know. . . ."

I nod, not knowing.

"It isn't malicious. With you, especially. And she can act that way with me as well."

After a respectful pause, during which she stares at a point beyond my left shoulder—a sure sign the conversation is about to shift—Carole delivers her standard opening: "So, David, how *are* you?"

"Just fine."

"I'm interested."

"I'm leaving for China in thirteen days."

"So?"

"We're moving further apart."

"Don't try to be mean."

"It doesn't work?"

"It's not you."

*I murdered the fucking dog, didn't I?* I almost say. But I'm too tired to issue the challenge. When I reach across the table for the cake, my hand quivers through the air like a shot bird.

"Don't you worry that by going over now you're lending credence to the Chinese government's version of what happened last spring?"

I smile.

"It's funny?" she asks.

"I think so."

"Simply by accepting a plane ticket, and taking the job, don't you risk signalling that the world has agreed to forget what happened on Tiananmen Square?"

Her accusation is so pretentious that I instantly recognize it for what it is: a boost to my spirits. I sit back in my chair. When Carole widens her eyes to command a reply, I summon images of us in bed. No aspect of our separation feels more false than this denial of past intimacy. Is it such a fleeting, forgetful bond? I don't find it so. My ex-wife by no means exudes sexuality, as magazines say of movie starlets. Most would find her too brisk in appearance and manner: the practical hair and business uniform, the crisp diction and hardy handshake. But I know about her freckled shoulders and muscular arms, the way sweat collects in the hollow of her neck, the sculpture of her thighs. I know that she scratches herself like a cat every evening before bed, until she raises goose bumps over her flesh, and that she melts—pardon the Harlequin vocabulary—when someone massages her scalp. I know about sucking her fingertips; I know about the soles of her feet.

Her hands lie palms open on the table. Until twenty-nine months ago, my duty would have been to slide my own hands between hers, and intertwine fingers, and gently squeeze. That would have counted for communication. That would have spoken love. Now, I don't know what to do with my limbs, or with her thoughtless offering.

"I don't draw a crowd, Carole," I answer. "I don't turn heads. Haven't you noticed that before?"

"Everyone makes a difference."

"Everyone is important."

My laughter is happy, if a little manufactured. The sound emerges a raspy chuckle; my gut no doubt jiggles.

"How I love that laugh," sighs Carole. "I think I miss it more than just about anything else."

"Lise misses my eyes," I comment.

Now it is her turn to roar. For someone otherwise so controlled and tight, my ex-wife has a laugh that is curiously loose, even girlish. "Yes, she does," she says.

"There are still lots of body parts unspoken for."

"You know what we mean."

I do.

"Natalie will miss all of you," she obliges.

"She'll barely notice I'm gone."

A mistake. I realize it at once, and scramble to stop her from responding. "You don't have to—"

"The girl is confused."

I wait.

"Children can't be expected to understand these things. She's probably better off with one father, rather than one and a half."

The remark is like a cattle prod to the rib cage. Carole's eyes are no consolation: I opened the gate, she is walking through it. Reaching for the plate, I stuff cake into my mouth.

"Who's the half?" I ask.

She sighs a second time. "A year of seeing only Jean-François as a father figure will be good for her. She'll be able to think of herself as an ordinary kid, like the other kids on the block. She won't be so confused."

"Is he moving in?"

"That's not really your business."

"Don't get officious with me. I'm not some underling in your office."

Her hands curl into fists.

"Are you going to file for sole custody while I'm in China?"

"You offend me."

"You just called me half a—"

"Let's stop this."

"Are you going to try to take her—?"

It comes on swiftly. I should have gone somewhere for a bite to eat. I should have asked Carole for a sandwich. As it is, I feel panic, the urge to stand up and flail my arms, but also exhaustion, the desire to lie down on the floor. I close my eyes.

"David . . . ?"

I am silent.

"Are you . . . ?"

"Shh."

I hear her sit back, shift in her chair, then lean forward again. When she speaks, it is in a chastened tone. "Please don't be concerned," she says. "Natalie will always be your daughter. Go help those people. You need to. I understand that. I've always understood that impulse in you."

Though not yet ready to declare the seizure under control, I have to answer. "It's not what you think," I say slowly. "I'm going over for myself. No one else. I couldn't care less about helping the Chinese."

The silence is so lengthy I finally look at her. Her features have gone slack. I recognize the expression—she is presently hating herself—but am baffled by it. Carole scours the kitchen with her gaze, as if in disapproval of her own house. "We were different people back then," she says. "Different context. Different time."

Carole Lapointe was always a closet materialist, unable to acknowledge, deep down, property as theft, prosperity as exploitation. Unable, I suspect, to even truly accept the ideals we were touting, never mind live them. For all the years we were together, these contradictions undermined her resolve, jabbed at her conviction. For all those years, I exploited her ambivalence in domestic warfare, knowing full well that she was, in her own way, as committed as anyone. Now, of course, I see her failure to express an allegiance to abstractions as the sign of a healthy intellect. I also see my critiquing of her behaviour as hypocritical. Should I tell her this? Funny, now she needs reassurance.

"I know you," I say.

"You do not," she answers. "Maybe once. But no longer."

"Then I see you."

"Bullshit. You see who I was. You see who you'd still like me to be."

"Carole!"

"Sorry, David. It's just true."

The shifts are dizzying. The guessing and half-intuiting, the misunderstandings and calculated woundings: no wonder people are drawn to declare pets their best friends.

Natalie calls from the living room.

"Just a second, honey!" Carole and I both answer. The same words at the same moment with the same inflection. Naturally, we laugh again. Then she reaches across the table and covers my cupped hands in hers. Just like that.

"We've only the loan of them, anyway, haven't we?" she asks, her eyes brimming.

I do not know what she means. I do not, to be honest, know what any of this means. Still, I nod.

In the front hallway I thank Natalie for her gift—a travel guide to China—and help her don one of my presents to her: a hand puppet of Kermit the Frog. In keeping with the mood of the visit, I fight off tears as I wallow in the sheer beauty of my child—her natural sheen, her innate wonder. I ask for a kiss. She offers a peck. I demand a hug. She scrunches her eyes, exactly like Carole, then makes a face, similar—no!—to one of Adele's expressions. Undaunted, I repeat my request, and she acquiesces.

"Kiss Kermit, too," she demands.

"Want me to turn him into a prince?"

"Silly. He's a frog."

I kiss the puppet.

Carole and Lise, standing arms-crossed in the hallway, applaud my gallantry. Jean-François, shy in the background, says it is like a fairy tale.

"So it must have a happy ending," he decides.

We all agree.

"Say hello to Adele from me," adds Lise, as I turn to face the frozen sunset.

I knock on Lena Buber's door at six o'clock. She should be frying up a gloomy Christmas feast right about now: a kipper and eggs, tea with condensed milk. I have a fruitcake in my fridge that I will insist on unwrapping in her kitchen, along with a glass of cognac from the bottle I stole out of Adele's cupboard this morning. I will suggest we wait until later in the evening, once we've both eaten, and will beg her to let me tune her radio to the CBC, to brighten our festivities with music.

I knock twice more.

Partway up the staircase, I notice a letter sticking out of my mail box. I recognize the handwriting and barely keep myself from opening it in the dark. I do tear into the envelope in the front hallway, my hat and coat still on, the door still open.

Her script is gnarled, her French is precise. I can hear her smoke-brandished voice in every word.

> *David,*
>
> *Please buy an answering machine. The walk over to your place with this note will probably send me to bed. You know how bad my cough gets.*
>
> *All right, I forgot. My schedule has been manic lately, a blur of meetings and deadlines. No excuses, though, and I apologize. What a pity, too: I spent the day with some dreary faculty members, a husband-and-wife team devoted to every good cause imaginable, and to quite a few beyond my limited intellectual resources. These people are the new fundamentalists. They have no children, but are experts in*

child-rearing. *No pets, but are stern advocates of animal rights. Neither has ever slept around, but both scold wrongdoers, sigh at the general decline in morals. They've never been abroad, except to study Spanish in Guatemala, but speak with great authority of the lunacy of World Bank policies, the evils of U.S. economic imperialism. They have*

*their faxes and modems and computer links, and they bond with the likeminded, and increasingly set the agenda, dominate the discourse, without ever* seeing *anything, without ever being humbled by the strangeness of experience, the stark difference of skin.*

*At least my generation had kids. Pets. Travelled whenever we could. At least we smoked and drank and screwed each other! One should live first, and then devise theories on how to do it right.*

*I rant. Probably to deflect attention from my lapse today. But your attention won't be diverted, will it?*

*Was not telling me of your illness a punishment for my sins? Poor boy: lunging at shadows still. If Carole had not confessed her dismay at your decision to go off your medication in 1987, I'd never have known. Imagine a mother's hurt on learning years after the fact that her only child was afflicted. If it is any consolation, you did wound. A manly thing to do.*

*You want to know more about Jacob? About the only person, you claim, I've ever loved? You little shit. You are so much his son. I'll tell you soon. Promise.*

*Merry Christmas, David. Try not to smoke as much as you did this morning. And go easy on the cognac: your head will ache for days.*

*Adele*

*PS: Have you a copy of Jameson's* Marxism and Form *on your shelf? I can't find mine. Leave a message on the machine.*

Remarkably, I cross the room to the shelves, frightening the sill pigeons in my haste, and scan the rows for the title. Still in my winter ware, slickening the hardwood with melting snow, I grab Fredric Jameson and head for the phone. It takes some fortitude, and a lot of self-name calling, to make Mother wait until the morning for her book.

# 6

ZUO CHANG KEEPS CLEARING THE HALLWAY MIRROR WITH HIS handkerchief. Overcome by the cold two blocks from the apartment, he sprinted the rest of the way, unaware of the effect frigid air can have on the lungs. Catching his breath took five minutes. Stopping the burning in his cheeks and earlobes is taking even longer. He massages the ears while smoothing his hair, now grown into a baby ponytail. Zuo stands puzzled before the glass, as if the obstinate fogging perturbs him. He wears an expensive Nehru shirt and grey wool pants. His aftershave is subtle. His handkerchief has been ironed.

Five months have made all the difference for my teacher. Back in September, he turned up for our first lesson in standard Chinese-in-exile apparel: an ill-fitting plaid shirt, highwater polyester pants belted as tightly as possible, white gym socks. The uniform—of poverty, not bad fashion—instantly put me at ease. I could sympathize, empathize, with this man; we were both of a sort. Now, I am less comfortable. Zuo Chang has become someone else, someone sophisticated and stern, or else more likely has simply regained the stature natural to his demeanour. Montreal is open-armed that way; adopt a recognizable persona, play a certain part, and you will be welcomed. For Zuo, taking on the role of the distinguished artist and teacher, the handsome French-speaking emigrant is easy: he is simply playing himself.

My compassion is of no use to him now.

"Last lesson," I say. "Then I'll have to sink or swim on my own."

"Swim?"

"Sink, more likely."

He frowns, and I explain the expression. I also pour the tea.

"Zhou Hong is very interested in English expressions," says Zuo in Mandarin. "She keeps a notebook full of them, which she takes with her everywhere."

Of late, a lesson has not gotten far without at least one reference to Zhou Hong. For a man otherwise guarded about his personal life, he is oddly forthcoming about his wife. So pronounced and severe are his opinions of her that I keep summoning clichés, straight from bad movies, of an Asian ice queen, a smoker of opium and thin cigarettes, a thrower of tantrums and Ming vases. Their relationship seems far from perfect. Though she is eleven thousand kilometres away, Zhou Hong still manages to irritate her husband daily. On certain nights, he gives the impression that he has come to Mile End straight from a quarrel with his wife in West Beijing.

"I guess she likes the language," I reply. Speaking in Mandarin reduces me to brief, banal statements.

"But English is not her business. Not English, nor music. Her job is in the Foreign Affairs Office. Yet she still pretends she is a student: learning more vocabulary, buying new cassettes of music."

"She uses English at work?"

"Only with foreigners. Her colleagues all speak it terribly. No one cares. What counts is politics. Everyone else knows this, and devotes their time to making allies and fighting enemies. Only Zhou Hong wants to talk as well as an American. Only she focuses on her duties. People criticize her lack of seriousness."

Is he joking? I fear not. Equally strange, of late I have

taken to defending this stranger. "English is the dominant foreign language in China," I counter in French. "You said so yourself. Maybe improving her skills *will* help her career."

He flashes me a look suggesting relief that this is, indeed, our last lesson. "You will understand once you are there," he says.

The admonishment rattles in my memory. Last November I went down to a gallery on Sherbrooke Street that was exhibiting two of Zuo Chang's paintings in a group show called "Brushes of Fire—Chinese Artists in Tiananmen Exile." It was an odd event. Though the gallery catalogue, and the *Gazette* critic who wrote up the opening, described the show as a protest against the June 4th massacre in Beijing and the ongoing suppression of human rights in China, I had trouble locating much politics in the art. A huge canvas offered a collage of crushed bicycles and mangled tents, torn banners and bandannas smeared with screaming blood-red ideograms. That one I got. Likewise a painting by a woman showing a police line-up of young Chinese men and women against a backdrop of a rising sun, its red once again suspiciously dark, almost vermilion. Their body language was languid, code for defiant; their facial expressions were neutral, code for alienated. But aside from these works, the half-dozen other artists in the show, including Zuo, filled their canvases and scrolls with the usual bending bamboo and scuttling crabs, cone-shaped mountains crowned in mist. Columns of black ideograms lined each painting, but from what he had told me, these were usually poems written hundreds of years ago or aphorisms extolling the beauties of nature. A few of them were even titled *After Qi Baishi* and *From Xu Beihong*, references to dead masters. When I clumsily expressed my confusion about the "fire" in the brushes, he did not snap back—as I had expected—but rather smiled patiently. "These are painted as our hearts and souls need them to be," he said in French. "As our sense of ourselves as individuals, but also as inheritors of great traditions, dictate. Their politics is their apoliticality. Their public protest is their privacy. We are alone in our rooms when we work, and are unbothered and happy, proud to be Chinese." I had never heard Zuo Chang sound so relaxed. I mentioned this, and he smiled again. "You will understand why I am this way once you are in China."

"Your story," says Zuo now. "Please tell me it."

My final assignment for our tutorial involved creating and then narrating a story. I spent days looking up verbs and casting sentences, even polishing the tone of the piece. Now, for no good reason, I suddenly doubt the wisdom of my tale.

"A man lives with his wife on a farm in Heilongjiang province," I begin. "His father lives on another farm ten kilometres away. One morning he decides to visit his father. It is winter, and the weather is bad. He dresses in his warmest clothes to protect against the wind and the snow.

"The man is gone all day. His wife cooks and cleans. Also, she paints their bedroom door. Later on—"

"Paints their what?"

I repeat the word.

"A farmer in Heilongjiang province would not have a door to his bedroom," says Zuo. "Only a piece of cloth, perhaps. Such privacy is not permitted."

"Not possible?"

"Not permitted."

"Anyway," I say, "later that day a neighbour visits. He is an attractive man. The weather gets worse. The wife invites the neighbour to stay for dinner. They decide the husband won't be able to return that night. Not with the cold and snow, the darkness. So they go to bed together."

"To bed?"

I anticipated trouble here. "Together," I repeat.

"Share the bed?"

"Sex."

"Okay."

"During the night, the wife dreams that her husband comes into the room. Next morning they find his body near the farm. He is dead from cold. Only the wife really understands. She sees the paint on his fingers."

I hold up my hands, rubbing my fingertips against my thumb.

"He had entered the house, found her with the neighbour, and touched the door?" asks Zuo.

"Exactly."

"And then killed himself?"

"More or less."

Zuo Chang's face is especially handsome when he is pensive. Creases vanish, lines smooth. His eyes, too, often shot through with fatigue or anxiety, drain of emotion, an attractive emptiness.

"If you had been the husband," I ask, switching languages again, "and discovered your wife in bed with another man, would you have returned to the blizzard to die?"

He answers at once: "Yes."

Though startled, I go on. "And if you'd been the neighbour, would you have tried to seduce the woman?"

"Was she pretty?"

"Their lives were hard and lonely. Where they lived was inhospitable. And that one night was all they would have together. Their only chance to feel sensual again."

That word! For a concept I rarely ponder, it sure flies out of my mouth often enough.

"I'd have seduced her," replies Zuo.

"Why?"

"Fate."

"Even if a tragic ending is likely?"

He stops to consider this. To be honest, I am astounded that he is treating my questions not simply as serious but worthwhile. I was sure he would find them foolish.

"Tragedy *is* fate," he answers simply.

"What about the wife," I say. "If you'd been in her position, what would you have done?"

"The wife?"

"Would you have let the neighbour make advances, or even made them yourself?"

"How can I reply?" says Zuo with abrupt impatience. "I cannot speak for her."

"But imagine you *were* her. Knowing what she knew about the past and the future. Imagine you had the chance to—"

He rises, declaring the question nonsense and the lesson ended. I follow him to the hallway.

"Sorry if I offended you," I lie.

He shakes his head.

"Don't you have something for me?" I ask, watching him don his new wool coat.

"I don't think so."

"I offered to bring a package to Beijing for your wife and daughter. Remember?"

He blinks. "No need for gifts for Ying," he says. "She is joining me here soon."

"Oh?"

"The paperwork has begun at this end. All Zhou Hong must do is arrange her passport and visa."

"Can she travel alone?"

"Why not?"

"She's five," I feel obliged to mention.

"Strangers will be kind to her," says Zuo, without so much as a blink.

"And Zhou Hong?"

"What about her?"

"When will the paperwork be done for her?"

I regret the forty-watt bulb in the hallway fixture. I need a better look at Zuo.

"I do have a package for my wife," he says after a pause. "It slipped my mind. When do you leave?"

"Day after tomorrow."

"Tomorrow night I will try to—"

"I can pick it up," I interrupt. "Your friend's apartment is down off St. Lawrence, isn't it?"

"Yes, but—"

"I'll call first."

In the light, Zuo Chang's face is impossible to read.


"The guy was lying," I tell Ivan. "About his feelings and his motives. What he's going to do. How he's going to act."

"You see right through him?"

"Hardly."

"Then . . . ?"

"So tell me," I say. "Given what I've explained, tell me what Zuo is going to do."

"He's going to look after himself."

"But not his wife?"

"*Sauve qui peut*," he says with an infuriating shrug. "It's the age."

"Fuck that."

"I don't make the rules, David."

"But you abide by them?"

"If by 'abide' you mean spend a year nursing Jacques while he died, and then abase myself begging Denis not to leave me, and now devote most of my energy tending to my own inexorable demise, then, yes, I suppose I am a slave to the age. How conventional I must be. How weak and superficial."

"Okay," I say.

"And you," he adds. "Are there no rules of the times that you are following to the letter?"

"I said okay."

"Regarding your response to, say, every bad thing that's happened to you? Classic child from the broken family. Prototypical victim of a loveless parent. Cliché of the abandoned husband. Stereotype of the grieving father whose—"

"I apologize, Ivan," I say, wiping my brow. "Profusely."

"Apology accepted."

We fall silent. Around us, Remys shares our pensiveness: the café is empty except for a bearded guy reading a book in a corner, and Chantal glancing at one of the French papers at the counter. Most afternoons the poolroom hosts a crowd of men nursing warm beers and bummed cigarettes in the hope that Remy will disappear for a few hours to get laid, so they won't end up thrown out into the street, driven back into their dismal St. Urbain flats where wives and kids and grandparents huddle, the TV on, no jobs to go to. Guatemalans and Peruvians, guys from Caribbean islands, even some local Italian and Greek dropouts: they chatter and laugh and shout across the small chamber. Silence, especially the absence of smacked balls or a rattling fooz-table, is unnatural here, like a film without sound. The café still stinks of smoke—the aroma is its natural body odour—and still looks as if most of the furnishings have been put in storage, in order to commence a renovation. That air of anticipation, of imminent but perpetually postponed improvement, is, I suppose, the essence of Remy Fidani's operation.

It is also the air Ivan and I have been breathing for so long that I wonder if we'll be able to adapt to atmospheric conditions elsewhere. Though the analogy is far from obvious, it keeps impressing itself on me: we are prisoners facing the prospect of parole. China as my liberty? Death as his? The thought is twisted. The thought is best kept to myself. The conversation, meanwhile, which started off light—jokes about disbanding the Groucho Marxists, advice to my subletter on living above an ill-tempered octogenarian and below kitchen-table sex fiends—has been gaining weight as both the afternoon dims into twilight and empty beer bottles, studiously ignored by Chantal, transform our table into a ten-pin bowling lane after a messy split.

"Should I be bothered that you care more about the fate of your Chinese teacher's wife and kid than about me?" asks Ivan.

"I do not care more about Zuo Chang's family."

"It's all you talk about."

"I'm concerned."

"You're obsessed."

"What Zuo is doing is terrible. He's going to tear apart his daughter and destroy his—"

"You don't fucking know these people!" he shouts, his eyes straining from their sockets.

"Calm down," I say.

"Am I making a scene?"

"Ivan. . . ."

"It'll all be over soon enough, darling. Don't worry your pretty little head any longer."

"It would have helped if I could have gotten hold of you these last two weeks," I say through gritted teeth. "Didn't you get my phone messages?"

"Did my machine record your voice?"

"How should I know?"

"Guess."

"Probably," I grant.

"Then I must have gotten them, musn't I? Got the messages, but made up my own mind about who I wished to speak with—no one, as it happened—and who I didn't wish to speak with, which proved to be everyone, including you. I chose and followed a course of action. I made my own fate."

"You're drunk," I say.

"I'm Terry Fox."

I must look surprised.

"Don't you see the parallel?" slurs Ivan. "A young man, also ill. Decides to challenge death. To defy it."

"Terry Fox had cancer," I point out. "And one leg."

"I know that."

"He jogged across Canada. . . ."

"And I'm going to languish in bed in your apartment."

"Sorry?"

"My challenge to death," he says, as if to clarify. "My act of defiance."

"To rot inside a crappy Plateau apartment?"

"Think the media will follow my every move?"

"You're potted."

"I'm a national hero," he answers.

I digest this assertion. "Who else didn't you return calls from?" I ask, anxious to anchor the conversation.

"Guess again."

"Denis?"

"With Max wailing in the background. Being tortured, probably. What a shit he is."

"The cat?"

"The fag."

"And your parents? Any word since—?"

"Not from Gregor, needless to say. Titania tries to leave messages, but they drown in her weeping and peasant Russian, which I can't follow. She places containers of food outside my apartment door every afternoon, like I'm in quarantine."

I ask a foolish question.

"Silly boy," says Ivan, rubbing his eyes raccoon-style. "Don't you know your Old Testament? Falls from grace are always permanent. Ongoing, too. Once you start, you never really stop."

When he sat down at this table three hours ago, I studied him, I thought, with some acuity: we hadn't seen each other since Christmas Eve, when Denis had just left and Ivan was complaining of the flu. During the interim, thanks to the single call he accidentally picked up—he was expecting to hear back from a medical lab—I learned that his coming out to his parents had gone off with a bang. Within an hour of hoisting a vodka with Gregor and Titania, Ivan was wrapping his neck in a scarf and fighting off tears while proclaiming in mongrel Russian-French that, in contrast to what his father had just proclaimed, it was they who were, to all intents and purposes, dead. Ivan Fodorov was alive, thank you very much, but was an orphan—naturally without inheritance. Titania wailed at this parting jab; Gregor tossed a glass at his ex-son's head. Ivan spat on the slammed door, shuffled home to his empty apartment, and there bawled like a kid who *had* lost his parents, in a car accident or an army invasion. Even knowing what I knew and guessing what I guessed, and bearing in mind his theory of human inattentiveness, I still treated my best friend to a shoddy examination, because, in plain brutal fact, I was too busy mulling over my final words with Zuo Chang and too busy pondering my two-week-old conversation with

Carole and too busy thinking—God knows why—about last summer when Natalie, having her second go at the "Otter" swimming course at the south shore "Y", finally did summon the bravery to keep her head down and her bum up, and traversed the shallow end of the pool with the instructor walking beside her; and I, one of *those* parents, clapped and whistled and declared her the bravest girl in the world. My daughter won't drown! was my crazed analysis. She'll live forever! If memory serves, I sized Ivan up this way: fashionably gaunt, purposefully aloof, and maybe—maybe—a little tired.

Here is how he really looks today: starving and exhausted, so distracted by death that a hooded figure with a scythe might as well be seated next to him, and be demanding the ashtray in order to fire up another cigar. Because his jeans and collarless shirt cannot conceal, as his billowy clothes usually do, a stomach so concave his hips jut out, like a science-lab skeleton. Because his cheeks have collapsed into a permanent pucker and the sacks beneath his eyes are purple-black, ready to explode at a pinprick. Because his skin isn't Montreal-winter pasty—we all resemble Bela Lugosi in January—but rather is splotchy, marked by faint scars that could be the glow of freckles that exploded a million years ago.

All changes in the last thirteen days? Hardly. Try over the past twelve months. I just haven't noticed. For which I would apologize to him, ask his forgiveness, if that wouldn't sound foolish, and be met—rightly enough—with the usual banter about our willed estrangement.

But he is clairvoyant, or else I've simply been staring too long. For, dropping his elbows to the table and cupping his chin in his hands, Ivan begins to weep. Not in dismay over my assessment of his appearance, I don't think, but simply as expression, gesture. The tears roll down his cheeks, hesitate at the cliff edge of his jawbone, then plummet. Our position near the blinded window shields him from gazes. It also paints his face with slats of waning light. I am transfixed by the light and by his stillness: he does not slump or shake. His action is dignified, and I feel flattered, even honoured, by the confidence.

"I'll remember," I promise.

"You're a prick to be leaving me," he says without rancour.

"Do you still miss Jacques?" I ask.

"Do you still miss Carole?"

"Not her," I reply. "That was probably inevitable. But losing Natalie, inch by inch, birthday by birthday, is a nightmare. It makes no sense. I've done nothing to deserve it."

"Amen," says Ivan, wiping his cheeks.

We count our collective cash against the empties. Thanks to a testy computer, I still have no bank card. Ivan is flush, though, and we prepare to assail the counter, and Chantal.

"Should I try another anglo joke?" I ask.

He rubs his eyes again. "How do I look?"

"Like shit."

He pats down his hair.

"Who are you trying to impress?" I say.

"Watch."

As we near the bar, I examine the waitress. Though still in punk uniform—the fashion is on the rebound, I'm told—she is transparently clean, hair washed and clothes laundered, and transparently, if unsmilingly, happy. Absent are the glazed eyes that fuelled speculation about substance abuse. Absent is the aggression, raw as skunk smell in the night, and inchoate anger. Chantal, I recently learned, is all of twenty years old. At least her manner now better matches her age: sharp movements, a jiggly foot. Bracelets on her wrists clack. Rings on her fingers drum the counter to a jazz cassette.

Ivan pays the bill, then does something odd: he places a hand palm-upward on the cash register. Chantal slides her hand into his, squeezes, just as quickly withdraws. The exchange lasts a second, and goes unnoticed, except by me. I cruise both faces. His is deadpan but, yes, she is smiling. Timidly. Crookedly. Revealing teeth yellowed and snaggled: a reflection, if not the source, of some deep and deeply unfair shame the young woman must feel.

"Show him Remy's latest masterpiece," Ivan tells her.

Remy often works on a drawing during slow periods, especially if the subject is in the room. I noticed him at the counter last week, sketch pad open, eyes all over me, and assumed I was about to join the gallery. Chantal pulls the pad out from below the coffee machine, checks that the "scumbag" isn't around, then flicks pages.

My face stares back. Quite a mug it is, too: the thick black brows of the ponderous, the sad mouth of the defeated, the bird-infested beard of the socially exiled. A reasonable likeness, unfortunately, if also exaggerated and mean-spirited. But this caricaturing pales in intent next to Remy's vision of my corpus. My head lists atop a gruesome body. I have no neck, no arms or legs, and a tubular torso notable for the patches of hair upright as pine needles.

"What am I?" I have to ask.

"A worm," says Chantal.

"A caterpillar," corrects Ivan.

The waitress and I examine the drawing again. Having a will of their own, my starved senses immediately shift their focus to Chantal: her studded earlobe and long neck, the bone protruding from the top of her shoulder, the vaccination scar still visible on her arm. Her nut-brown skin and freckle splotches. Her scent—of perfume, or maybe just deodorant—and faint body heat. My anarchic senses, especially the smell, see and touch ones, want nothing less than to jump her. In my mind's eye, her belly is exposed, revealing muscles juxtaposed with flesh, the pushed-out button poking from its cavity, the smooth surface beneath. The backs of my knees go soft; my groin tingles. But I also reconfirm how young she is, how much of an effort it is for her to simply stand beside me, engage in this exchange. And I notice above her left eye a not-so-tiny scar that emerges below her heavily—and purposefully, I now suspect—pencilled brows only when she is animated, and that undermines her tough punk mask with the fact of her having once been cut.

Do we communicate? Probably not. *I am a gentleman*, I would want her to know. *I trust your decency*, I could imagine her answering me. To which I would add that, as ever with men, decency and gentleness are perceived of not as qualities but flaws, not attributes but drags on success. Nice guys finish last. The best lack all conviction. Sticky, shadowy stuff, I grant, and outrageously self-serving. The presumed way of the world, however; the presumed truth about malehood. All very well to mock it, challenge it, seek a healthier self-definition for the species, but suppose the old, unhealthy self-definition, rippling with testosterone and machismo and—according to Ivan—suppressed homoerotic impulses, is still king of the mountain? Still kicks sand in faces? Still gets the girl?

"At least I'm not a worm," I say to her gently, decently.

"This drawing will help me remember you," she answers in slow French. For a moment, I can't figure out why her words so move me. Halfway out the door I get it: I have never heard Chantal speak a full sentence before.

"Explain," I order Ivan on the sidewalk. The air finishes the sobering-up job begun at the counter. My head aches.

"Too cold."

"Explain!"

He looks ready for mummification: a down jacket puffed by two sweaters, the kite-tail scarf, an earband under his hat. Only immigrants from warmer climates—i.e., elsewhere on the planet—and sick people dress like this in Montreal. He exhales smoke genii. "She loves me," he says feebly. "What else can I say?"

"I can think of one or two things," I answer. "Like, for example, that you're gay."

"Remy has treated her like shit. Most men have treated her like shit. I don't want to fuck her. I don't want to possess her. I won't cause her much harm."

"I don't get it."

"Neither do I."

"Are you going to be, you know, a thing? Walk around Mile End arm in arm? Use the plural when accepting invitations to parties?"

"Don't be ridiculous."

"Then . . . ?"

Ivan grimaces unironically, a sign both that he is grappling with my question and is feeling the effects of alcohol evaporation. "She says she loves me. That she wants to take care of me. I tell her she's nuts. I tell her it makes no sense. But she insists. . . ." He stops, bites his lip.

"It doesn't seem fair," I gently point out.

"You've still got a hard-on for her?"

I shrug.

"Poor David."

"Lucky Ivan."

Before embracing in stiff goodbye—our jackets hug, not us—I hand him the extra keys to my apartment, with tips on the hot-water supply and the sill pigeons. When Ivan asked again during our phone conversation if my flat was still free, and then offered to sublet it himself, I was initially just surprised. Only after I hung up did the truth sink in: he was presuming that he would soon be unable to work, and need to save money, keep expenses down to a minimum. I, in turn, had no choice but to presume that my friend was intending to die in my place, so to speak. My "home," such as it is.

"Will Chantal be—?"

"She moves in the day after you leave. I join her at the end of the month."

"Another sex-free environment," I kid.

"Smoke-free, too."

"I'll make sure Adele drops in to see you."

"She can light up on the balcony," says Ivan.

Our parting is hastened by the arrival of a half-dozen Central American men who are padded in pointless layers of cheap garments, and who look cold and unhappy, and would, one suspects, accept repatriation at this moment, regardless of the raging generalissimo or rampaging junta awaiting them in their homeland. In their haste to escape the Canadian winter they drive a wedge between Ivan and me, mumbling apologies in various languages. We accept the schism and go our separate ways.

## 7

NO ONE I KNOW IS HOME. NO ONE IN MILE END OR THE Plateau, downtown or the southshore suburbs. More accurately, no one I know in any of these places is picking up. Some of them could be right there in their houses or apartments or rented rooms. Some could even be listening to incoming calls. But all are screening and deciding against acceptance, against contact. More accurately still, all are screening my calls, judging my voice, the worth of my message, and deciding against acceptance and contact. Deciding, I suppose, against me. Paranoid? Facts are facts. Carole should have left her office an hour ago, collected Natalie at the day care, and now be well in the door—reading the mail, making dinner. But I get her machine. Adele, mildly contrite about Christmas, assured me she would be in this evening—my last night on the continent—for a possible quick visit, at least a good chat. Machine once again. Ivan, I know, has a shift at the restaurant, but I left a message with his boss, and was told that he hadn't shown up. Earlier attempts at contacting the assistant manager who promised to consider my unsponsored credit-card application and the ticketing agent who assured me a place on another flight both ended unsuccessfully: the bank never called back, the airline put me on hold for ten minutes, then cut the line. Even more traditional attempts at communication, like dropping by a café or popping into a local shop, failed: Remy was away screwing someone and Chantal had the day off; Zera guarded the counter, and couldn't, or wouldn't, say where Firoz was. So desperate was I for someone to talk with that I hopped onto the No. 80 bus down to Collège Plateau, where I found a new receptionist who barred me from entering the staff lounge, and then, once I blustered my way past her, a stranger correcting tests from my English course at my desk. Some guy with a beard and a gut, a broken marriage and an unfinished novel in his computer.

Imagine, then, my hysterical delight at the sight of Lena Buber, a ghost since well before Christmas, dragging her shopping cart out to the sidewalk. Lena in her black fur coat and *Dr. Zhivago* fur hat, her red rubber boots and useless cane, her poker face and fuck-you attitude towards everyone on the street and, most astonishingly, her resolutely ungloved hands that turn first pink, then alabaster, then the hue, simply, of death. Lena, the hunched figure out of children's stories—Natalie knew at once that she was the Wicked Witch, and to this day inquires after my infamous neighbour—who inches up the centre of Esplanade to the shops, indifferent to car horns and curses and threats to call the cops, except to occasionally turn around and, showing her detractors a mask of splotches and folds, cataract-milky eyes riven with judgement, make a disdainful whoop of her cane, as if she is shooing a begging dog.

Who could ask for better company? I throw on my coat and, leaping over a snowbank, catch up to her.

"Going shopping, Lena?"

"My Boy Scout," she replies. She never shows surprise at my interventions. They are inevitable, I gather, like the ongoing deterioration of the century.

"The road is icy," I say.

"So what?"

"Should I take your arm?"

"As you wish."

"Do you mind if I walk with you?"

"If you must."

As I wish, if I need to, if I must: Lena's mantra of non-compliance and non-gratitude. No doubt she is making some point about the self-interest that underlies most acts of courtesy. No doubt she is right to be cynical. No doubt, either, she is a sour old woman. There is even some doubt as to whether Lena was ever an especially sweet young woman. Temperaments may not be immutable, but neither are they eternally protean, especially, I suspect, for people who hail from what we "over here" call "over there." My neighbour is definitely an Old Worlder: born and raised in Romania, an adult prisoner first inside the Soviet Union and then a Nazi death camp, a brief pioneer in the transmogrifying Palestine, and finally a forty-one-year-old immigrant to Canada, though in reality just to Montreal. Yehiel Buber was already dead when I met his wife. Lena was ancient three years ago. Fed up, too: wanting to be done with it, to suffer no more. She told me so, often, without prompting. Fed up spending her days listening to English radio—her command of the language is perfunctory, but her childhood French is long forgotten—and sewing dresses for the same woman on The Main that she has worked for since 1952; fed up eating the same food and sleeping the same hours, and almost never dreaming: not since Yehiel died, she once admitted. I assumed her body would acquiesce to her mind's request. Especially during one of our six-month winters, when enclosure and isolation graduate from being temporal states to metaphysical conditions. But Lena lives on, her decay stalled, her decrepitude levelled. And her mind? Sharp as a decade ago, she sighs. Sharp as twenty-five years ago, she sighs the more. I joke about her subconscious wish to see the century out. A who's-tougher-than-who wager. A to-the-death bet. She shrugs, not an answer. She calls me her Boy Scout, not much of a jibe.

At the corner, a motorcade of puffing vehicles in our wake, we veer onto the sidewalk. Lena nearly falls on black ice, her habit of leaning on her cane for support making it worse. I hold her arm until the door to the grocery shop, where she shakes me loose. Her eyes tear involuntarily; her nose runs.

"I leave for China tomorrow," I say.

"I know."

"When did I tell you?"

"In December."

"I missed you on Christmas Day," I foolishly say. "Have you been sick lately?"

"Of winter, yes. Of people, yes. Of living, for sure. But otherwise I am fine, sorry to announce."

I pull open the door. "A friend will be staying in the apartment," I offer, my goodwill dissipating. "Ivan Fodorov. You'll like him."

"Is he a Boy Scout also?"

"I don't think so."

"Good."

"Goodbye, Lena."

She dismisses me with a whoop of her cane, too. No bon voyage or handshake or, God forbid, peck on the cheek. Slightly miffed, I decide against following her into the grocery to buy food for dinner. Instead, I continue up St. Viateur a block to another *dépanneur*. It is a hopeless operation, permanently understocked and unkempt—regardless, it seems, of who happens to be the owner. I go in there once a year to remind myself that Firoz Velji's place is far from the bottom of the barrel. To read the price on a tin of soup I have to wipe away the dust.

To pay for the soup I must endure the furious stares of the teenager working the cash register. The boy, who looks Lebanese, bags the tin, takes my money and makes change all with the same inexplicable hostility, underlined by an equally mysterious fear, on his face. I do not engage him in idle chat.

Twenty minutes later, the soup simmering on the stove, the tape player emitting a barnyard chorus of Chinese vowels— *waaa . . . uuuh . . . waa-uuh-laa*—which I mimic, my lower jaw dropping to my chest to get around the orotund sounds, I answer a knock on the door. I am hoping it is Ivan; I am worried it might be Adele. It is the police. The Montreal Urban Commission police, to be exact. Three MUC uniforms crowd the snowy landing. As if a photo-op for the new multicultural force, the crew includes one standard small-eyed guy, a young cop-of-colour, the shade being the varnish hue of South America, and, amazingly, a bottle-blonde woman. Though impressed by the spectrum, I am still leery. Cops, or at least small-eyed Montreal cops, beat innocent people up, sometimes badly, and occasionally shoot them, always accidentally.

"Did you just buy a tin of soup in a *dépanneur* on St. Viateur?" asks the cop in French.

"Tomato soup," I answer in English.

Why that language? Instincts tell me it is prudent.

But my reply leads the police to invite themselves into the hallway. The woman and the allophone slip past me. They seem busy with their hands. I am about to provide a French version of the answer when the senior cop grabs my arms and wraps them around my back. I am too surprised to react— the idea, no doubt—and dumbly permit my wrists to be bound. I feel a pull, then a tightening.

"The store owner has identified you," he says.

"What?"

"You're under arrest for armed robbery."

"I am?"

The remark is stupid; clearly, I am under arrest; clearly, I have done something wrong. Despite my years of street activism, which included the inevitable demonstrations-gone-awry, I've never been handcuffed before, nor faced the prospect of jail. I should be thinking about this. The metal cuts into my skin—a strong focusing mechanism—but still my mind wanders weirdly. The small-eyed officer's French is amazing: thickened with joual and anglicisms, driven by rolls of *rrr*s and *grrr*s of such thrust his mouth twists to spit them out. Working class, for sure, East End or maybe Verdun. As pure an expression of the local idiom as could be imagined. An accent I know intimately—to this day, Adele eases back into it when expressing solidarity on television or radio—but have all my life abjured. In its place is an almost idiom-free French, the diction and cadences of someone who acquired the tongue early on but whose allegiances ultimately lie elsewhere. Are these ties so incarcerating? For sure, I feel no allegiance to my actual father, whom I barely knew. It seems, though, that, contrary to what I told Zuo Chang, I *have* chosen his language over my mother's, and remain locked to it, and it to me.

Matters proceed briskly.

"Where's the gun?" asks the joual cop.

"The what?"

"Speak French."

I repeat the query in French.

"It doesn't matter," he says, directing me to the door. "We can come back for it."

Suddenly, the allophone officer, stiffening as the air fills with sound, draws his revolver. The action is so startling and terrifying—he aims the barrel into the living room—that I shrink away. This, too, is a mistake. I am shoved at the back of the head and in the ass by his partners, landing chin-first on the hardwood. My teeth jam together, a sickening crack.

"There's someone else here," says the one with the gun.

"Who is it?"

I am unaware that I am being addressed until a boot taps my left shoulder.

"No one," I answer.

"Listen!"

We all listen.

"*Waaa . . . uuuh . . . waa-uuh-laa.*"

"What the—?"

"It's a cassette," I interrupt, talking to the floor. "In the kitchen. In the tape player."

"Check it out," says the senior cop. Literally: "*Checkez-là*" is his command.

I mention the soup on the stove, and the young officer agrees to turn it off. Next the phone rings. First time in almost seventy-two hours, I silently calculate. Curiously, the police ignore the sound. As I am being hauled to my feet, I count the rings: five, six, seven. Who would have been so patient? Not Ivan. Not Adele. It must have been Carole. With the receiver to her ear and Natalie by her side. The child watching her mother, waiting to be told to take the phone and say hello to her dad, wish him adieu and farewell and even *zaijian*, the Chinese expression I taught her.

"Hey, buddy," says the small-eyed cop. "You stoned or what?"

I return to the matter at hand. "You've made a mistake" is all I manage.

He has been waiting for this. "No mistake," he says. "Armed robbery, two counts. We have it on videotape."

"Videotape?"

"We know who you are."

To slide into the rear seat of the first of two cruisers blocking the street, I must follow instructions: lower my head and relax my upper body, let the woman guide me under the door frame. To avoid the spikes of pain that drive into my shoulders the instant I sit, the weight should remain on my legs. Any shifts and it hurts. The problem is space. The front seat is pushed back and my knees are pinned up against my chest. I try to keep still. Glancing out the window is a bad idea; the old Italian couple two doors down are on their stoop, watching. Across the road, the balcony smoker leans over the railing, his usual look of grim resolve replaced by one of ironic fatalism: another troublemaker rounded up.

Off we go, sirens silent but cherries flashing, through the streets of Mile End. The lead car slows at stop signs and accelerates into changing lights. Obviously, the police are carrying dangerous cargo. Were I observing the procession from the sidewalk, it would provide a pleasant sensation, a glimpse of lives lived on the edge. From the back seat of the cruiser, the scene corresponds to no reality I can identify with. It isn't happening. It can't be.

I close my eyes until the station.

The reception area is glaring. Though I am now uncuffed, I am also surrounded by a scrum of uniforms, including the three arresting officers. The senior cop, even more grizzled in the light, demands my shoes and sweater, watch and belt. A woman behind a counter takes down my name and age, address and occupation, mother tongue.

"English?" she asks. "With a name like LeClair?"

"He speaks French," says the officer.

"My father is anglophone," I answer. "A Montreal Jew. I learned English from him."

"A Jew called LeClair?"

"That's my mother's name," I lie.

"What's she, Greek?"

"She died when I was a kid."

Thankfully, she does not note this information. Instead, the desk officer rubs her brow with the nub of her pen. She has the big bones and broad smile of Adele's relatives in St. Henri. I trust the look: such faces are honest and upstanding. The woman seems tired. She probably has a husband and a couple of kids. She probably wishes she was home with them right now.

"Bullshit," says the joual cop. "He's francophone. He's our guy."

"Can I make a call, please?" I ask for the usual North American reason: watching police shows on TV.

"Do you have a lawyer?"

"No."

"Better call them," advises the woman. She points to a sign for legal aid.

"I don't need a lawyer."

"Yes, you do."

"You have a video of the hold-ups?" I reply. "Look at it. I'm *not* your guy."

I am expecting a retort. But her attention is on the forms, and she merely indicates the phone.

Naturally, no one picks up. There I stand, left hand gripping my pants to stop them from falling to my knees, right hand juggling twin tasks: keeping the receiver cradled against my ear, and punching the keys. Punching, I might add, despite a pronounced tremble. I am disappointed by the lack of cool, the clichéd evidence of guilt. But I am appalled by the memory that floods my inner retina, like a dike hole no Dutch boy could possibly plug: Adele in her chair in the

Clark Street apartment, fixing me with her Medusa stare as I fumble to keep the heavy black phone to my ear while scribbling down a number and a name. My unsteady hands becoming spasmodic if the caller is male—perhaps even a particular male voice—while my childish mind is assaulted by more snow drumlin images: hair tonic in the medicine cabinet and aquamarine bottles of aftershave; overflowing ashtrays and piles of boxing magazines; a couple dancing to music from a walnut-finished radio: a golf club—no, a baseball bat—being swung indoors. Despite the reminiscence, Mother gets phoned first. I show the receiver to the desk officer to let her hear the tart message, but she declines. Next I dial Ivan, cutting the line the instant I hear his machine click in. No way I'll phone Carole. No way I'll provide her with the ammunition. Now thoroughly rattled, I dial a number without a clear idea of who it belongs to.

Zuo Chang answers.

"Zuo?" I say, switching reluctantly to French. "It's David. David LeClair."

"Yes?"

"I've been, let's see, I might be late picking up the package from you tonight."

"What package?" he asks in Chinese.

"The package!"

He repeats the question.

With even greater reluctance, my gaze fastened on the countertop, I switch to Mandarin. "You know what I mean," I try to say. "The things for your wife. But I can't really talk now. I'm in a bit of trouble. I need a few hours to—"

"What kind of trouble?" he interrupts.

On learning what kind, his tone changes. I can picture him flinching in distaste, as if a sock was being waved under his nose, while pushing a bang of black hair back up atop his skull. Of course, I can also feel the fear through the phone line: the natural, healthy immigrant fear not of authority as such, but of the arbitrary use of authority against the vulnerable. At this moment I happen to look up, past the woman at the counter, to a series of monitors on the wall. The screens offer bird's-eye views of the holding cells.

"It's a mix-up," I continue. "They think I'm someone else. I should be free—"

"Please," interrupts Zuo again, his voice strangely hushed. "I cannot become involved."

"I'm not asking you to. I was just wondering—"

"I must go."

By now, the cop is staring mouth-agape at me. Again, I recognize the expression from Adele's people: half astonished, half amused. I also know why she is looking. Which doesn't, unfortunately, mean I keep cool, though my anger is actually aimed at Zuo.

"What language was *that*?" she asks once I hang up.

"My own business."

"Suit yourself."

"And I'm an anglophone."

"Whatever," she shrugs.

My cell measures eight-by-four and has a wooden bench, a stainless steel toilet, a caged video camera mounted below the ceiling. Surfaces glow bright pink. Walls, ceiling and bench, even the concrete floor, are all painted my daughter's favourite colour. The only thing missing is paper patterned with teddy bears or balloons. The pink door is plastic plated. The pink walls are graffiti-decorated. Most of the artwork, chiselled with fingernails, makes no sense. I distinguish a swastika, a human eye, an erect penis.

My escort to the chamber informs me that I will have to wait until the on-duty detective has finished his dinner. A proper meal, I'm sure: meat and potatoes, salad and bread. The chief's dining might end in an hour, two hours, or not until the morning. In the meantime, I should reflect on my misdeeds and compose my confession. Also listen to my stomach growl. Swallow hunger burps.

Thinking I have time to kill, I lie on the bench, hands folded across my chest, eyes resolutely closed to the—I presume—confession-provoking pinkness. My heart thumps and my thoughts blow around like a newspaper on a subway platform, but otherwise I feel self-possessed, in control—not close to the edge at all. The cell, if anything, is nicely quiet, and the lack of options obliges me to do what I probably ought to: relax, calm down. In my head is the sound of the camera lens advancing from its socket as authority figures zoom in on my face for clues. They must see nothing—without the eyes, there is nothing to examine in a human face—for the scrape of shoes in the corridor soon jars me from my repose. A key is inserted. The door swings back.

"Get out," I am instructed.

The detective identifies himself as Jean Desjardins. He also identifies his suspect shortly after sitting across a table from me in an office up a flight of stairs and down another corridor. The office is no bigger than the holding cell. Though it isn't pink, it also isn't decorated, except for two posters on the walls. The posters, curiously enough, extol the tourist pleasures of China. One features a photo of the Yangtze Gorges, the other the Temple of Heaven in Beijing. Jean Desjardins is a fortyish man with hair plastered to his skull and an Adam's apple that rises and falls in his throat with mechanical regularity. His face should not be so lined. He should not cough the way he coughs, nor squint the way he squints as he reads from a file. His hands should be steadier; he sure shouldn't light up two cigarettes in five minutes.

"Your name is Pierre Clermont," he reads in French. "You're twenty-nine, five-foot-ten, one hundred and seventy pounds. A juvenile offender and reform-school flunky. A drug addict and petty thief. Twice you robbed that grocer on St. Viateur on the same night, waving a hand gun, taking only cigarettes and beer. Not very smart, Pierre. Not very ambitious."

"I'm thirty-four," I reply in English. "Five-seven, two hundred pounds. Didn't you check my wallet?"

"You had only a medicare card."

"So?"

"Easy I.D. to fake. No credit cards, eh?"

"I have a passport in my apartment."

Detective Desjardins lowers the file. "Why do you need a passport?" he asks.

"To travel abroad."

"What?"

I repeat the answer in French.

"See," says the cop. "You speak French."

"But not as my first language."

"Bullshit," he asserts, reading again from the page. "It says here that Pierre Clermont is unilingual. You can't even speak English, let alone claim it as—"

"I can't speak English?" I interrupt.

"Not according to the file."

"But I'm—"

"Wipe the smile."

I wipe the smile from my face. Two factors encourage me to do so: the muscle in the detective's jaw that jumps when he becomes agitated, and his sheer proximity, which would allow him to launch a punch without having to stretch. Not that the man appears coiled for violence. He appears coiled for another cigarette.

"You don't speak English and you don't have a passport under the name of LeClair," he summarizes. "Unless it's fake as well."

"Just look at the video," I say.

"We have."

"Then you know it's not me."

"But it is you."

"What?" I blurt in French.

Jean Desjardins reclines in his chair. Deliberately he taps his pack of cigarettes until two sticks pop up. One he places between his own lips. The other is tossed across the table at me. My hands remain in my lap. As a result, the cigarette bounces off my forearm and falls to the floor.

"Don't smoke," I explain.

For the next two hours I contemplate the idiocy of that lie. Maybe I can hide the fact that my mother is alive and well in Outremont. But a two-pack-a-day habit? Surely I smell like an ashtray. Surely I look like an ashtray. The stained fingertips and sallow skin, the putrid clothes: short of an arm tattooed with track marks, my addiction is among the most difficult to disguise. No question, I need a cigarette now. No question, the cell is getting to me. Efforts at regaining the Zen calm I had before the first interview fail. Efforts at *not* mulling over the pinkness that swarms my senses also flounder. As for my attempt to pee beneath the camera's gaze, it ends in disaster. Stupidly, I refuse to let my pants sag down around my ankles: too much cheap vaudeville. So I unzip and hold the fabric in one hand, the wick in the other. But then I feel the lens, acting like some Sistine Chapel deity, bear down on the activity. Hands are raised to block the sight-line. Pants collapse like a tent; wick goes mad as a sprung garden hose.

Thinking about Natalie often saves me from wallowing in my own consciousness. Lots of Montrealers I know defer, or even pass on, having kids because they're sufficiently entertained by their own various selves: sexual, emotional, intellectual and so on. They're confident they make good company. They're happy to join clubs that would have people like them as members. Children, they correctly guess, make you not only lousy company and get you kicked out of clubs, they also pick fights with your precious inner companions. They rope-a-dope the emotional, wear down the intellectual, KO the sexual. They leave you punch-drunk. They knock the self right out of you. For many, the fight is a mismatch, a rigged card. They didn't see it coming. They weren't properly trained. For me, the primary appeal of having a child was precisely *to* get walloped this way. So inadequate were my various selves that I secretly longed to have my bells rung, my slate wiped clean. Thus, baby and parent could discover the world together.

Only I forgot one thing. I was thirty when Natalie was born, and even when politely asked, the past doesn't accede to the present so easily. Full of crap and the same old complaints, my pre-dad consciousness hangs tough, daring me to pretend I'm any different, mocking private measures of change. But if the coat can't be thrown out, it can at least be relegated once in a while to a closet. Musing about my daughter allows for this. Usually, the thoughts swirl around images of flow and fragility and the temporal beauty of human connection. Most often, I draw on songs and stories for the sentiments. Not true: I use these sources to uncover the self I know is there. As one who has tried to pretend the past away, I'm ready to declare that my real problem may simply be accumulation. The daily traumas of living—the deeds and disappointments, the errors and misjudgements—pile up as I age, like a basement of unwanted belongings, obscuring even my ability to locate the part of me that is capable of recognizing how glorious any life is. That blurred self, I declare, is the real one: it is who I'd be except for the mess. A poem I studied in high school describes a boy dancing with his father in a kitchen. The kid is waltzed around the room atop his drunk papa's feet, and though his ear scrapes against buckle and his dad is a rough, perhaps violent, man, he is still thrilled. Of course he is. A child's unconditional love for his parents is so moving. His faith wrenches the heart. Because it can't be otherwise, can it? The perspective, the relationship: all fixed in time, all beyond reclaim. The image brings tears to my eyes. Lying on the bench in the cell: fat drops that well up until they trickle down into my beard. I weep not into a sleeve or from behind a web of fingers but in plain camera sight, my expression likely contorted.

There is a similar line in a song I listened to years ago: a young girl, again recalling her youth, summons a vision of her daddy smiling as he swings her in his arms. For me, this tableau also contains overtones of tension, possibly of menace. The father is under great stress. The daughter is all sweetness. Despite the complications, they swing; despite the mess, they are lovely together. The song never fails to weaken my knees. I twirled Natalie in that manner. Before Carole left me: before the girl turned two. How feathery she was. How—I'm sorry—angelic. In the wide, high-ceilinged living room on Waverley Street, during afternoons of parenting punctuated by husband-wife fights, I would raise her to my belly, instruct her to wrap her legs around my stomach—"You have the moon in your tummy, Daddy!"—and commence spinning around and around. Our bodies fastened. Our gazes locked.

Faster and faster I would turn, the room and the apartment receding like taillights in a rear-view mirror, until we were truly alone: a parent and child adrift in some primal ocean. Not of flesh and bone, skin and hair, but such stuff: dreams and wishes, hopeless longings.

Are we really at once so vast and so tiny? The universe small enough to be contained by our imaginations but the cosmos too girdling to even notice our existence? I cannot reconcile these contradictions. I cannot figure out my place in any of this.

So I bawl. Whimper and sniffle, use my sleeve as a rag. To hell with the camera. To hell with whoever is passing judgement.

"Christ, you're a wreck," says Detective Desjardins. We are back in the office. The break has done nothing to improve his appearance. The delay has done even less to endear me to this farce. "Pissing on yourself, crying like a baby."

"Mind your own business," I reply, to my own surprise.

"You don't think—?"

"Do you have me on video or don't you?"

His smirk, never especially convincing, withers. "I was just looking at it," he says.

"And I'm robbing that *dépanneur*?"

"You're buying a tin of soup."

"Tomato," I agree.

"The kid in the shop told us his parents had tapes of the previous robberies. When we asked to see them, he said they'd been lost. Then he admitted that his father only installed a camera *after* the last hold-up."

"Is buying soup a serious crime?"

"The boy is positive you're the guy," says the detective, running a hand through his hair. "The parents are sure you're not the guy. I'm sure they'd make useless fucking witnesses."

"Can I leave now?"

But the cop, it seems, needs to talk. He lights himself another cigarette, incinerating a half-inch of stem with a single drag. "That store has been robbed five times in the last three years," he begins. "All the local grocers have been hit. The whole island is out of control. Too many drug addicts and punks. Too many foreigners."

"Where do you live?"

"Longueuil."

"My wife and daughter live there," I say, finally switching to French.

"Yeah? You should join them."

"They haven't invited me."

Detective Desjardins nods. He also does a mime: indicating the ring-finger on his left hand, he removes an imaginary wedding band and tosses it over his shoulder. "This job," he says glumly.

I am escorted, uncuffed, back to the front desk. My belt and sweater, watch and wallet are returned to me by the same woman.

"Does Pierre Clermont have kids?" I ask the detective.

"What?"

"Does the file mention children?"

He squints at the paper again. "A boy and a girl," he reads. "Ex-wife lives in Hull. Why so interested?"

I shrug. "Do you really think he has any credit cards, either?"

The desk officer asks me to sign a form. I should refuse, or else study the document closely, but all I do is borrow her pen.

"Want to tell me what language you were speaking on the phone before?" she asks.

"The queen's English," I reply.

"Co-operative," she comments.

At the door, Jean Desjardins suddenly grabs my arm. "Think this is a joke?" he asks tersely.

"You arrested me for—"

"A word of advice, friend," he says, bruising my skin. "Next time, don't fuck with us. We speak French or English with anyone who comes in. No problem with that here. But don't lie about your first language because you think we're too ignorant to get by in English."

Softly, respectfully—the muscle in his cheek slithers like a water snake—I mention that I wasn't lying.

"*Bonsoir, Monsieur LeClair*," he sneers, releasing me.

# 8

OF COURSE I KNOW HOW LUCKY I AM. I KNOW THE DATE, January 14, and the year, 1990. I know that Chinese dissidents, most of them kids, were sentenced to anywhere from three to fifteen years for their peaceful insurgency last spring, and now rot in prison; I know that the schoolteacher who tossed ink-filled eggs at the portrait of Chairman Mao on Tiananmen Square was sentenced to life in jail. I know these people were convicted in kangaroo courts lorded over by a system of justice that is little more than a mechanism for state control. I know the prisons of Ceausescu's Romania will soon begin emptying out, and that thousands of citizens, their lives in shambles, will peer at unwalled daylight and unblinkered vistas for the first time in years. I know the Soviet Union, even with Gorbachev and *glasnost*, is probably still holding legions of its people in prisons and gulags, individuals rounded up way back when on the most absurd pretences—buying tomato soup, say—and railroaded through some bogus procedure, then dumped into a shed or upright coffin in a camp rimming the Arctic Circle. I know Nelson Mandela is still not free; I know the ayatollahs hope to keep Salman Rushdie a hotel prisoner until one of the faithful, and fervent, can get to him. I know a little of what is out there. I know it, in part, because of what I've read and watched on TV and who I've spoken to. I know it as well because of the citizens who are *here*, in this city and state: citizens who were either born or else grew up terrified of their own cities and states, and had to flee, relocate. I know where most of the world lives. And, no ostrich, I accept that shameful incidents sometimes occur in Montreal police stations and prisons.

But still, the menace doesn't truly reach down to me. Down to the sweat pores in my scalp. Down to the pit of my stomach. Possibly this is because I am white and ought to be middle class. I believe bad things can happen anywhere but I don't believe that things themselves can be wholly, irredeemably bad. An ex-Marxist who queries systemic rot? Worse, a humanist who doubts that states are capable of collective evil? Ask Andrei Sakharov. Ask Wei Jingsheng.

Or Zuo Chang? I am, after all, hurrying along St. Lawrence to his place. It is near midnight; it is minus twenty-two; the wind blasting up the boulevard is arctic gulag. I will, moreover, be waking my Chinese teacher up to, what, collect a package of soaps and perfumes and perhaps some cassettes of music?

I have the address memorized, and count off the three-storey walk-ups on Villeneuve Street until reaching, I hope, the right one. Suzanne-the-UQAM-professor owns the building, Zuo Chang explained, and occupies the ground floor. I knock on the door, not hard, not like the police. Then I knock again, still not like the police but like someone freezing on the front step. My third knock, arguably, is one of *those* nocturnal summons. By now I am praying I heard him right: 23 Villeneuve. I am praying because virtually across the road stands number 32, and it is also a walk-up, also has a ground floor flat.

The door opens. Mercifully, the face that greets me is his, albeit a frowning version. He wears a white bathrobe and slippers. His hair is in disarray, his eyes are dull with sleep. Not too dull, though: before greeting me Zuo closes an inner door, limiting my vision to the foyer.

"I didn't think you'd come," he says.

"I was delayed."

As if just remembering our phone call earlier this evening, he stares past me to the street.

"It was a mistake, Zuo. Everything has been cleared up."

"You were arrested?"

"All cleared up now," I repeat.

"Impossible," he says.

"What?"

A voice calls out from within the apartment. I recognize Suzanne from her answering-machine message. At once, I know I'd better keep shuffling my feet: I won't be getting invited in.

"Come back to bed," she commands.

"In a minute," he answers with a look that is far from inscrutable.

Not waiting for a welcome, I step inside the foyer. Zuo can hardly object; the breeze is furling his robe. I am anxious to study his face, but he is anxious to study the floor.

"The package is in the kitchen," he says softly. "Stay here, please."

So distracted, and possibly embarrassed, is Zuo Chang that he fails to shut the inner door properly. When trapped air reopens it, I intrude on the dimness. Five metres of hallway are faintly visible, enough, based on experience, to size up the apartment. Once a collection of boxy rooms off a long corridor, home to a pre-Quiet Revolution Catholic or Jewish brood, the flat has recently undergone a baby-boomer renovation. Walls have been knocked down to blur useless kids' bedrooms into a single living space. The original brick has been exposed and remortared, without worry of chalk or crayon markings; the hardwood floor, a mess if scuffed with heels and grinding toys, is all varnished glitter. A kitchen, its design oblivious to tiny hands and flaring burners, centres the main area, along with a standing fireplace, positioned without undue fretting over who might brush against it. Besides the self-contained master bedroom, the only other chamber is a small study at the back. It is ideal for weekend guests. Light from the street illumes a spare refinement to Suzanne's decoration. Plenty of sleek electronic gadgets. Plenty of nice bought-on-trips-abroad things.

Where, I briefly wonder, will five-year-old Zuo Ying sleep? Her first days in Canada, away from Beijing and her mother, in the house of a woman she cannot communicate with, but who is clearly important to her father, and therefore to her: where will this bewildered youngster rest her head? No doubt Professor Suzanne will gladly give her study over to the girl. With pleasure! she will say. The poor child must be so disoriented. She should call the room—and the apartment— home. For the time being, at least. Until other arrangments can be made. . . .

"I didn't have a chance to wrap it," says Zuo, handing me a plastic bag tied at the top.

I hold the package up, unimpressed.

"Practical stuff," he continues. "What she cannot easily find in China."

"You mean the bag?" I ask.

He grins weakly.

"Is there a letter in there?"

"We talk on the phone."

"I can wait," I say.

"For what?"

"For you to write her a letter."

"No need."

"No need or no wish?"

"Take what is here, please," says Zuo. He pulls the robe tight across the chest. I should let him return to her bed. I should leave it alone. But, still pumped from the arrest, I am in a fierce mood.

"We never talked about Tiananmen Square, did we," I say. "Not once, in all the months. You must have been horrified by what happened."

"We cannot discuss this tonight," he replies, reaching for the partially closed door.

"Sure we can."

"It's late. I'm very—"

"Your opinion interests me. I'd really like to hear it," I add, barricading myself inside the foyer.

Zuo Chang sighs. Abruptly, and for the first time, he looks his full thirty-eight years. "I was horrified but not surprised," he says. "It is what usually happens in my country."

"Oh?"

"When individuals try to do things. I mean, things other than the personal. Other than what they can manage for themselves, to keep happy, to forget. When they try to change society. They get hurt, and sometimes killed."

"Is that all it was?"

"When someone is arrested in China," he adds, finally meeting my gaze, "the problem is never 'cleared up.' His life is never the same. Never again normal."

I absorb the criticism without a flinch. "If you'd been in Beijing during the student movement," I ask, "would you have joined in the demonstrations?"

"Most of the professors at my college marched once or twice. Especially the younger ones, those without adult memories of the Cultural Revolution. Staff led the school contingent onto Tiananmen Square one day, carrying placards and shouting slogans."

His tone is neither triumphant nor condescending: it is resolutely neutral, as if he is describing TV news footage.

"So you would have, too?"

"Of course."

"And would you have gone back into the city on June 4th to fight the army?"

He makes a sound like air escaping a balloon. "Only a few professors and faculty did that."

"Crazy people?"

"Brave crazy people."

"But not you?"

He shakes his head.

I shouldn't, but I do: "Why not?"

"These are good questions, David. A little simplistic and cruel, but good. Too bad you are not asking them in Mandarin."

"Nothing personal," I say.

"Of course."

A smile edges Zuo Chang's lips. It could just be the cold, though: we both wince as a gust of wind blasts into the foyer. Suddenly weary, taken aback by my own aggressivity—my impulse is to demand that he step outside for a proper fight— I decide I'd better go home before I actually *do* commit a crime, and merit a hardball interrogation and pink cell.


The Velji apartment upstairs is dark, but a light glimmers within the shop. Not one of the fluorescent tubes: a yellowish blur near the front. Still a half-block away, I see the light as the welcoming candle in the window of an isolated farmhouse.

My first knock on the door goes unanswered. So does my second. I am about to hammer on the glass when it occurs to me that Firoz may have a good reason for not answering his door in the middle of the night.

I call him by name. I identify myself.

The door is cracked. A head sticks out. "My friend," says Firoz gently.

"Midnight inventory?"

"Come in," he replies.

The light emanates from a lamp on the floor beside the cash register. Next to it is a mattress made up as a bed. I stare down at the mattress. I also inhale the curry essence, my stomach emitting the low growls of a cat warning a dog.

"No longer welcome in my own bed," he says. "Outcast from the house of my wife and children."

"What happened?"

"Nothing so unexpected."

Firoz wears his usual sweater and baggy pants. The expression on his face remains sweet, but his smile is brittle and his eyelids keep drooping—in shame, I suspect.

"You and Zera had a fight?"

"She has had enough. Of my incompetence and failure. The poor woman. How she must pain."

"But you're the one sleeping in the store?"

"Shh!"

We both glance down the aisle to the back door, and the stairs to the apartment. I, at least, silently curse our impulse.

"Consider her position," says Firoz, restacking a display of paper towels that has been the same height since last October. "Twenty years invested in a marriage, in a man. What has she to show for it?"

"Four kids," I answer angrily, "a home, a business."

"The children, yes. They are a blessing."

"And a husband who isn't in prison," I add. "Who's around, helping out, doing his best. Who puts up with his wife's—"

Wisely, I stop. Firoz thanks me with a nod.

"The recession will end soon," I say.

"Not soon enough."

"Everyone's having trouble making the rent."

"Everyone doesn't matter."

I note the sharpness in his answer. It is, unfortunately, anomalous. "You're a good person," I say honestly. "I admire you." *And*, I add in silence, also honestly, *you're probably fucked*.

He shakes his head in resignation. Once more overcome by exhaustion and hunger, I find nothing to add. In a feeble gesture I lay a hand on his shoulder.

"She might leave me," he whispers.

"Don't think it."

"Didn't your wife—?"

"Yes."

"It can happen," he adds, "to men like us."

My hand slips off. Perhaps my body language stiffens. I say farewell to Firoz—a year will bring major changes to the Velji household, I predict—and return to the cold.

## 9

IN THE MORNING, I DON'T BOTHER. CALLING PEOPLE, I MEAN: listening for the dreaded hiccup ring, waiting for the commencement of the "You have reached . . ." or "*Vous êtes bien au . . .*" and only then hanging up out of annoyance and frustration. Not that I'm happy to be departing in silence. Quite the opposite: I'm dying to tell friends about the arrest. Now that the tale has a happy ending, Carole should hear it and sympathize, then pass on a version to her taciturn sister, Lise, who maybe will finally find a kind word for her former brother-in-law. But Carole should also let me recount the story to Natalie, and do as any father would: exaggerate and enlarge in direct proportion to the widening of her smile, the darkening of her irises, until it is a proper yarn thick with heroes and villains and perilous adventure. And certainly Adele, a born hater of cops and soldiers and authority in general, would love to have the anecdote at her disposal, in order to illustrate in her next column or television appearance that right here and now ordinary people are being trampled on, taken for fools, by a system that pretends to be in their service, but in actual fact serves the interests of the. . . . And so on. Missing the chance to tell Ivan is especially galling. The pink cell is good for a laugh. The cop behaviour is daily Montreal news. What would intrigue him is the issue of collective guilt; how, while languishing in the cell, I managed to produce a shortlist of 'crimes'—misdemeanours, more likely—of which I was guilty, and for which I deserved some form of "punishment." He would love to play with that awkward truth about divine versus human justice, and spin it around until, once again, at issue was our failure to examine either ourselves or each other, and accept what is there.

But what I would really like to tell him about the arrest is. . . . Well, why not? One call. Knowing his chatterbox friends, I'm sure he keeps his machine on unlimited message mode: at least I won't get cut off.

Sure enough, the "This is Ivan, but I'm not here . . ." business comes on. I wait it out.

"Ivan," I begin, "are you home? If you are, please pick up. . . . Okay, listen, something interesting happened last night. I was arrested, accused of being an incompetent robber named Pierre with a wife and kids in Hull. Nobody roughed me up, and I got to spend a few hours in a cell decorated by a real queen. But that's not what is amazing. I finally got it, you see—about me, about going to China. I realized that, if I'd wanted, I could easily have convinced the cops that I *was* this guy who is five years younger, four inches taller and forty pounds lighter than I am, and who can't even speak English. I could have convinced them because they wanted to be convinced. They wanted me to be someone else."

I pause to catch my breath and to order the thoughts that are tumbling from my mouth.

"This afternoon I leave for Vancouver. Tomorrow morning, I continue on to Toyko. Who steps off the plane at the airport in Beijing? The Chinese expect to see a distinguished professor of translation. Fine. I'll be that man. I want to see a different me: someone confident and self-possessed, who makes things happen, who has the look of success. Fine again. Because I'll be in a different city in a different country on a different continent. So I'll be different, too."

I get dressed and wait, and pack two suitcases and wait, and tidy the apartment and wait, and even exchange morning coos with the pigeons and wait, but the phone still does not ring—not once. Only faintly aware that my neurons are preparing to misfire, I finish my preparations by ignoring a self-made promise and unknotting Zuo Chang's care package. Inside the plastic bag are three sets of underwear and two bras, fingers of lipstick and a tube of facial cream, a box of Tampax. Underneath these items is a softcover book called *Apprendre l'anglais dans trois mois*. As a gift, the book is a conundrum. Those portions of the text that explain how to learn English in three months are written in French, not Chinese. Zuo can read the text to understand how to correct English errors, but is helpless to detect the mistakes themselves. His wife, in contrast, will recognize her English faults in the italicized portions, but lack the necessary French to address them. A mutually futile exercise in language improvement. A bad Global Village joke. I, of course, am an automatic master of *Apprendre l'anglais*. But I am also headed off to a country where my ability to communicate will be reduced to that of a two-year-old, a healthy levelling.

I spread the contents of the bag over the kitchen table and study them like tea leaves, seeking even a trace of affection, a vestige of respect, in Zuo's purchases. A pang of sympathy for Zhou Hong—yes, for a woman I've never met—grows into a stitch of anger at her husband's callousness, and, calculating the remaining time, I throw on a coat and walk out to Park Avenue. The No. 80 puffs at the intersection, and I ride it four stops. At a music shop on Laurier Street I ask the salesman to select six cassettes of nineteenth century music, preferably Dvořák and some lesser known Schubert. Handing over the cash I had allotted myself for a final restaurant lunch, I return to the apartment for a last round of bagels and cream cheese, a meal I will not miss. I also reassemble the package, now slightly thicker, and bury it inside my suitcase.

And I have a seizure. On the living-room floor, shortly before noon. First there is the deadening sensation in my limbs. Then comes the nausea. The chasm looms up out of nowhere, like the camera eye of a helicopter that, flying fast and low, bursts upon the Grand Canyon. Earth dissolves in shock: sky opens in astonishment. Over the edge I fall, without a fight, without much concern. I think briefly of Carole but more of Natalie, losing in the descent my name and age, height and weight, occupation and language. I sense that my hands are moving, that I am lucky not to be holding a cup or fork; that lying down in the middle of the room, away from the furniture, the moment I first felt it coming, was wise. All I need do is empty out. Calm breathing, a regular beat.

Afterwards, I open the window next to the bookshelves and, mimicking some movie I saw as a kid, declare to the sill pigeons that they should "fly away" and "be free!" They are not interested in either proposition, and instead trill in fear, their feathers ruffling. The birds more or less demand that I shut the window and leave them be.

Which I do. Then I lie back on the floor. A few minutes later, the taxi honks from the street. I rise from the hard earth, brush away the snow and ice and set off across the frozen field. The sun is an egg-yellow blur. The moon is twice-ringed.

## 10

"In China," says Zhou Hong in her private voice, "people say not what they think. Not even what others want them to think. They say what must be said, in order to be free of dangerous thoughts."

"Free of all thoughts?" I ask.

"Just the dangerous ones."

I ponder this distinction, impressed by Hong's ability to channel her soft voice onto only me, despite the setting. "Then should you have even said that?" I wonder.

She laughs easily.

"Our secret," I promise.

She turns away. The table seats a dozen, and she should be seen speaking with all the guests, including those with whom she shares no common tongues. The Soviet professor, for example: a privately devastated, publicly obsolete woman whose unilingualism, and disregard for other languages, including the host-country's tongue, is almost touchingly self-destructive. *I am a goner*, her appearance and manner cry out. *Give me alcohol.* A school banquet—the first of several this week, my tenth in two months—is a highly choreographed affair. Everyone has a part to play. Everyone has a function. My function, I have learned, is to smile while being served sea slugs and beef tendons; my part is that of grinning, multilingual foreign teacher. Despite her status as the only representative of the Foreign Affairs Office who shows any interest in foreigners or, presumably, their affairs, Zhou Hong's primary banquet function is internal: to entertain the fossils at head table. Her error is to be lovely, and lively; her downfall, I gather, is to be capable of carrying on a conversation with anyone and anything—mammal or otherwise.

The fossils are otherwise. Nine weeks ago, I might have declared these old men important reminders of the bold revolutionary days. Perhaps a little long in the tooth. Perhaps a touch reluctant to hand over the reins. But otherwise pillars and sages, living history. Then time passed, and this dozer awoke. Not much time, admittedly, and not from much of a sleep. Revived by conversations and observations and facts of a startling rawness, I quickly adjusted my wide-eyed awe first to the blink of the dismayed, then to the squint of the outraged, and finally full circle to the doe-sized twinkle of the cynical. A loss? I don't think so. A gain? I don't think so, either. Simply a newfound alertness and—I hope—a helpful edge.

Take the college elders. How could one not be skeptical? These ancients, all vice-presidents and chairmans and heads of various committees at Beijing's top foreign languages college, and all gathered today to welcome another foreigner onto the teaching staff, speak no foreign tongues themselves. Half of them, country-boys-made-good under Mao or Deng Xiaoping, are rumoured to be unintelligible in Mandarin as well, so hardscrabble are their local accents. Nor have they ever been abroad. More piquantly, they display at every opportunity a frank hostility towards the idea of meeting a foreign teacher, let alone welcoming him or her to the college. They, too, are at the banquet to be served sea slugs and beef tendons, and be entertained—i.e., flattered—by the likes of Zhou Hong. The fossils, after all, are men, and Hong, unlike some older female comrades, is clearly a woman. Not that they're likely planning any lecherous advances. Their energies, once devoted exclusively to sex and power, no doubt, now appear channelled in a single direction: death avoidance. Assigned by senior party mandarins to absurd academic postings around the capital to assist them in dying— out of boredom, most likely—this generation of former ineffi- cient military officials and corrupt, inefficient government offi- cials eat as much as they can and drink as little as they can and sleep whenever, and wherever, they can, simply to hang on: to not die; to never, ever permit the country to be run by anyone other than fossils like themselves and fossil protégés, such as their fifty-year-old children. As for youngsters like Zhou Hong, they are held in high suspicion. They cause trouble, as during the Turmoil, and show disrespect, as during the Turmoil. But at least she isn't a stinking academic. At least she evidences no wish to overthrow the government, reduce the nation to chaos. Besides being lovely, she is merely a suspiciously efficient, suspi- ciously bilingual administrator whose husband did a bunk because of Tiananmen last year.

If the fossils are the rock, the foreign staff are Zhou Hong's hard place. Extracting herself from head table with a smile and a laugh, she sets off to rally the three tables of culturally attenu- ated foreign teachers, cheer us up with encouraging words about the grass dumplings and chicken-fat-in-oil, promises of additional outings to the Great Wall. She also softens us for the imminent spectacle of a fossil-speech. Before the festivities are over, we will be obliged to listen to the same discourse delivered in some form of Mandarin by a different trembling, slurring gentleman, and duly translated—with purposeful disinterest in off-the-cuff remarks found in the original, she once admitted to me—by that same Zhou Hong. The words will be as they need to be: how honoured the vice-president is to welcome another distinguished foreign professor onto staff; how such exchanges not only enrich the intellectual life on campus but show further proof that friendship can easily bridge the great divide.

Zhou Hong starts up a conversation with the German teacher seated next to me. "Professor David is already famous," she says, her voice now public. "Professor Mueller tells me she heard the story from her own students."

"The story?" I ask modestly.

"You tell your students you are not America," says Professor Mueller.

"I said I was no Boy Scout," I correct, speaking quietly to encourage Hong to lean over. "First day in class, I wrote the word *boy scout* on the board and explained what it meant. Then I told my students about the time that Boy Scouts fanned out around Montreal to earn merit points by helping old ladies across city streets. At intersections everywhere that day, elderly people were seen being dragged against their will, sometimes into oncoming traffic, by kids in uniforms. Thinking they were being molested, some of the women fought back. One bit a kid in the arm."

I pause for effect.

"I explained to my class that the Boy Scouts weren't really interested in helping old people. They only wanted to get merit points and earn badges. I said that I wasn't a Boy Scout, and they weren't old or needy. They were college students and I was their teacher. Someone with a class to give, not a message to deliver. Ideas, but no ideology. They'd have to cross the street all by themselves."

"You are not America," repeats Professor Mueller.

I am not fond of this woman. "It never occurred to me to see the parable that way," I say.

"But it is obvious."

Zhou Hong intercedes by retying her hair. Looping errant

strands between her fingers, she outlines a hook mark behind her right ear. Always her right ear, I've noticed. Like the way she runs her tongue over her upper lip when she is impatient, her lower lip when she is uneasy. And the way she blinks rapidly when speaking, but slow and measured when listening, as if in beat with her own heart.

"The students all remember the story," she summarizes, "and repeat it in their dormitories. This makes David famous on campus!" Her laugh is forced.

"Humph," says Professor Mueller.

Zhou Hong excuses herself. Offering no excuse to Mueller on one side or Professor Ishikawa on the other, I follow her across the room. For a moment I worry that the college's oldest fossil, Wu Tong, rumoured to have been a close friend of Mao Zedong before Liberation, and known to have been a repeat victim of the Chairman after 1949, is staring at me. Certainly, his ancient, aquatic eyes appear to trail my movements. I am about to change course for the toilets when Hong, having stopped a few feet ahead, draws me in with her hand.

"Blind," she says.

"What?"

"Comrade Wu is blind."

"Funny, it looks like he's—"

"For many years," she adds. "He was made vice-president of the college during the Cultural Revolution to protect him against purges in the army."

Usually, I ask right away. I know I shouldn't. It is like inquiring after a long-institutionalized family member. First, you make sure he isn't dead. Then you ask, discreetly, if he's still crazy. And always will be? Today, sensing the wisdom of indirectness, I try to phrase the correct question.

"Could Comrade Wu see before he came to the college?"

"People say so."

"And he stopped being able to see during the Cultural Revolution?"

She nods, her gaze elsewhere, as if we are strangers waiting at a bus stop.

"He lost his sight during an interrogation?"

"People say so," reiterates Hong. She blinks. I attempt to count the flutterings, check my own heart for correspondences.

"How is she today?" I ask.

"Who?"

I wait.

"Fine," she lies.

"Any word from—?"

"No need for him to call," she interrupts. "Everything is arranged for the girl."

"He's made sure of it?"

"Of course. Only three days left."

"And as her father," I say, "Zuo Chang naturally wants what is best for—"

"*All* of us," she interrupts again. This time, she challenges me with her gaze. I back down. But Hong also goes to retie her hair once more. Except that no strands fall over her eyes, and she tucks air behind her ear.

"Are you all right?" I foolishly ask.

She still smiles. *The whole room is watching*, her expression now communicates.

"Thank you, Zhou Hong," I say for the record.

Back in my seat, I hear her hearty laugh at the table behind me, imagine the bright expression on her face.

"Did you hear about the teacher Wang Hua," asks Professor Mueller. "What people are saying about him?"

"Who?" I reply.

She humphs again. Elaine Mueller possesses a repertoire of humphs, pshaws and uh-ahs that intend to communicate a variety of sentiments, but end up implying only one: arrogant incredulity. Her arrogance, though unattractive, stands to reason; her incredulity, well, is hard to believe. After all, Professor Mueller has taught at the college for six years and lived in China, off and on, for more than three decades. What fresh hell could she possibly be encountering in 1990? A youthful Leninist, she first came to Beijing, then still called Peking, in the 1950s. Her part was to serve the revolution as an international comrade; her function was to teach selected mandarins the important, if bourgeois, German language. Ten eventful years followed. At the outset of the Cultural Revolution it was strongly suggested that she leave. Refusing, she encouraged her inquisitors to assign to her the same punishments they were handing her Chinese brethren. That request earned her four years soft labour in a Beijing machine shop *and* an explusion order in 1972. More than a frustrating decade in exile followed this travesty. But her return to the new China of Deng Xiaoping proved disappointing. Not just because of the corruption and materialism and intellectual vacuity. What stung Elaine Mueller the worst was the gradual reduction of the official ideology from coal-fired state engine to museum antique. Her frustration at a boiling point, she began in the mid-eighties to introduce her graduate students to other books by the famous nineteenth century German revolutionaries, a line she would not have dared to cross when Mao was alive, despite the huge portraits of Marx and Engels that decorated Tiananmen Square each May Day. Her ready excuse—that they wrote excellent German— stayed ready semester after semester, year after year. Because no one criticized her selection. Not her dean, on extended leave at a university in Frankfurt since 1983, nor her vice-dean, employed full time by a German firm in town, nor her students, whose queries about courses centred on whether they could study translations of Ian Fleming and Stephen King.

Elaine Mueller is sixty-something, sad and bitter, with nowhere to go and no place to call home. Of course I recognize her: Adele Guy with an adventurous streak. I understand that she was offended by her mild punishment during the Cultural Revolution, and is still deeply hurt by the non-criticism of her intellectual rebellion. I understand a life committed to ideals; I understand what it feels like to have that life mocked, made irrelevant. And, by chance, I am extremely interested in what gossip she has to share about the Chinese teacher Wang. She knows I am, too: hence the humphs. But I simply do not care for the woman.

## 11

IN MY BATHROOM MIRROR IS THE FACE I HAVE BEEN WEARING since I landed at Capital Airport in January. It is, first of all, clean shaven. Stuck in Vancouver for a night on the way out, I dulled two razors and bloodied a sink erasing on impulse sixteen years of manicured growth. Staring into the hotel mirror afterwards, running a hand over my roseola skin and abruptly swollen jaw, I had to lean on the counter. For a moment, I was a teenager again and the bathroom was in the Clark Street flat. For a moment, the future was clearly mine and the past was cleanly buried, and I had no disease. I snapped out of this state quickly enough, but still decided that to shave every morning while in China would serve to assert the supremacy of the malleable present. A rejection of the indelible. A commitment to the self-stylized. Further assertions were pondered—dying my hair black or getting a buzz-cut—but I settled on a curl-killing trim and a tube of gel, the scent of which immediately triggered that same stubborn Mile End memory of Vitalis in the medicine cabinet and a bottle of Aqua Velva atop the sink, a shaving brush in a mug, a half-dozen combs in a glass.

The Vancouver-born face belongs to a professor of translation in Beijing. He is a non-smoker of cigarettes and a besporter of sunglasses. A husky but dapper man—I've lost fifteen pounds to date, and always wear a tie in public—he seems somewhat of a mischief maker, even a tease. This teacher began his first class with a parable, and often interrupts lectures, under the guise of translating stock phrases and received opinions, to ruminate on consumerism and the collective, gerontocracies and the military state. He says whatever comes into his head, more or less, but with a studied nonchalance: knowing, as he does, that he is immune from consequences. His students, in contrast, often act like merely listening to such blasphemy will land them in trouble. To their frowns and squirms, fake smiles and shocked stares, he merely grins and, straightening his tie, declares himself a humble conduit of the material needed for intellectual discourse. To encourage reflection. To expand minds. No cant or creed, he emphasizes. No sales pitch or snow job.

As for this professor's past politics, they are irrelevant. Political theory here appears a means to the end of acquiring power; political practice looks to be the art of maintaining that power. Face to face with realities of a severity—or perhaps simply a *real*ness—unimagined back in Montreal and unimaginable, he suspects, for most Canadians, he is less mute about formerly held beliefs than he is bashful and, increasingly, without clear memory. He should be more surprised by how easy it is to forget. He should certainly be more disturbed. A complex ideology eliminated with less effort than a beard? But then, unlike his mother, he never truly inhabited any belief system. The hair, in contrast, was very much his own.

In private, I am a toss of emotions and a jumble of impulses. I also light one cigarette off another to make up and rub my chin raw out of habit. Synapses have been short-circuiting in my brain like defective fuses. It hasn't been this bad since the accident with Potemkin, and the breakup with Carole. The seizures occur almost daily, usually in the evenings, after too much food and beer. As a result, I rarely go out at night, and keep apart from the foreign community. Scholarly devotion, I imply: alcoholism, others likely assume, tallying my daily beer purchases from the building cafeteria or the shop outside the south gate. Only two people visit my apartment regularly, both Chinese, both compromised by the friendship. From one friend I have learned attitude; from the other, I hope, concern. One provides the familiar, if edgy, pleasure of male company, the other the delight, and eternal strain, of female companionship. With one I can usually chatter in universal guy code. With the other, despite her excellent English, finding a common language is often difficult, and I am generally the problem. As for what these people get from the friendship, it is less clear. One, an all-consensus troublemaker, displays a provocative affection for my dwelling. A love, even, for my TV and cassette player, the cafeteria delicacies and bottles of Qingdao I provide him. Despite her mild manner and undisputed loyalty, the other may actually be taking the greater risk, courting the worse peril. I know this sounds far-fetched—and I hardly dare believe it myself—but she may love me.

English department dean Feng Ziyang loves Marlboros. Single cigarettes, yes, and packages, naturally. But entire cartons? More than his Chairman Mao button collection. More than his wife. The dean, as Zuo Chang warned me back in Montreal, is a chain-smoking-survivor-of-the-Cultural-Revolution intellectual. I have no argument with the first point: twenty minutes in Feng's office equals at least three cigarettes, each partially inhaled, partially showered over sleeves and documents and partially crushed into ashtrays to emphasize unclear points, refute—as far as I can tell—unmade accusations. As for Feng Ziyang having "survived" the Cultural Revolution, I'm doubtful. No question, the man is still chief of his department, despite chronic "health problems" that predate last spring, but have by all accounts never been worse. No question, either, he is still a husband and father. But he is also, by his own dementedly frank admission, a physical wreck and spiritual shell. Even the intellectual tag no longer holds. "A non-practising intellectual," he once described himself to me.

My meeting with the dean is in ten minutes. At the front door of the residence I turn up my jacket collar, don my glasses and greet a Beijing spring morning. The sky is low and smeared; the air has a sulphurous odour and a chalk taste. Under my feet is a sidewalk alive with patterns of red dust. A faint breeze, the stirring of air brought on by shuffling legs, dissolves the existing shapes: any settling or stillness soon creates others. Dust on the ground is one thing. Dust plugging the nose and drying the mouth, rasping a perpetually sore throat, is something else again. Dust in northern China is the Gobi Desert, sweeping down from Inner Mongolia to blight the capital, offering the spectre of breakers unfurling over fields and exploding against buildings. Dust is spring in Beijing, I'm told, and this being the case, the muggy, mosquito-swarmed summer that locals speak of so despairingly cannot come too soon.

To reach the English department, I must cross a field—a sports ground, in fact—to a red-brick building. I make the journey riding the lip of a wave, head bowed, pants splayed against my legs. Once within the shelter of a wall, I hawk a wad of spit and blow my handkerchief bloody.

The department offices occupy the top floor of a five-storey structure. Still winded, I climb methodically, my coughs resounding in the stairwell. Secretary Shen sits alone in the room. She greets "Teacher David"—she quite rightly confers the title *jianshi*, meaning "senior," only on older faculty: the rest of us are *jiaoshi*, "juniors"—announces in her non-English that Dean Feng will be back in a moment, then orders me to sit in a chair near her desk. I oblige. The secretary's struggle to use English would be more charming were it not a reflection of her profound conviction that I cannot speak, or understand, Mandarin. Her belief flies in the face of some hard empirical evidence, including my conversations in Chinese with other staff and my interruptions of her comments to Dean Feng to clarify a point. But Shen's conviction is made of sterner stuff. Namely, she is convinced that no foreigner, regardless of his skill or devotion, could possibly learn Mandarin. Her reason? She gave it once, with reluctance, to her exasperated boss, and it is a model of clarity and a kind of reason. Outsiders cannot speak the Chinese language, claims the department secretary, because we have not suffered enough.

Now in her sixties, Shen began her professional career in 1949 by learning Russian, including a year of study in Moscow. Her sojourn abroad led her to be labelled a reactionary during the first anti-Rightist campaign, and she was dismissed from her teaching position and sent to the countryside for re-education. Once rehabilitated, she abandoned the now out-of-favour Russian tongue for the suddenly vital Korean language. Fluency in Korean coincided, regrettably, with the initial Red Guard rallies at the college in 1966. Along with most of her colleagues, including the junior teacher Feng Ziyang, Shen was humiliated by her students, beaten and imprisoned in a bicycle shed, and eventually returned to rural China to once again "learn from the masses." In her case, the learning process involved harvesting rocks from a Shandong shoreline and depositing them in a pile a kilometre inland, where another work unit awaited to transport the cargo, also on foot, in the direction of what appeared to be a different stretch of Shandong shoreline. She performed educational tasks like these for seven years. From the age of thirty-eight until shortly before her forty-fifth birthday. While her children, back in Beijing with their grandparents, grew up into strangers; while her husband, a physics professor at Qinghua University, died of pneumonia, learning from the masses in Shanxi province. Still another rehabilitation provided Shen Yuan-fang yet another opportunity to acquire a foreign language. Declared too old to be considered for an "important" foreign tongue, and subsequently turned down for Spanish, French and Italian, she agreed to have a go at Arabic. In the early 1980s, apparently—I am getting all this from Zhou Hong, who arrived at the college in 1981—Secretary Shen was one of two Beijing intellectuals, self-taught using books and audio tapes, fluent in this difficult language. Until, that is, an actual Arab was hired. And couldn't be understood by the Chinese experts. Nor understand them. Barely a sentence, hardly a word.

After which, Shen renounced foreign languages completely, going so far as to deny speaking any herself—making her, I suppose, a non-practising linguist. Mandarin was enough for her. Mandarin was more than enough for China. School administrators, at a loss what to do with the veteran teacher, appointed her secretary to a department. Their choice, the mighty English faculty, was especially suitable: Shen, it was presumed, truly did not speak that language. Once, though, merry on rice wine at a department New Year's banquet, she confessed to a table of professors that as a teenager she had dreamed of devoting her scholastic life to the English language, and its literature, after watching David Lean's film adaptation of *Great Expectations* at the British Embassy with her father in 1947, two years before Liberation.

Another Adele Guy? I see similarities. The small frame, the

tight mouth and—for sure—the hard, judgemental eyes, the thinning grey hair drawn taut into a bun, as if to highlight the ravages of experience on the human face. Their careers run parallel, as do the dates. What they appear to share most in common, however, is what actually distinguishes them with utter finality. Mother has always chosen to view the world in black and white: a single-minded struggle, a war without prisoners or casualties. Shen Yuan-fang came of age in a culture that viewed itself, and the place of those within it, in such terms. Adele chose not to recognize and certainly not to enjoy the plurality of things, and of her own selves; Secretary Shen never had any choice but to toe the totalitarian line about the individual and society. Even language learning became a dreary duty for her, nothing to do with expanding her private world, nothing to do with any sense of joy or belonging—the blue dome of sky over us all. So the woman contracted, her skin a tightening vice, until she shrivelled. And Adele's skin? By her own definition, it has been an equally incarcerating force in her life. By her thinking, class *is* skin, and it distinguishes who does from who gets done by. Thus, there is no real difference between the plight of a sixty-one-year-old Chinese scholar and her counterpart in Outremont, Quebec. Thus, workers of the world are united, if only to show each other their chains.

But what does Mother really know about constriction and disappointment and how history mauls people? What could she possibly know about imprisonment? She has not suffered enough. She, too, could never speak Mandarin.

"Hurry, please," says Dean Feng, darting across the room to his desk. "So busy today!"

I switch to the chair of the desk in front of him. It is the workstation of the vice-dean, Professor Wu, last seen boarding a plane for Dallas, Texas, in May 1987. The desk, everyone informs me, still belongs to the AWOL academic. The piles of unmarked essays, the memos to Dean Feng—the two men were not on speaking terms for years beforehand—the scribbled notes about an upcoming lecture on British idioms, even a thermos containing his wife's special tea, prepared for her husband each morning: all remain in place thirty-five months later, as if Wu might poke his head through the office door at any moment to collect the essays of students who have since graduated, dash off to give the lecture in a course now taught by a twenty-two-year-old, or just retrieve the thermos for a refill from Madame Gao, who continues to live in their campus apartment with their son, despite administrative efforts to have the family evicted. I always sit gingerly in the vice-dean's chair, anxious not to show disrespect. Despite the proximity, I see only Dean Feng's head and shoulders, the smoke signal from his cigarette. Everything further below is blocked by skyscrapers of documents.

"You want to speak with me?" asks Feng.

"I don't think so."

The dean cackles.

"You called *me*," I point out.

"I did?"

"Last night. At my apartment. You said we needed to talk. You said it was urgent."

"So busy!" repeats Feng. He laughs again. When implying amusement, Feng Ziyang's laugh is a nervous bark; when relating frustration or unease, it is the yelp of a dog that has had its paw stepped on. He drags on his cigarette.

"Okay, okay," he says. "I remember now. Things are still bad here, understand? Still not safe. You have ever been in trouble back in the States?"

"Canada."

"Okay, okay."

"What do you mean 'trouble'?" I ask, conjuring the TV monitor and pink cell.

"Bad business. Bad news. Meaning, you're screwed. Meaning, you're fucked!" summarizes the dean. In contrast to Zhou Hong, whose English is pared of grammar only when she is upset, Feng Ziyang speaks in permanent abbreviations. Life, I gather, is too fraught for complete sentences. His English is nearly flawless, but is kept choppy by bad nerves and a fondness for American slang.

"Tell him about Wang Hua," says Secretary Shen in Mandarin. "Tell him to keep away."

"Quiet," says the dean.

The secretary, recording marks in a ledger at her desk, does not blink.

"Trouble in other places is not like trouble here," continues Feng. "Here, trouble is BIG." He demonstrates with his arms. "Is BIG, and never goes away. Lasts for lifetime, maybe longer. Understand?"

"Not really," I lie.

"Look at me. Look at my—" He stops, hammers his cigarette into—I imagine—an ashtray on the desk and frisks his jacket. "You have any . . . ?"

I produce an unopened pack of Marlboros from my pocket. "Keep it," I say, lobbing the pack over the skyscrapers.

Feng nods. Secretary Shen glances up, her eyeballs bobbing above the rims of her glasses.

"I am still not safe from last year. Still could lose my job or be arrested. Why you think I wear these clothes?" asks the dean, fingering the lapel of his Mao suit. "Comfort? Fashion? When the political officer interrogated me after Turmoil he mentioned my situation in 1966, at start of Cultural

Revolution. This incident still in my file! Incident where I was roughed by students and locked in that room."

He makes a darting gesture in the direction, seemingly, of a supply closet across the hallway from the office.

"In there?" I ask.

The dean twitches.

"You were imprisoned in that closet?"

"What are you talking about?" asks the secretary, her brow furrowed.

"Nothing."

"That is none of his business, Feng," she scolds.

"Of course," answers the dean, sheepish as a schoolboy caught whispering about the girl in the next seat.

"Just tell him to keep away from Wang Hua."

"Tell him yourself, Shen Yuan-fang. He understands what you're saying."

"No, he doesn't."

"Why should I keep away from Wang Hua?" I interject.

"See!" says Feng.

"See what?"

The dean turns to me. "Say something in Chinese, please. She doesn't want to believe us."

"I don't speak any Mandarin," I say in that language.

"I know," she answers.

"I don't understand what you and the dean have been saying about Wang Hua, either."

"He's a foreigner," says Secretary Shen to her boss. "What can you expect?"

Dean Feng lights a Marlboro. Though forty-six, his boyish face and wiry frame lend him the look of a new, sleep-deprived parent. An overwrought parent, too: the piston legs and twitching mouth, the breathless speech lovingly mimicked by his students. A shock of hair falls over his eyes, obliging him to clear them with a hand nearly always pinching a cigarette. Ash falls are common; once the dean apparently singed a brow. Burst capillaries high up on his cheeks betray his actual age, along with the splays of lines, deep as knife cuts, at the corners of his eyes. Being an intellectual, even a non-practising one, he wears black-rimmed glasses. Being an intellectual over the age of thirty, his lenses are as thick as my baby finger.

"Tell, eh—what's his name again?" asks the secretary.

"Don."

"David," I correct.

"I thought it was 'Clear' or something."

"That's his other name."

Shen absorbs this information. "Tell whatever-his-name-is about Wang's background, his activities during the Turmoil. Tell him Wang isn't even—"

I miss the word.

"Wang is only half-Chinese," explains the dean to me, still in Mandarin. "His mother is Tibetan."

Secretary Shen *tch-tch*es, her eyes still glued to her ledger. I study her waxy skin and melanin-spotted hands, the bald patch at the top of her skull. My compassion for the woman vanishes.

"So?" I say.

He yelps. "Okay, okay," he says. "Just be careful. Wang visits you too much. Stays too long in your room. These things are noticed. Commented on. People talk!"

"And mention the woman, too," she says.

"Quiet!"

"What woman?" I ask, my voice rising.

"Shen speaks nonsense," lies the dean.

"He will get her into trouble. BIG trouble," adds Secretary Shen, using the foreign word.

"Very, very busy," says Feng, on his feet. "Must ask you to leave now."

I glare at him.

"You're no Boy Scout, remember?" he says.

"But I am a friend. I *have* friends here."

This time, his yelp is nearly a cry. "See my new button?" he asks hastily. "Very rare. Three-D, like in movies."

Though Cultural Revolution memorabilia is the current rage in Beijing, a boon for government warehouses rumoured to be bursting with millions of buttons, banners and Little Red Books, Dean Feng began his Mao collection almost a decade ago, when it was neither fashionable nor especially prudent. Once he journeyed to Hunan province, where Mao Zedong was from, and found a picture of the Chairman that plugged in, the better to illuminate the dreams of the faithful. He loved the object but balked at the price. Besides, Feng was disciplined—buttons only. He owns more than fifty, kept in a box in his apartment, with the latest discovery on display beside the phone atop his desk. I examine the button, which is actually a hologram, holding it up to the window light until the figure emerges. The sage sits in an armchair, the still centre of a storm of dark gold and crimson red. On his face is a familiar Mao expression: relaxed but remote, informal but condescending. Daring disagreement. Mocking human concerns.

At the door, I point across the hallway to the storage closet. "Were you really locked up in there?"

"Another era."

"What are you being investigated for now?"

"A mistake," answers Feng. "Authorities think I was leader

of school march on Tiananmen Square last May 16th. They think I was organizer!"

"Why would they think that?"

"Exactly. The Turmoil was made by thugs and unemployed workers," announces the dean to the walls. "Not students. Not intellectuals."

Who made the "Turmoil," as the democracy movement and subsequent army crackdown are being called? According to my sources—Wang Hua and Zhou Hong, naturally—the culprits numbered in the millions. The army tried to overrun the city. The city defended itself. The army killed. The city died. Among the corpses were some unemployed workers and hooligans. Mostly, though, the bodies were of employed workers and law-abiding citizens, retired officials and fearless teenagers. Dozens were students at third-level institutions. A handful were once their teachers. Most of the dead were Beijingers, proud of the city and protective of it, outraged that tanks and troops would be used to squash a peaceful, albeit prolonged, protest. "The People's Army doesn't kill the people!" they shouted, incorrectly. A minority of the corpses came from out of town, young people who had raced north to the capital to witness the birth of the new China. They vanished from their villages, houses and bedrooms; their parents suffered the disappearance of a son or daughter without seeing a body or receiving a word of confirmation. The Turmoil, my same sources maintain, caused two undergraduates to vanish from our college. But these students, both women, had never been declared dead. Only missing, no longer registered for classes. Still possessing dormitory beds and rights to ration tickets, however, plus lockers full of stuff. Clothes and shoes, tapes and books. Unfinished letters. Unclaimed mail.

Their names are often scrawled onto sheets of paper and

posted at night on announcement boards around campus. I stood in a crowd one cold February evening studying a poster. Astonishingly, the snippets of whispered conversation around me centred on the quality of the calligraphy. Cafeteria staff noted the hasty radicals and lavish strokes. A group of librarians nodded at the bold execution of one particular ideogram, comparing it to a master. It was agreed that the author had made no attempt to hide behind generic penmanship; the style was personalized and could be traced. I, too, stared at the poster, thinking of Zuo Chang's passionate art, but remained at a loss to truly appreciate the work. The courage of it I understood. The approach of a school official scattered the critics. Only I, playing the foreigner, stayed to watch the man remove the sheet. Not tear it: the paper was carefully folded and slipped into a briefcase. Posters rarely survived until dawn, but so far no culprit has been caught putting one up.

The six weeks of demonstrations that preceded the massacre were also created, claimed Wang and Hong, by the multitudes. All Beijing protested. On the biggest days, students constituted merely a segment of the marchers, some voices in a resounding chorus of disapproval. Three-quarters of the undergraduates at the college paraded onto the square at least once; half the faculty joined in, most notably on May 16th, the morning the president authorized the use of school buses to transport protesters downtown. The college marched east along Changan Avenue towards Tiananmen, banners fluttering, plain-clothes police snapping photos of the vanguard. At the head of the contingent, a megaphone in his hand and a bandanna around his head, walked Dean Feng, hoarse from shouting insults at the nation's leaders, pink-faced from the heat and strain and the pounding at the back of his skull. He suffered a nervous breakdown four days later, the morning martial law was declared and the school administration began to issue statements denying it had ever supported the insurgents, let alone loaned them vehicles. Three other department heads linked arms with Feng Ziyang and a phalanx of undergraduates, approaching the square with bold strides and no apologies. The students variously graduated into unemployment, spent the summer in detention, or else simply baby-stepped back to campus in September to endure daily apology sessions—called "re-education"—and punitive stints of army training. Two of the department heads who marched with Feng are no longer department heads. The other is dead, a suicide.

Only Feng Ziyang is still a dean. Everyone on campus agrees that the man has luck; fewer are certain, however, if his luck is good or bad.

Except for Wang Hua. He is certain that Dean Feng is crazy, and that crazy people have excellent luck. Crazy people watch terrible things happen, have terrible things happen to them and even do terrible things themselves, with an impunity rooted in a syllogism. Feng Ziyang is crazy; Feng Ziyang is Chinese; therefore, to be Chinese is to be crazy. Logically, to be Chinese is also to *be* Feng Ziyang. When I pointed this out to Wang, he merely agreed—hardly a clarification. But Wang Hua isn't denigrating the dean. He means the craziness as a compliment. He usually says it while drunk on beer.

I return from the meeting to find him watching television in my living room. His feet scuff the coffee table, his hands massage a bottle of Qingdao.

"Come in, Wang," I say.

"Make myself comfortable?"

"Of course."

"You shouldn't leave a key above your door. Let in all the ruffians and bad elements."

"Like you?"

"I am not a ruffian. I am an intellectual. Watch me think," says Wang. He inverts the bottle over his mouth and pours beer down his throat. Most of it gushes back up, soaking his cheeks and neck, staining his shirt.

I join him on the couch. "I found out the real reason for your bad behaviour this morning," I say. "Secretary Shen told me."

"Shen is a witch."

"She said you were—"

"A thug?" he asks, using the Mandarin term.

"Only half-Chinese."

He closes his eyes.

"Only half-civilized."

"But I told you this a long time ago, David."

"I blocked it out. Too shocking," I add, pretending to shiver at the revelation.

"This half is Han," says Wang, dividing himself at the waist. "The shit and piss part. The other"—he moves up to his heart and head—"belongs to a barbarian minority."

"I'm of mixed blood, too. Half English, half French. Also half Catholic and half Jewish."

"Half of man is woman," he intones. "Famous proverb. Known to all Chinese. I wonder what it means?"

I wait.

"Once the yellow crane is gone, it will never return!" he says, mugging his reflection in the bottle. "Very meaningful, I'm sure. Beautiful Chinese expressions. Beautiful words."

"How many of my beers have you drunk, Wang?"

"Only half."

Two bottles: barely a toe in the water. Wang Hua's threshold is famously high. Mere exuberance requires three to four beers. One bottle more introduces ribaldry into his manner. Scandalous carry-on kicks in at the five-to-six mark, after which his moods can become unpredictable, ranging from sullen silence to deranged chattiness and punctuated by long bouts of unconsciousness, his body splayed over the couch, his snores ripping the air.

Not a pretty sight. At his best, Wang is a handsome man, with almond eyes and high, swollen cheekbones. The cheekbones and copper skin identify him as either a southerner or, more likely, a minority. Until today, the eyes were obscured by a bang of oily black hair, the fashion signature of the most anti-academic, pro-hoodlum persona on campus. A persona suitable for the college's token bad element. Wang is that element, or else pretends to be, or else doesn't care what others think of him. He is twenty-nine, a 1984 graduate of an institute that he loathes, who has taught English vocabulary and "film studies"—inserting a video in a machine—at that same school since graduating, under the thumb of the same dean he thinks crazy, alongside the same colleagues he lost all respect for while a student, eating in the same squalid cafeterias, showering in the same filthy communal baths. Not to mention the accommodation; not to mention the pay. Wang has endured these ignominies for a single reason—to retain a residency permit for Beijing. Not to be reassigned back to his hometown in western Sichuan province. Not to be banished from one of the few places in the country where rock music is available, foreign novels go on sale and magazines from New York and London can be obtained, pored over and then circulated among friends.

Wang Hua recognizes the inconsistencies in his thinking. He revels in them even, further proof that he, too, is crazy.

Beijing sure doesn't like him as much as he likes it. Beijing considers his cheekbones and misshapen eyes suspicious, despite belonging to a Han-surnamed, Mandarin-speaking young man whose wardrobe is devoid of the embroidered belts and *chuba* tunics favoured by official Tibetan groups in the capital. Nor does he go out of his way to befriend the class of burnt-skinned Tibetans who apparently turn up on campus each May for summer language sessions, except to give them coaching in the Mandarin obscenities necessary to deal with any who might show disrespect. Wang's wardrobe, in fact, is a flea market of torn jeans and oversized business suits, ballooning T-shirts and sweat tops boasting the names of Bible-Belt colleges, plus his prize possession—a black leather U2 tour jacket with the words UNDER A BLOOD-RED SKY emblazoned across the back. The jacket was a gift from a fleeing English academic the previous June, and is known not only on campus but the length of the city's university corridor. Known among students for its foreign sheen and mysterious message. Among clothes pedlars for its potential black-market value. Known, too, among security police and institute spies for its distinctiveness, so easy to pick out of a crowd, a mob captured on video tape.

This morning, Wang Hua sports neither the jacket nor the hair. He visited an outdoor barber downtown last night. Visited him drunk and determined. The barber cut off all his hair and then shaved his head. Shaved it smooth as an egg, shiny as a Buddha.

"How does it feel?" I ask.

"Naked."

"Have people said anything?"

"Not to my face. All behind my head."

"Back, you mean."

"No, head."

Wang's smile is crooked. His English is *that* good.

"I wore a beard for sixteen years," I say, rubbing my chin. "Shaved it off the day I left Canada."

"To be free of your past?"

"To appear different."

"Have people said anything?"

"They don't know," I say.

"Ah."

There is a pause.

"You do look like a prisoner," I finally grant.

The smile straightens. Incarceration is Wang Hua's favourite topic. Prisons, he maintains, are like Chinese boxes: varying in size, infinite in number. From skin pigment to language to history to propaganda: race does not define, it confines. Does not bolster the self, but annihilates the self: not foster personality so much as crush it, the way a tank crushes a miscreant. In Wang's opinion, residency permits and passports, special economic zones and national borders, even penal institutions and labour camps, are all timid versions of this greater constriction.

"You want to look that way?" I guess.

"Prison barbers are incompetent, I hear. Shave unevenly. Draw blood."

He raises his empty bottle.

"Maybe you are going to the cafeteria for lunch?" he inquires.

I collect two bowls from the kitchen, plunk a fresh Qingdao on the table for Wang and shut the door. In the stairwell I hum the nursery song that my Mandarin teacher, a graduate student in Japanese, is teaching me. Unlike the stairwells in every other building on campus, the landing is bright and clean, devoid of bicycles and cooling woks. Unlike most college corridors, the one that leads from the stairwells to the reception area is freshly polished, the floor still damp from its latest mopping. The foyer, meanwhile, with its plush chairs and low tables covered in red cloth, resembles no other campus foyer, and the cafeteria—decorated with traditional paintings, the plates of bone china and the chopsticks of lacquered wood—is unique.

This is the Foreign Experts Building, after all. Occupants of the complex are declared experts in the languages we teach, though most of us have mastered little except the art of feeling, and acting, foreign. The building is our hotel away from home. It is where we retreat for a break from China. Apartments are spacious. Maid service is obligatory. Thermoses of hot water are delivered daily to the door. A laundry service starches shirts overnight. All amenities worthy of jealousy; all special treatments. But aside from the flats, it is the cafeteria that arouses the most envy. The operation is lorded over by the school's official banquet chef and run by its official banquet waitresses. The leanest beef and plumpest chicken are served there, along with the freshest tofu and vegetables, the best quality rice. A thrice-daily feast: a three-star insult. The cafeteria is for residents only. The only building residents, of course, are foreigners. Guests are welcome, so long as they present themselves to the nasty daytime security guard, who is secret police, sign the register and surrender their work unit card to be photocopied, and then endure the wrath of the waitresses, who resent catering to locals even more than they do outsiders. Few Chinese have the appetite for the scrutiny. Few foreigners actually crave the cuisine.

I love the food, though, and for some reason it loves me back. No matter how much I eat, I am still peckish afterwards. No matter how inattentive I am to my waistline, I still lose weight. In the lobby I nod to the guard, greet some born agains from Florida and Arizona—as predicted by the guy in Montreal, the college had to hire a half-dozen Americans last fall, all but one of them Christians-on-the-make—and then start in on the cafeteria staff. I mock their nasal accents; they ridicule my tonal misfirings. I quip about their uniforms and slouches and permanent bad tempers; they mock my gut and ears and outrageously coloured hair. I never win. They never lose. But I am also served more generous portions of chicken and beef, warmer bowls of rice.

Back in the foyer, I react calmly to the security guard's request for a word. Deng Chen is six feet tall, with an imposing skull—high-ridge cheekbones, an escarpment jaw—and caved-in eyes. The face rarely changes expression. The eyes never fill with light. Though his English is monosyllabic, I make him use it.

"Any student in your room?" he asks.

"No student."

"Wang Hua?"

"Wang Hua is a teacher."

"He is in your room?"

I scan the register atop the counter, as if I can actually read the names. "Is his name here?"

Deng pauses. Wang Hua never signs in. Other, more friendly front desk staff—that is, those not employed by the police—appear resigned to his delinquency, and allow him to come and go. One rule only is inviolable: a Chinese cannot spend the night in a foreigner's apartment. Even Wang has not crossed that minefield.

"No name," admits Deng Chen.

"No name in the book, no visitor in the building," I confirm.

"Two foods?"

"I'm starving."

In the apartment I ask Wang to write out the ideograms

for DO NOT DISTURB. I trace his calligraphy into my own hand and tape the paper to the outside of the door. We eat in silence, the TV still on, our chopsticks clicking against the porcelain. He comments, as usual, on the food: it is ten times better than the slop served in the school cafeterias. Also as usual, Wang wonders aloud if I'll be wanting all my lunch. Once we are finished, he pours beer into his bowl, swishes it around like a priest with wine in a chalice, and raises the rim to his lips. Next he burps, twice. Then, to officially end the meal, he takes his chopsticks in both hands and, studying them with the mock seriousness of a kung fu master about to split a brick with his forehead, snaps them in half, a singu-lar—and jarring—custom.

It is *shoeshui* time. I keep a blanket and pillow behind the couch for Wang Hua, who has taken his afternoon nap in my apartment since a few days after I arrived. My friend lives, it seems, in a state of permanent bedragglement. His eyes are always cloudy; he yawns so often his jaw locks; he has been known to nod off while teaching a class. The problem, he explained back in February, is his room. Wang cannot sleep in his own living quarters. He is kept awake by his room-mate's snoring and the banging of doors in the corridor, the clanging of utensils a flight above and the drunken sing-alongs a flight below. He is kept awake by disputes on the pathway and music blaring from the next dormitory, screech-ing cicadas and probing moonlight. More than anything else, though, Wang is kept awake by the silence, especially in the small hours, when security police like to make their arrests while all campus lights are off, all doors are locked.

Early afternoons in the Foreign Experts Building are inno-cently calm. Staff vanish. Visitors are rebuffed. Residents either doze or else putter around their flats checking for electronic bugs, and writing letters home. Day or night, the police keep their distance. Even the previous June, I'm told, when army patrols roamed the campus following the massacre, the place was left alone. The undercover crew are still on the job, naturally, and the paid snoops and prying cleaning ladies; but, by comparison with everywhere else, the residence is exempt—perhaps its most envied privilege. "Not quite the Middle Kingdom," Wang once said, echoing expert foreign consensus about the compound. He sleeps like a baby here.

Except that, unlike the baby I raised, he favours the corpse position for his naps: flat on his back, blanket up over his face. Before covering his eyes, Wang asks me a question.

"I thought I'd wait an hour and then visit Zhou Hong," I answer. "Ying is supposed to teach me a new song."

"The girl leaves on Friday?"

"Morning flight to Tokyo. Transfer to Vancouver, then to Montreal. My route exactly, in reverse."

"Zhou Hong will be sad."

"There's still no date set for her to join Zuo Chang and the child in Canada," I offer coolly. "She can't even get a passport without some kind of invitation from Montreal. He needs to arrange that."

"Which he isn't doing?"

I shrug.

"An arrangement, in its own way," comments Wang.

We have talked about Zuo before, whom Wang knows only slightly: about his talents and achievements, his reputation for ambition, his apparent defection. We have discussed his decision to bring his daughter over first, an unusual, though by no means exceptional, procedure. Initially, I did my best to hint that Zuo's motives might be complex. But then, after several sly references to Suzanne-the-UQAM-prof,

I learned that Wang Hua, and virtually everyone else at the college, is *assuming* Zuo Chang is in the process of keeping his daughter while dumping his wife. The assumption is based, Wang once assured me, on precedence and personality. Also on the campus and city, the country: on how lives are lived, fates are decided.

"Do you know what happens to people who are treated badly in China?" he says. "Who suffer, are hurt, and then are made to suffer some more?"

I ask.

"The state looks after them."

"Thanks, Wang."

He speaks from under the blanket. "Once the yellow crane is gone, it will never return!"

I close the double doors that seal the living room off from the rest of the apartment. In the dining area I spend an hour marking tests and smoking cigarettes. Curious how cocky I am about the secrecy of my vice. No matter how carefully I conceal the habit—keeping the window open and a can of airspray on hand, returning the stick to the ashtray right after a drag—I likely do still smell of smoke, and do still display the addict's scars. But in presentation I am clean and, while not a health fascist, I make it clear to everyone that I find smoking filthy. Simply by presenting this familiar face with conviction, I seem able to convince other people to overlook the teeth and fingertips, to assume the stench is drifting over from elsewhere.

## 12

MOST CHINESE FACULTY LIVE IN A COMPLEX AT THE EAST END of campus, a half-kilometre from the foreigners' compound. The residences are stark and ugly, separated by courtyards of stubble and corrugated-tin sheds that, designed as bicycle garages, now house overflow families. Each building has four entranceways onto four stairwells. On every landing are four doors, half to apartments with two rooms, half to one-room flats. All the doors have numbers, as do the stairwells and residences. A family may live at 8-3-7: seventh apartment, third stairwell, eighth building. On the outer wall of the building is the corresponding number. Stairwell identifications are less visible: worn away or smothered in grime. With few exceptions, door figures have long disappeared. Occupants must explain to guests behind which one they live. Explain clearly, too, or else run the risk of having those guests interrupt neighbours or come and go without a visit.

Zhou Hong lives at 12-1-9. Her building is pressed against the brick wall that separates the college from the city, and her windows, three flights up, open onto a tree-lined boulevard packed day and night with cars and trucks, push-carts and bikes, pedestrians and playing children. Though Hong and her daughter live, work and attend school on campus, the view from their apartment is of a dusty thoroughfare in northwest Beijing. Though the Beijingers who reside along the boulevard gaze at the wall day after day, and wait for buses outside the east gate, and set up soft-drink stands and bicycle repair stalls in its shadow, and let their kids kick balls against the brick and stain it with their pee; despite this proximity, most have never set foot on institute grounds. Ordinary people have no business with intellectuals. No contact with foreigners. No complaint against the guards who man the gates in daylight and bar them at night.

Having crossed the near-deserted campus, leaving foot hieroglyphs on the paths, I slip into the stairwell. It doesn't make much difference, especially during the day, but an unobserved arrival at Zhou Hong's always feels like a small victory. Even presuming that the walls have ears and the doors eyes; even presuming that I can't possibly know who is watching. Departures, in contrast, especially during the evening, are best loud and highly observable.

The music reaches me on the bottom landing. It is Western, classical, nineteenth century: likely one of the tapes included in the package I gave Zhou Hong. That first morning, wobbly with jet lag and hunger—I missed breakfast in the cafeteria—I approached a woman at a desk in the Foreign Affairs Office and asked to see Mrs. Zhou; for, being the wife of Zuo Chang, she would surely also be stunning, with the regular features and slightly purple lips of Han aristocracy; for, being who she was, she would surely also be aloof. Instead, I met a woman with hazel skin, unchiselled features and a round, flat face. Her eyes were single-lidded. Her jaw was strong. That same woman had a sweet smile, a girlish laugh, and English surprisingly free—given what Zuo had told me about her note taking—of idiomatic expressions. Still, within moments of greeting me, she was already copying my words down in a small red pad not unlike Mao's famous pocketbook. Within moments of meeting her, I was already relaxed and happy, entranced.

Presented with her husband's gift, Mrs. Zhou ran her tongue over her lower lip and retied her hair. Then she felt the cassettes at the bottom of the bag. "I like these very much!" she said, clutching a tape to her chest. "Did Zuo send you some music?" I asked innocently. On hearing her husband's name, she sobered. We moved on to other business.

Now, climbing the stairs, I silently hope that neighbours in corridor No. 1, building No. 12, share her love of classical music. Zhou Hong owns a quality Japanese tape player. Walls in the residences are thick, but windows and doors, invariably ill fitting and cracked, permit conversations and music and TV babble to flow freely. I stop on the landing below and listen. Granted, I am not musical. Granted, I am rarely moved or taken out of myself by a song or a symphony. But she is, and I have witnessed her being washed over, even cleansed— so she tells me—by the experience. It is something to watch. Something to feel, too, no doubt. I wouldn't mind. Not her experience of music necessarily. But of drinking from the same stream as Hong? Washing in the same waters? I wouldn't mind that at all.

"Ying isn't home yet?" I ask her at the door, knowing well that I am an hour early.

"Her final chance to see her friends."

"Was she okay this morning?"

"I don't think she understands," admits Hong.

"I don't think I do, either."

"Please come in," she says. "I will make tea."

Twelve-1-9 is a single room flat. One room, a galley kitchen and squat toilet, no balcony. According to city ordinances, the apartment is ample for a single-child family. Thanks to Zuo Chang's rising star in the French department, however, the couple were promised the first available two-room flat. A new residence was completed last month. But with Zuo absent without permission, the house committee reconsidered: the place went to someone else.

The room is rectangular, dark despite a window, and the ceiling feels only inches above my head. Against one wall is a narrow bed, a cot folded at its feet. In a corner stands a miniature table. Atop it is a droopy assembly of stuffed creatures: pandas and dolls, a slack-eared bunny. Half the area between the bed and the opposite wall is taken up with a floor-to-ceiling cabinet. On the shelves are a tea serving and four model terracotta warriors, books in Chinese and English, rows of music cassettes, and a small television with its screen hidden behind a cloth. When not in use, the tape player, perched on a tiny washing machine, is also kept under veil. A round fold-up table, the kind used for card games in legion halls, consumes the remaining floor space. Hong owns just two chairs: additional guests must sit on the edge of the bed. Like everything else in the room, the table is cheap and appears to have been manufactured some time in the last month. Even the "old" objects—the terracotta warriors and statue of Guanyin, the Goddess of Mercy—are crude fakes. Virtually everything at the college looks that way, in fact. Buildings and their furnishings, electronics and equipment: almost all brand new, almost all junk.

Because of her work, Zhou Hong's apartment boasts a rare and coveted household gadget: a telephone. It is red, made of plastic and resembles a life-sized version of what Barbie would hold in her hand for chats with Ken. The phone sits on the bottom shelf, haughty and proud. A topic of conversation among guests, Hong once admitted, if not exactly a facilitator of conversations. In my presence, at least, it has never rung.

Until that very moment when, agitated by a sound coming—I assume—from the tape player, I cross to the cabinet.

The ring is a gurgle that Hong, in the kitchen, would otherwise have missed. Hurrying to the phone, she focuses for some reason on the artwork adorning the walls. I, too, have a premonition of who the caller will be.

Her smile does not waver. By now I know to ignore her mouth and voice and concentrate on her eyes. When unhappy or perturbed, Zhou Hong's glaze over, as if her spirit has vacated her body. After thirty seconds of chat, she has ceased to be here, either for him or for me. I understand a little at first, and hear no mention of missing or being missed, love or devotion. Practical matters only: flight information, additional documents that need to be obtained. But then Hong begins to speak quickly and drop in phrases of her native Shanghai dialect, which Zuo Chang must know. The ploy works: a few words later, I have lost the thread.

Zhou Hong is not a Shanghai woman. That cliché, of severe beauty and worldly cynicism, refers to natives of the massive city near the mouth of the Yangtze River. She comes from a village in a county two hours away by bus, a day on cart or foot. "From the countryside" is the expression, and in urban centres it seems to apply to everyone from everywhere else. Such people are rarely asked to elaborate on their backgrounds. The inference, I gather, isn't that nothing happens outside the cities, and so the lives there merit only brief, shrugging mention, like a summary of a prison term. It is more that *everything* happens in the countryside, everything primordially, archetypically Chinese, and so the experience requires scant illumination. Who explains how one breathes or makes love?

Primordial to other Chinese, of course—not to me. Once, and once only, I got her to provide some details of her "from the countryside" upbringing. She was born in 1954. Her parents named her Hong, meaning "Red," but as a child she was called Hua-hong: "Red Flower." Though the name was common, after 1949 it took on special significance. Red was the colour of the revolution; a post-Liberation child was a flower of the new China. Red Flower actually got off lucky. She attended school with kids dubbed Red Soldier and Loving China, Liberation and Road to Russia. Her father was himself a teacher, her grandfather a rice farmer. Her mother, who sang in a local opera troupe as a teenager, bore three children in four years, only to die of a mysterious disease—malnutrition, Hong suspects—during the famine of 1959–62. The entire family might have perished had the father not abandoned primary school teaching, his true vocation, to become a cadre. As a party official, he helped educate the village about the workers' paradise. He also procured extra rations for his children. Later, his background as an educator led to the inevitable accusations of revisionism. Pure peasant roots spared him being persecuted, but not from being expelled from the ranks. As one of the tens of millions of minor offenders who couldn't be sent to the countryside to learn from the masses—he was already in the country, and already one of the masses—Zhou Hong's father wound up a labourer on a hydroelectric project three hundred kilometres upriver from the village, and from his children. He aged a half-decade for every year on the job, she estimates, lost the use of his right hand in an accident, and never recovered the vision sacrificed to dust and rock slivers. After the Cultural Revolution he remarried and is now retired.

I complained about her summary. Don't tell me about the politics, I said: tell me what it was like growing up when and where you did. Zhou Hong smiled, perhaps a little indulgently, and resumed. Her grandmother did not have bound feet, but was known by only a single name, as was the old custom. She also had black teeth and fine grey hair. Hua-hong's favourite outing was a visit to her grandparents' farm inland from the river. No buses serviced the marshy terrain; no real roads, for that matter. They either walked, rode bikes or caught lifts on carts pulled by water buffalo. She remembered the bright air and sunlight, the clusters of red peppers outside the farmhouse, the congealed blood of a slaughtered chicken in the yard. In the village, they lived in a wooden house, with an aunt as mother substitute and a widowed grandfather as patriarch. The house had two rooms, one atop the other, linked by a ladder. The kitchen was a coal fire in the back alley. The toilet was a bricked-in ditch a block away. Summer heat was oppressive; columns of insects encased the one streetlamp. The laneway was narrow, but still wide enough for banners and marches and spontaneous rallies. She recalled watching men and women, many her father's age, being paraded past the house wearing sandwich boards and hangdog expressions, in the hands of strutting Red Guards, many not much older than herself. Afternoon *shoeshui* was often impossible, thanks to the loudspeaker installed on the post; nights, she was frequently kept awake by "meetings" outside a nearby shop. First, her father was sent away, returning only twice a year for visits. Then an uncle got into trouble and vanished. He died in a camp. Her oldest brother helped expose the uncle as a reactionary; she joined her elder siblings in denouncing her father's former profession.

A model student, a flower of China, Hua-hong joined the Junior Red Guards at thirteen. She loved the uniform. She loved the songs. More than anything, she loved Chairman Mao, who was the sun, moon and stars; who was the good earth; who was China. At fourteen, she tried to board a train for Beijing to attend a rally on Tiananmen Square. Again and again, older teenagers pushed her off; her final try, she twisted an ankle on the tracks. The girl did participate in several rallies in Shanghai, though. She did sing the songs and shout the slogans and wave her Little Red Book. She wanted to fight the enemies of socialism. She wanted to destroy the Old Ideas and Old Culture. Finally, at age seventeen, enrolled at a university where no classes had been taught in years, she learned of a once-in-a-lifetime opportunity, and used all her charm and skill and doggedly memorized ideological fervour to avail herself of it. She was appointed head of a unit to be sent on a special mission to a special place, a hard case, where ideals were badly needed and much work had to be done. In that place, she would meet her future husband. She would also become not only an instant adult but a stranger to her childhood self, her own given name.

In 1971, Zhou Hua-hong went to Tibet.

Of course I was astounded. Of course I wanted more. But by now her expression was plaintive, and I let it be. Alone in my apartment, I asked the question out loud: Hong's story was too archetypal to merit telling? Too much like a million other stories? Since then, not a day has gone by when I haven't mulled over that staggering possibility.

She hangs up and retreats into the kitchen to fix the tea. Her walk is measured, her cheeks are flush.

"This is hard," she says.

"Did you tell him I was here?"

"No."

"Why not?"

"I'm not sure. Talking on the phone should not make me so uncomfortable. He is my husband."

"He's trying to take your daughter away."

"What?"

Swallowing, I repeat the accusation. No potential truth about the situation has troubled me more: suppose Zhou Hong is as aware as everyone else of what her husband is doing, and is still letting it happen? Wang Hua has dropped hints to this effect. So, I suspect, has Dean Feng. By my own definition, for her to know, and intend to do nothing, constitutes an admittance that the ending to all this will be tragic. For me to know that she knows, and also to do nothing, would amount to submitting to tragic inevitability. Funny, but I'm no longer so gung ho about having stories wind up this way. Even Ivan's sour alternative—a farce perpetrated by fools—sounds more appealing.

Again, she reties her hair, pausing with her fingers still crooked around her ear. "Not my daughter only," she corrects gently.

"Okay."

"She has a chance to leave. Everyone here wants that. Zuo has had good luck; now he is sharing it with the girl."

"But not with you?"

I apologize at once.

"You are very sweet with Ying," says Hong.

"I'm in love," I answer.

"Like with your own daughter?"

I feel heat in my cheeks. Her smile puts me at ease.

"Love for our children is so easy," she says. "So natural and uncomplicated. With Ying, I never worry that I am making a mistake or speaking foolishly. I am confident, at ease. Do you not wish it could be this way with adults also?"

"Only all the time."

"I like talking with you, David."

I return the compliment.

"Chinese people often find it easier to talk with foreigners than each other," observes Hong. She holds her cup to her mouth, though not necessarily to drink from it. She does the same with chopsticks, pressing their tips into her lips until her skin turns crimson. "Not so many barriers. Not so many rules."

"Not so much at stake?"

"Probably," she admits.

"I can't picture you as a Red Guard," I say.

Her expression suddenly goes blank. "I was someone else then. Not who my father taught me to be. Not the person I was comfortable pretending to be. I only wanted to please Chairman Mao. To do that, I would say or act—"

"I became a Marxist to please my mother," I intervene. "Studied for years, joined groups, organized protests—all to get her to think better of me. Know what really stinks? It didn't even work. She still found reasons not to be proud of her son."

"I was a disappointment to Chairman Mao as well."

I look at her. She laughs. Relieved, I join in. Soon I am emitting a proper belly rumble, my first since leaving Montreal. Hong's eyes widen at the merriment until she, too, bursts. Two adults, one male and one female, one a foreigner and the other a national, carrying on behind closed doors? The sound drifting, no doubt, through window seams and air vents into other apartments and down corridors? Not prudent, I'm sure. Not practical.

A good moment, though. "Hong," I say, hoping the right words will materialize. "I've been wanting to ask you something for ages."

"Ages?" she replies. "Like generations?"

"For a long time."

"Okay."

She leans across the table in interest. I am, unfortunately, seated on the edge of the bed, and the sensation of the fabric, especially when I rub my moist palms over it, is enough to fire messages down to my groin. *Come on, words*, I silently implore. Meanwhile, her shirtsleeves are hiked halfway up to her shoulders, revealing a mole on the right biceps. Carole's shoulders were mapped with moles. During pre-Natalie afternoons of lovemaking, seated naked atop the bed sheets with our arms entwined and her hand below my waist, I would trace the familiar route from mole to mole with my lips, tonguing each growth until it glistened, diverted only when her trembling—as much from laughter as arousal—knocked me off course. It was a natural progression from the shoulders down to her breasts and then, slowly, each inch of skin covered, further below to her magnificent belly, still my prototype of flesh and muscle, folds and cavities. *Say something*, I counsel myself, trying not to look at Zhou Hong's arm, not to conjure her stomach. *Get anything out.*

"Yes?" she asks.

Her eyes are bright. Her arms are lovely. Can sexual tension of this thrust be completely one-sided?

"Is there any chance . . . ?" I stammer. "What I want to say is, we've known each other for a while now and—"

It rings again. The phone, I mean: the red plastic thing with the chirp. What are the odds? This time, neither of us glance at Zuo Chang's art on the walls; neither of us appear to have a clue who the caller might be. But then the voice of Dean Feng, launching into his diatribe before she can even say hello, bursts from the receiver. I hear my name mentioned and I am angry. I hear Wang Hua's name and I feel sick.

The conversation is brief.

"How did he know I was here?" I ask.

Her shrug renders the question moot. "The dean wonders if you have seen Wang Hua today."

"Why does the dean want to know?"

"People wish to speak with Wang."

"People?"

Zhou Hong, the receiver still in her grasp, examines a shelf of cassettes. Her face is in profile, leaving it unreadable. The music still plays, and is nice and emotional, but I feel no urge to cast the scene in a more poignant or romantic light because of Antonin Dvořák. This is no movie: no *Ordinary People* or *Death in Venice*. I formulate my next question with care.

"If I see Wang," I ask, "what should I tell him?"

"To keep a toothbrush in his pocket" is her hushed reply.

"Pardon?"

She shuts off the tape player. "I must return to the office for a moment," she says in a voice made huge by the hollowed air. At the door, she switches to her own language. "I hate this," she says to no one. "I hate this!"

Outside the building, in full view of the community, I arrange to visit Ying in the morning, and to talk again with Hong, using public words and faces, at still another banquet for an incoming Australian at noon. She even has the composure to remind me about the concert on Friday evening. I repeat my assurances that she can back out, and I will understand. After all, the girl's plane will have barely lifted off the ground. Hong will just be home from the airport and, though stunned and grieving, will also be in the first throes of examining her twice-emptied apartment, surveying her twice-narrowed life: a devastating process, I can say with some authority. Fighting shame, warring with self-pity and hatred and the desire—in me, at least—to commit a random act of violence, she will be preoccupied, wanting time on her own. To make a fool of yourself, I joke. To avoid making a fool of yourself in front of others.

But she is adamant. She very much wishes to attend the concert: she needs to, really. I do not ask her to repeat what she told me once, with even more reluctance than her child-hood reminiscence, about her relationship with music. I don't need to ask: I remember her description word for word. She said that music envelops her, lets her float freely outside her body, outside her self. That while listening she feels beyond time and place, worry or awareness. That in such a state she believes she is held safe, the water warm. That music grants her a welcome detachment from all things, but also a pleasing connection to them: a sensation of solitude, but also of being united. Happy. Better, somehow. And that when the tape clicked off or the performance ended she emerged raw and clean, momentarily unable to recall where she lived, her own name. Ordinary sights and sounds staggered her. Ordinary encounters felt strained. Others told Hong that it was she who acted strange after a concert or an hour with a cassette: prone to staring off into space, likely to mumble words to no effect. Friends found it amusing. Strangers thought her peculiar.

Ring any bells? I couldn't get over the similarities between her reactions and my condition. I can't get over my certainty that, perverse as it may sound, we are talking about the same basic experience.

What I do ask Zhou Hong to repeat is the particular reason she is so determined to fight her way into town on a Friday night to attend one of the frequent performances at the Beijing Concert Hall. She does so happily. On the bill is a famous violin concerto composed by two students at the Shanghai Conservatory in 1959. Based on Shanghai opera and a local legend, but written in Western symphonic style, *Butterfly Lovers* suffered the consequences of Chairman Mao's late-life manias. Like virtually all other musical forms, except a select group of revolutionary operas, it was banned during the Cultural Revolution. Especially galling was the concerto's synthesis of Western and Chinese influences: an affront to purity of race and ideological purpose. So memorable was the principal melody, however, that people hummed it in private for years, while riding bicycles and hanging wash, tilling fields and working lathes, as they did the arias from beloved, and also outlawed, operas. *Butterfly Lovers* became part of the national ghost repertoire, to be enjoyed alongside the phantom book library and shadow theatre, the spectre art museum. Now, of course, it is once more a shining example—along with the discredited operas and paintings, the books and plays, the temples and gardens—of the enduring national culture. Cassettes from Hong Kong fly out of shops; live performances are the hottest tickets in town. Though Hong will not admit as much, preferring to emphasize how beautiful the music is, it sounds as if the concerto has become freighted with cultural import. It sounds as if people are hearing all kinds of things in the notes. As if they want the music to stand for something else, something inside themselves: resilience and sadness, beauty. As if *Butterfly Lovers* is supposed to be China.

It sounds as if I'm in for a gloomy concert experience. But a proper night out with her—our first, really—when circumstance will bring us closer than ever.

Dust coats the campus floor like insecticide on fields. Invisible only because it is everywhere, covering everything, the powder will continue to form breakers and swirl and crash until a rain meshes it once again with the earth. Indoors, the dust will re-emerge as a pepper on foods and a smudge on facecloths, a tickle in the throat that keeps one awake coughing. It will need to be wiped off plates and silverware, swept off tables. It will need to be hacked up and spit into bathroom sinks.

## 13

FIFTEEN MINUTES TO CURFEW, AND WANG HUA ISN'T MOVING. Earlier, I brought him some dinner from the cafeteria. I also slipped out the west gate to stock up on beer in a local shop. Only the evening security guard observed me cross the lobby with two bowls of food; only a few foreigners saw me—the pathetic boozer—haul a half-dozen more bottles up the stairwell. The guard, a pleasant woman whose three-year-old spends his mother's shift watching TV in the lobby until he falls asleep on the couch, did ask a question, but it was about a word in an article in the *International Herald-Tribune* she was reading. All the security staff—except the secret policeman, I assume—keep the party-line *Renmin Bao* visible atop the desk blotter, and a week-old *Herald-Tribune* or *South China Morning Post*, given to them by one of the born agains, invisible beneath it. All the staff are learning English; all want at least a better paying job in town, at most to leave the country. Few, if any, wish to find God in their hearts. Beware those gifts from Billy and Sue Ellen and Roy and Lavina! I should warn them.

Now, Wang and I are hanging out on the back balcony beneath a starless sky. The front balcony off the living room faces a student residence. That curtain has not been drawn all day. But the charmless cement terrace entranced from the dining area affords an overview of the neighbourhood beyond the south gate, and a detailed perspective on the alley directly outside the wall. For all its triumphant downtown boulevards, plenty wide for revolutionary parades and columns of tanks, and its vaulting Hong Kong–wanna-be office towers, plenty fancy for unimpressed foreign staff, most of Beijing, I've learned, comprises streets flanked by apartment blocks, themselves a post-1949 façade behind which lie centuries-old tangles of alleys—called *hutongs*—that open onto traditional courtyard compounds and often end at inexplicable and untraceable canals. In daylight, our laneway offers the usual dreary state shops and lively private markets: butchers hacking at slabs of meat, old men smoking behind peanut mounds, women in Mao suits hawking plum-sized oranges and squash-sized pears. Competing for space are streams of bell-ringing bicycles and horse-drawn carts piled high with construction rubble, kids—almost all boys—adjusting their oversized Red Army hats as they wave wood pistols, plus the occasional penned-in automobile, its passengers inscrutable behind smoked glass.

The alley provides, in short, a glimpse of the vast "out there"—West Beijing, northern China, the cradle of Asia. The part of the world that I am in owns the next century, apparently. The China I am a resident of is perhaps the most closely watched nation on the planet. The city surrounding me, meanwhile, is that nation's nerve centre: the heart of the colossus, the omphalos. It is also a highly sensual—olfactory, especially—presence in my daily life. But I still don't have much to do with it. I've always had to keep my sights narrow in order to cope. While living an outright lie is proving downright consuming. No energy left for anyone or anything else. Just you and your shadow. You and the bathroom mirror.

The back balcony is protected from the gazes of those walking the on-campus path directly below. Only a Japanese teacher living next door can see over the cement railing. He teaches just two days a week at the school, though, and spends all his time with his lover—an overseas Chinese man, remarkably enough—in another part of the city.

Still, given that I've already fibbed about Wang Hua's whereabouts, I would have preferred to stay in the living room. He insisted, and now the main door to the building is due to be chained. On the railing are bottles of beer, an empty peanut bowl, two sets of feet. Again, Wang has made no attempt to conceal his presence on the balcony, nor to modify his voice. He has been drinking all day. I have been drinking since dinner. Three times I've excused myself to pee. Not once has he stood up from his chair. The phone has rung twice; twice we have let it ring away.

"I guess I do need an answering machine," I say to myself after the second call.

"A what?"

"A machine that records messages. So you can hear who is phoning and decide whether or not to pick up."

"You can pretend you're not home?"

"And then call the person back later," I agree.

"Or not call them back?"

"Exactly."

"If you are *still* not home?" asks Wang.

"That's the idea," I agree again, uneasily.

"The lie, you mean."

"The lie, I mean."

"Because you're right there when they call, aren't you?" he asks, his voice innocent.

"Right where?"

"In your room. Watching TV or listening to music. In the privacy of your imagination and the safety of your mind. No one bothering you with knocks on the door or phone calls. No one intruding on your stupid fantasy."

"You understand the technology, Wang," I say to end the conversation.

He brushes non-existent hair back from his eyes. "And there is a tape, too? A tape with voices on it. As evidence?"

"You mean the voices of the callers?"

"I mean the evidence."

"What evidence?"

"Of the crime."

"Calling someone up on the phone isn't a crime," I say, the sentence clanging in my memory.

"It can be," answers Wang. "If necessary. For the good of the state. For the good of the people."

With that, he empties his seventh bottle of Qingdao, mostly into his mouth.

"Almost finished," he announces.

"I thought I'd bought plenty. Of beer and cigarettes," I say, holding the inverted pack of Marlboros over my eyes to count the remaining sticks, as drunk people are wont to do.

"You smoke too much," says Wang. He picks one cigarette out of my hair, where it now nests, and another from my shirt collar. The third stick plunged over the railing.

"I don't smoke at all," I reply. "Do I look like an intellectual-who-was-persecuted-during-the-Cultural-Revolution?"

"Do I look like a hooligan?"

I offer him back a surviving cigarette. Immediately, Wang pops it into his mouth. After several seconds of chewing, his expression neutral, he leans forward and spits the mulch off the balcony. Then he gargles with my beer. His spreading grin is sardonic. His eyes, even in the dark, swim.

Minus the hair, Wang Hua's features are in stark relief. With the strong cheekbones and flat nose, the liquid eyes and baby skin, he could easily pass for a woman. An attractive woman, too: I conjure television images of Tibetan nuns—in the news, I shamefully add, because they are being imprisoned and beaten and sometimes raped by Chinese soldiers—heads shaven to emphasize their self-abnegation but also to unintentionally highlight their thin-air sculpted beauty, as ethereal as the mountainscape that produced them. Astoundingly, the mere thought, in vague correlation with Wang, gives me a partial hard-on. I would be dismayed, rather than bemused, with myself were the connection not so ludicrous. Wang Hua is definitely a man, and is presumably heterosexual. To the best of my knowledge—and with due respect to Ivan's fashionable theories about androgyny—I, too, am these rather conventional things. Besides, Wang's stained T-shirt and baggy pants are male prisoner garb. His behaviour, meanwhile, is classic Bad Element—definitely a guy thing in China.

"I'm dangerous," he declares.

"Just hungry, it seems."

"The food was delicious, but now it is finished. The peanuts were tasty, but they are also gone. And the beer was wonderful to drink, but only you have any left. Almost finished," he repeats ominously.

"Let's go sit in the living room," I say, ignoring the echo.

"This balcony is perfect. We are above China. China is below us. We can see people. People cannot see us. I never want to leave."

"Okay."

"And I *am* finished," he continues, sliding his feet off the railing. "No more thoughts or ideas. Just beer and food and sleep and this—"

He indicates a solitary sexual act. I nod.

"Once I really was dangerous, though."

"Last June?"

"Last June I was stupid," corrects Wang. "I mean in 1967. In 1967 I lead the revolutionaries at my school in marches to denounce the Liu Shaoqi clique and root out the enemies of socialism. We marched around the town looking for enemies. When we found them, we burned their belongings and smashed their houses. Sometimes, we beat them with sticks and rocks, but not often. Older revolutionaries got to do the fun stuff: hurting and torturing, killing an old man who taught my father history before Liberation. We watched the activities and cheered our comrades. I was given a special Chairman Mao button as a reward."

"Like one of Dean Feng's?" I ask for no reason, except that I'm half-potted.

"He has the same button, yes."

We are silent for a moment. I hear the wind through leafless branches, a radio in a nearby dormitory, the scrape of feet on the path below.

"I was six," says Wang softly, "and full of certainty. Also of hatred and violence. And I was dangerous!"

"When I was six," I counter, "or maybe a little older, I lay in the snow on our front balcony pretending I was with my father. Doing stuff together, I guess, just being together. Funny, I remember him a little. Not what he looked like or even his voice, but the smell of him, the sensation of his hands squeezing my shoulders. . . . But that's impossible. He left when I was a baby. I must have invented those memories. On the balcony, maybe. *That's* what I was probably doing out there, besides having fits."

"Fits?"

"Of doubt," I add quickly. No one—not even Zhou Hong—needs to know about the epilepsy. *Sober up*, I warn myself.

"Are you drunk?" he asks.

"You made me."

"China made me," says Wang. He raises both arms to heaven, like a preacher. "From the mouths of young people you can get the truth."

"Okay."

"At seventeen there are no ugly boys or girls."

"Got it."

"Can I stay here tonight?"

"Is that another proverb?"

"It is a question."

"Of course," I reply. My stomach starts to churn.

Wang drops his arms. "I never want to leave this apartment," he says. "I never want to go outside again."

"Zhou Hong shouldn't let Ying go," I announce.

"Hmm?"

"Ying is her daughter, her child. Zuo Chang has no rights to the girl. Not now. And once she goes, she'll forget her mom. Kids do. They don't mean to. But you become the past. Something finished. Something fucked up."

"Totally fucked up," says Wang.

"You remember them, of course. Every sight and sound. Every touch. For sure, every ki—" My voice breaks. No joke: a full-scale crack in the tone, the fatal first step towards blubbering. "And you grieve," I continue, tracing my own palm lines. "For yourself, for your relationship with your wife, for the child. Like when you see her already building walls. Already feeling abandoned; already learning to defend herself. A protective shell of stuffed animals, for God's sake. As if Kermit-the-fucking-Frog is going to keep the. . . ."

I sigh, suddenly exhausted. I also wait, eyes downcast, for Wang to laugh or belch at my speech. A hand brushes against my shoulder.

"Some mercenary, David," he offers.

"Who said I was—?"

"Last week, also while drunk. I had to look up the word in a dictionary. You said you shaved your face to present a lie and wear mirrored sunglasses to hide the truth."

My head is clear enough to be embarrassed by Wang's summary of this conversation, which is not itself sharp in recall. "I'm changing," I say. "I mean, I've changed."

"Your appearance?"

"Don't make fun of me."

"I change my appearance, too," he says. "Even my hair. Makes no difference, though. Not to the police, not to China. I'm still me. Still who I must be."

"Of course. I'm not saying—"

"And you sound like who you must be, too," he adds, his eyes sly. "Nice man. Good father."

We are cut off. Not by a jangling phone, at least, but a chain being pulled between the handles of two doors. "No going back from here," I say, rising.

"Know what the definition of a friend is?" he asks.

Unlike the recent exchange with Wang, Zuo Chang's definition of the concept burns bright in my memory. "Someone who can do something for you?"

He smiles and shakes his head. "A friend is someone who has no choice but to join you in your cell, but still asks permission to stay."

"Please stay, Wang," I say.

The phone rings again.


I don't sleep well. No surprise: Wang's snores make for harsh counterpoint to the usual cicada symphony. Curiously, in timbre and inflection, most notably when they rise to a crescendo, his snores sound like monks chanting mantras in East End Montreal accents. The analogy is demented but, once made, holds me in its thrall. What a glottal roar my imagination composes. It is like a packed Forum, seventeen thousand saffron-robed fans murmuring away; it is like, I suddenly suspect, the Clark Street apartment when I was a boy. Who was cracking the air with the whip of his snores then? Except for the lost night with Remys waitress Masha Cloutier, it has been almost three years since I've slept with another human being. Obviously, the lumpen figure on the couch doesn't qualify as the full experience. Still, he is blowing his dreamworld horn, and I, two doors away in the bedroom, cannot make peace with the melody.

In the bathroom I cup my hands beneath the faucet. After barely a trickle, the flow sputters. Pipes shudder and squeal; the water ceases, not to start up again until dawn. I scrub my face anyway. Since I can't sleep to dream, I return to the balcony to smoke the final cigarette and mull over two recent reveries. The first, which appears part of a series, was in French, despite having no dialogue. I suppose I *dreamt* it in that language, which sounds odd, I know. I sat at a kitchen table wearing only a bath towel. A stove light failed to keep the room from darkness. An open balcony door failed to circulate the still air. From the back alley came the clink of silverware on plates, cat disputes, love-making. From further away, carried in the still summer night, drifted in strains of pulsating live music. A woman—Carole, surely—slumbered in a bedroom up the hall, and her low, regular breathing reached my ears strong as a heartbeat. I listened to the breathing, and the music, while slowly eating slices of melons and kiwis, oranges cut into quarters. Pools of juices glistened on the surface. A knife glimmered atop a counter.

The other dream, which is reoccurring, returns me to English—without, once again, any dialogue—and to Beijing. Twice now I have set off to explore the city's canals. For centuries the network of palaces in and around the capital was linked by waterways. Equally important, the city itself, perched on the edge of a desert steppe, was hooked up in the thirteenth century to the Grand Canal, vital provider of grains and supplies from central China. Many of the waterways remain, but are in disuse, filled in or choked with garbage and sewage. Both my outings ended without much success; what water I found was, if not frozen over, then inert and foul smelling even in the cold. In the dream, though, the canals are clean and the water is the blue of certain bird shells. Naked, I float downstream on my back, arms outstretched, vision blinkered by stone walls. Overhead is a tall sky, cirrus clouds drifting by. Around me are never swarms of people, never the living city, but bird flotillas and lilies that brush my fingertips, tickle my buttocks below the surface. I am weightless, of course, and feel at once within my corporeal body but also outside it, gazing back down, gazing back up. All sounds are blocked. Only what is within my head is audible; only those inner voices, often cause enough for concern. But even they fall silent, and I simply float.

## 14

AMONG MY BACHELOR HABITS, NONE IS A BIGGER SECRET THAN a favourite clothes-washing technique. Most laundry days in Montreal I stuffed my duffel bag and trundled over to the laundromat on St. Viateur, where guys like me exchanged *saluts* and once-overs and not much else. Occasionally, though, I found the prospect of such a night too dispiriting, and so I invented an alternative. Filling my tub with six inches of water and stirring in a cup of soap, I would dump in my underwear and socks, T-shirts and pants. Next I would switch on the shower and derobe. Then I danced over my clothes. Stomped on the jeans and ground heels into the shirts. Swished the socks and kneaded the underwear. Sometimes I would perform a bogus native dance, complete with whoops; more often I sang songs that had no direct associations with washing, but that seemed appropriate: "Dance to the Music" by Sly and the Family Stone and James Brown's "I Feel Good." It did feel good, swooshy and steamy and wet, though had Ivan or Adele or—God forbid—Carole walked in on me during the act, I would have withered in embarrassment: more so, I suspect, than had they caught me masturbating.

Imagine my delight, then, to discover in China a billion other people who also wash their clothes this way. Even in Beijing, the majority of citizens still thump with sticks and soften with knuckles and, in summer apparently, slap against walls or enamel basins their shirts and pants and undergarments. My confidence at an all-time high, I rarely use the machines behind the cafeteria. In fact, at 6:56 the next morning, I stand naked in the tub, my feet being massaged by fabric and warm water. Noticing the hour, I hastily towel off and throw on some clothes. It is Thursday, and the cleaning lady will be knocking on the door in four minutes. Madame Chai cleans my apartment first thing every Tuesday and Thursday morning. Once she has landed a perfunctory knock, there will be no stopping her from letting herself in: no cries of dismay, no bare flesh in the dining area, no sleep sounds from the bedroom. Even a sign, even in Chinese—like the one Wang and I co-authored last night—will not put the woman off.

By 6:58 I am at the door, ready. I hear her enter the stairwell and begin to climb. By the fourth floor she is out of breath; struggling to locate the correct key, she mumbles to herself. Oddly, she inserts the key and turns it part way before knocking. That tips me off, and I swing the door open more or less simultaneously with her hitting the wood. Madame Chai tumbles into my apartment, her face astonished, the chain dangling from the lock.

"I'm sick," I say in Mandarin, indicating the sign. "Need to sleep. No cleaning today."

"I have to check the living-room drapes."

"Not now, please."

"But—"

"Thanks, Madame Chai. I'll tell the security desk once I'm better. You can return then."

A squat, pie-faced woman who mops floors with a vigour that could be mistaken for rage, Chai strains to peer beyond me to the glass doors leading into the living room. I block her path.

"You kept your drapes shut yesterday," she says.

"Thanks," I repeat, backing her into the corridor.

I listen again. As expected, she does not make for Professor

Mueller's apartment across the landing. Instead, she retreats down the stairs. I crack the door. At the bottom the puffing cleaning woman whispers; "He's sick. What can I do?" When a male voice responds brusquely, she tells her tale.

With the DO NOT DISTURB reinforced, and Wang Hua still asleep in the living room, I slip out. A curved mirror angled above the main entrance permits desk security to survey the corridor without having to get up. Security staff, in turn, are observable by anyone approaching, and are often on view eating or watching TV, resting their heads on the blotter with their eyes closed to the columns of *Renmin Bao* newsprint. As I near the exit, my reflection expands hideously in the mirror—neck stretched, legs squished beneath a bloated torso—while the parallel image of Deng Chen suffers a painful narrowing. Deng fixes me with his zombie glare and makes a move. Before he can even get around the counter, I am through the door into a windless grey morning—perfect for sunglasses and an upturned jacket collar.

Zuo Ying waits on the front step of corridor No. 1, building No. 12. The child's perfection fills me with a wistfulness that is, I readily admit, clichéd. She has an exquisitely shaped face, flawless features and milk-chocolate eyes. Already her pencil brows arch over their sockets; already her profile is haughty. A quality of her gaze, at once introverted and curious, belongs to her father; I am not surprised to hear that, though she can write only a few characters, her paintings of bamboo stalks and butterflies are attracting notice. From her mother Ying has inherited a laugh almost against her nature. Zhou Hong laughs readily and easily at anything. Her daughter is more cautious, or perhaps less convinced. The results are giggles swallowed like bad medicine and smiles so strained they reveal her gums—a tiny blemish in what is otherwise a priceless porcelain statue from some forgotten dynasty.

"Hi," I say in Mandarin.

"My mom is upstairs," answers Ying in her helium voice. "She said I should wait for you here."

"Want to go for a walk?"

She wears the yellow tracksuit I bought her last week. A bowing Mickey Mouse smiles on the back; a marching Donald Duck and a tripping Goofy beam from respective thighs. The images are pirated and the suit is a cheap fake. The girl kept it on for five straight days, and still uses the top as bed clothing. My doubts about the propriety of the gift vanished before this obsessive delight, as they always did with Natalie. Yes, I think of them together. As friends, sisters. Some days they skip rope on the college sports field; other times they monkey around on the couch in Carole's basement. They read books in English and chat in Chinese and play hopscotch using French. I am guardian to both. Not alone: Carole and Zhou Hong linger in the background, arms crossed, smiles bemused. As steward, I bring the girls cookies and mooncakes and cook them pasta with meat sauce, dumplings with soy. I give them a bath, which they share, and then ready them for bed. First we play a game. Though I taught it to Natalie when we all lived in Mile End, until recently every trip to Longueuil, regardless of the hour, included at least one version. Using extra blankets, I slowly tuck the child in, adding layer upon layer until exploding with the final covering, shaking the mattress as she screams in delight. I do that to both girls. Then, encouraging them to prod my belly, I let rip a Santa Claus roar that leaves them helpless with laughter. Next we sing one of Ying's lullabies, learned from her mother: "The gods on the rooftree guard pigeons from harm/And my little pigeon is safe in my arms." Finally, pillowing their heads with my shoulders, I tell them a story that has some odd twists and a few scary parts, but an ending where everyone lives happily ever after.

What is going on here? Already, Hong admits, people on campus have begun to talk. Already, other foreign teachers have wondered aloud about my sticking my nose in this matter. For my own part, I am comfortable with my actions and, to a large extent, my thoughts. Of course I am substituting; of course I am interfering. Not for the child's sake, either. Nor exactly for her mother's.

We start off for the sports ground. Ying hums a song that I don't recognize.

"What are you singing?"

"A song for the airplane rides," she answers. "My granny taught me it."

"Can you teach me?"

"Are you going on an airplane?"

"Not tomorrow."

"It's only for—"

I don't understand the word, but presume she says "travellers" or something similar.

"Then can you sing it?"

"I just did!"

No question, she is different from Natalie: less fun loving, more serious. As we near a campus street, I reach for her hand. She surges ahead, implicitly rejecting the help. When a supply truck roars past us, churning up dust, my heart tries to leap from its cage.

"You'll be with your father very soon," I say, carefully casting the sentence in future tense.

"He lives in Montreal."

"I know. I live there, too."

"No, you don't."

"I mean, I did," I correct. "And I will again. I might even see you in Montreal."

"You live in the foreigners' building," says Ying. "Mom says you speak many languages and have a bathtub."

By chance, a recent conversation with the cleaning lady about a blocked drain introduced me to this word.

"Does my father have a bathtub in Canada?"

"Maybe."

"I thought you were his friend."

"I'm sure he has," I amend.

"Good. I want to—"

I repeat back the unfamiliar verb.

"Paint pictures," she clarifies. "With my brushes. Like these. . . . " She indicates the Goofy stencil.

"In the bathtub?"

Ying traces her earlobe with her finger, as if to loop strands of her short hair. Then she gives me a brisk nod. At once I am convinced that Zuo Chang's lover should prepare herself for watercolour paintings on the sides of her tub, along with, I hope, plenty of other messings of her child-free abode.

"Do you love Zhou Hong?" asks the girl.

"Sorry?"

"My dad doesn't. They live apart now. They can only have respect for each other."

"That's not true," I reply, trying to sound emphatic rather than distressed. "Your mom and dad are still. . . . Where did you hear this?"

"Everyone says it."

I want to ask more. I wait, hoping that Ying, like every other five-year-old on the planet, will soon have no choice but to empty her mind of all thoughts.

Giving up, I scan my mental thesaurus for available verb choices. I know the words for *love* and *hate*, *like* and *dislike*, *beautiful* and—thanks to the girl—*respect*. Not many options, unfortunately.

"I respect your mom, too," I say.

"Respect?"

I nod feebly.

"Then no one loves her," she decides.

We are now on the track. Early mornings and evenings, the college sportsground is packed with strollers. At first, I found this puzzling; the campus is latticed with laneways, many reasonably secluded, where couples or friends could enjoy greater privacy. The pull towards the track, a terrain exposed to wind and rain, devoid of shade, antagonistic to intimate conversation, seemed to go against better judgement. Within a week of arriving, however, I began to understand its appeal. Walking the sportsground required no decisions. Leisure-time goals needed not to be outlined; the risk of destination was nonexistent. Many evenings, tired and overwhelmed, I also found myself drawn to a non-decision and, rather than navigate campus laneways or—perish the thought—the streets of the neighbourhood beyond the gates, I wound up on the track. In such a context, the presence of other equally addled strollers acted as consolation. The circle closed, I realized with some amusement. An internal Chinese matter.

The oval is empty now except for a scrum of old men spotting the ground with sunflower seed shells. Birds land near them, stabbing at the food, alighting. A bleary orange sun hangs in a corner of the sky.

Ying finds a stick and begins to sketch on the clay surface. One drawing is so interesting I ask her about it.

"Earth," she says.

"You can write ideograms?"

"My mom is teaching me before bed every night."

I ask her to draw another.

"Sky?" I wonder, studying the result.

"Good!" she agrees, exactly as Zhou Hong must do. "You do one now," she adds, handing me the stick-brush.

"Me?"

"Can't you write?"

"Not well," I try to explain. "In Chinese, at least."

She frowns. "What other way is there?"

I attempt the simplest ideogram I know. Still, she puzzles over my work. Where Natalie crooks her head, Ying squints; where my daughter is compelled by her nature to speak, regardless of how pre-sensical her words may be, Hong's child clings to a silence that is innocent but often feels strategic. No question, two of the three members of this family push the right anxiety buttons in me. The third, too, has a pronounced effect on my behaviour.

I try again. This time, Ying nods and, taking the stick back, draws a companion ideogram.

"Fire and—?" I ask.

"Water," she answers.

"You write very well, Ying."

"I'm only five."

"That's what I mean."

"How old are you?"

I tell her.

"Then you should do much better!"

Angling back across the field to the residences, I look ahead to Zhou Hong's corridor, in the hope that she might be observing us from the window on her landing. She isn't but others are: old ladies on benches, security guards leaning against walls.

This is pointless and nearly impossible in Mandarin. It is also none of my business. "I want to tell you how people live in Montreal," I begin, already stumbling.

The girl looks up at me. "Why do you wear those glasses?" she asks, a frequent question.

"I want to explain something, Ying. About men and women. Love and respect. About your father and mother. I know I don't speak very well. But you can listen?"

She listens. I explain. It comes out mangled and hypocritical, transparently self-interested. Five minutes of this garbage and her expression is unchanged. She hasn't understood a word. She thinks I am a moron.

"Will my new mother have a bathtub in her house in Montreal?" asks Ying, blinking slowly, as if to count each one.

Thankfully, someone suddenly grasps my hand. We cross the empty road together.


Wang Hua sits cross-legged on the couch, swishing the dregs of a beer opened last night and staring at the television. The room smells of unwashed feet. I cross automatically to the drapes, think better of it, and settle on cracking a window. Without a breeze, no fresh air will enter the apartment—only more dust. Again, I silently question my friend's hiding techniques. I could hear the television from two flights below; Deng Chen saw me leave an hour ago. Even Elaine Mueller across the hall opened her door as I fumbled with my key to scold me about the volume. Her tone was charged with ill will.

The screen shows a man at a desk reading from a text. Behind him is a collage of newspapers and books.

"What's on?" I ask.

"Educational programming," answers Wang. He looks even worse than yesterday: complexion pasty and eyes puffed, stubbled scalp glistening. "The state is lecturing the masses on their accents. The state wants better speech from the peasants." He stops, absorbs a few sentences, translates. "'You are not using standard Mandarin. Your mispronunciations and dialects are hurting our great language. Please improve yourselves. We cannot understand what you say!'"

"Hear, hear."

"Foreign devil," he accuses, employing the Chinese term.

"Nothing else worth watching?"

"An American soap opera full of attractive white people with nice houses and large cars. Also tanned bodies and excellent sunglasses. It starts at seven o'clock."

"In the evening?"

"Right."

The phone rings.

"Six times since you left," says Wang. "Definitely need an answering machine."

I lift the receiver to a screech of static. Residents who are certain the interference is being caused by cheap bugging devices often hurl abuse into the void. I just hang up. This morning, detecting a voice in the hiss, I instruct the caller to shout. Dean Feng has good lungs: I end up holding the phone six inches from my ear. He needs a word with me. Could he—? Missing the rest, but guessing, I holler back that I will meet him in his office. Feng Ziyang counters that he would prefer to visit me at—"Can't hear you!" I say, slamming down the receiver.

"Better go," I tell Wang.

"Feng is crazy and Shen is a witch," he replies with a belch. "Believe everything they tell you."

"I have another banquet at noon. I'll steal you some food,

and maybe borrow a video machine from the building manager. Some of the born agains have tapes."

"Of being born?"

"Movies, Wang. Wholesome entertainment. Family viewing," I add, putting my coat back on.

"I am in a movie. Wearing my U2 jacket. Big star. Every theatre in Beijing will show it soon. Maybe even on TV."

For a moment, I am fooled. Then Wang blinks and grins, burps goodbye.

I run into the dean outside the building. He scurries along the path with his head down, tracing a set of footprints visible in the dust. Feng slows to match strides and stops briefly to analyse an odd jag in the tracks. Unless I am mistaken, the footprints are mine, left a half-hour ago. Even the jag can be explained: I was hastening home, my mind on Zuo Ying's comment about her parents, when I nearly collided with a bicycle driven by one of the kitchen staff. Looking up at me now, Feng Ziyang frowns. "I said I would come to you," he says.

"Is that what we decided?"

"Phones are so bad here. Junk, really. We can go to your room and talk?"

"Let's stay outside."

"Here?" he replies, as if I have just suggested lunch at the mouth of a volcano.

"Why not?" I bluff.

"Okay, okay," says the dean. "Wang Hua is missing for two days. He must be found. You can help?"

"Help?"

"This is politics."

"I don't teach politics."

"This is trouble. He can no longer be protected. I can no longer shelter him. Big mess now. Very bad."

"For who?"

Dean Feng waves his arms. "Me. You. Everyone! Do you understand?"

I can pocket my hands to hide their trembling, but am helpless to control a twitching right eye. "The dust," I explain, rubbing it with a fist.

Feng Ziyang's face, always animated, is so twisted that, for the first time, I, too, wonder about his mental health. He opens his mouth to speak, hesitates, then proceeds. "You were on track with Zuo Ying this morning," he says. "She goes to her father in Canada tomorrow. People ask: what was foreigner telling the child? Secrets to pass on to Zuo Chang? Maybe this needs investigation. . . ."

"That's insane."

"Not me saying these things. Other people. Same people who talk about you and Zhou Hong. Talk until there is trouble. Until it is too bad to fix."

"And then . . . ?"

He draws closer, perhaps to intimidate, more likely just to guard our conversation from some Japanese teachers walking past. "You are very serious?" he asks in a whisper.

Up close, his eyebrows sprout tufts. Hairs are half black, half grey. I try to look puzzled.

"Don't fuck around for nothing, David. Not in this place. Not at this time."

"My private life is off-limits," I answer in a voice that is, in my head at least, hysterical. "Unless it affects how I teach."

The dean produces a pack of local cigarettes and lights one, grimacing, I gather, at the mere thought of how it is going to taste. "When I was in that closet in Arts Building I had to shit in front of students who were my guards," he says. "No visits to toilet allowed. Only a pot, the door open, everyone watching."

"Yes?"

My tone convinces him to drop the anecdote. "A famous Chinese writer was asked to write story denouncing feudalism," he resumes instead. "The man was not sure. He called China 'room without windows or doors.' People in room are sleeping. Suppose he bangs on the wall to wake them up. 'You are all prisoners,' he shouts. 'Prisoners, and there is no way to escape!' Is he doing people such big favour?"

"I'm sorry your students locked you up."

"I'm sorry you are friends with Wang Hua."

"Will you stop Zhou Hong's daughter from leaving tomorrow?" I ask, not at all sure that I oppose the idea.

The dean goes to protest his innocence again, but abandons the defence in mid-sentence. He dashes into the building and heads straight for Deng Chen at the reception desk.

# 15

THE BANQUET HAS ONLY THREE TABLES TODAY. AT THE HEAD gathering sit bored administrators, distracted department heads—they have other jobs, I'm told, usually with one of the joint-venture firms, and are always in a hurry—and the fossils, preoccupied to a man with hearing aids and herbal remedies and the business of not dying before dinner. The second table is ruled by English. Americans dominate it, with sprinklings of Australians and Canadians whose accents are either fun and provocative or civil and unpushy, and even one English teacher, a wry Londoner named Clive, who is openly appalled by what he hears coming from the mouths of Floridians and Texans and is openly mocked by those very same Yanks for his own nasally, stick-up-the-ass manner of speech. Lively discourse there. As for the third table, it welcomes the internationalists, the polyglots—i.e., everyone else. Germans and Japanese, Spanish and French. Arabs from Damascus and Cairo. An Italian from Milan. The Russian teacher who is frequently indisposed—her weeping is audible from the bottom of her stairwell—and the North Korean who refuses, rumour has it, to mingle with capitalists. There is even an Indonesian gentleman, the collective employee of three Beijing institutions, who teaches at the college two mornings a week. Linguistically, this group shares only the levelled English learned by educated people around the globe. Most often, it breaks down into factions, though rarely does the seating arrangement conform. The result is babble:

Japanese to Japanese, French to French, German to Spanish or Italian. Days I am feeling the hegemonic anglophone, buoyed by my reasonable facsimile of an American accent, I find a spot among the English speakers. Days I am feeling not so much francophone as Canadian, the lower-in-the-food-chain neighbour of a grinning carnivore, I don my other hat and join the marginals, where if nothing else I can glaze over and tune out, focus on more important things—like Zhou Hong at the head table.

To the perpetually smiling Professor Moussa from Egypt I say hello, and exchange a brisk handshake. To the always grim Professor Pitof, native of Le Havre but resident in Asia since the French occupation of Vietnam, I confer a civil *bonjour, monsieur*, a greeting no longer followed by a *Ça va bien?* or the polite *Comment allez-vous?* because the professor, apparently, is never okay, never doing well.

So far, the banquet isn't faring much better. The problem is the guest of honour, a new language-lab teacher from Melbourne. He hasn't shown up. Zhou Hong, dispatched to the airport to collect him, isn't here either. Worse, when she does finally appear a half-hour later, she is alone. Hong pauses beside a piece of calligraphy in the doorway, flush from running, visibly distressed. Before she has a chance to compose herself, never mind cross the room and report to her superiors, the college president calls her name. She stops dead. He asks the burning question. She answers it in soft Mandarin.

"He is being refused entry."

The president, a middle-aged man who operated a coal mine in Hubei province until a few years ago, and who punctuates even the simplest thoughts with "ahem," as if he has given the matter considerable thought, clears his throat. "What?" he says.

"The Australian cannot get in," repeats Hong.

The president pushes his glasses back up his nose. "Ahem," he comments.

All of a sudden the blind vice-president, Comrade Wu, rises to his feet. Halfway up he teeters and is saved by the extended arm of Dean Feng, seated next to him. "Ridiculous," says the old man, slapping Feng's help away. "A foreigner can't get into the banquet?"

Zhou Hong, her hands cupped together like a child giving a musical recital, blinks.

"Talk to the security guard," advises Wu, his jowls quivering. "He'll let him in the room."

"Not the room," clarifies Hong. "The country."

"The what?"

"The Australian is being refused entry into China," she says with—I note happily—impatience in her voice.

"China?"

"Visa problems."

"You should have, ahem, made sure of these things, Zhou Hong," says the president.

"I thought I had."

"Obviously you were wrong."

"Everything was in order," she says. "At the airport, all his papers seemed—" The word is unfamiliar. "But the officials have a list, and he was on it. . . ."

Hong looks to Dean Feng for help. She has still not moved from her spot. Most eyes in the room are on her now, even those of foreigners unable to follow the conversation. Though no believer in telepathy, I offer her silent counsel: *Walk to the head table, Hong.*

Feng Ziyang stands. "Too bad about that," he says in Mandarin. "The food will get cold. We'd better eat."

"Not yet," counters the president.

"Some of the foreigners can understand us, Wei Peng," says Feng, a grin glued to his face.

"We can talk more privately at the table," agrees Hong.

"Forget about the foreigners."

"Better to discuss this—"

"Now!"

Both Zhou Hong and Feng Ziyang lower their gazes. The analogy, though unflattering, is unavoidable: they are being treated like schoolchildren. In turn, Hong and the dean are acting at once compliant and insolent—as would frustrated kids. The president clears his throat, adjusts his glasses.

"What are they saying?" whispers Professor Pitof.

I shake my head. At the English table, an American proclaims his desire to "get this thing over with." Waitresses, their manner subdued, pour soda and beer into glasses but delay serving the main dishes. Foreign guests shift in their seats; Chinese guests keep almost unnaturally still.

"Bad business," says the president. "First, the trouble with that teacher. . . . What's his name again, Feng Ziyang?"

"Huh?"

"Your teacher. The—" I lose several words. "You know, the one gone missing?"

"Wang Hua," says the dean.

My gaze remains locked on the college president. I do not shift or blink; in manner, I am unfazed and guiltless.

"First that mess, now this," continues the chief of the college. "The school looks incompetent. Full of troublemakers. All these mistakes—" I lose the thread completely. When I pick it up again, the subject seems to be different. "Zhou Hong, when is your husband coming back, anyway?"

The question sucks the remaining air from the room. Even the English table ceases to twitter. I do not want to make it worse for Hong, but I can't help myself; along with thirty other people, I stare at her.

"I don't know, Wei Peng," she answers, tugging on her right wrist. "He does not share his plans with me."

"Plans? What plans? He must return to his, ahem, position. His, ahem, country."

"His family?"

"Yes, yes—that too."

The hint of a smile curls her lips. Quickly, she suppresses it.

"Zuo Chang is my friend," says the man. "Someone I admire, someone I—" The words are new, or else spoken with a strong Hubei accent. "He had a future here. On my apartment walls are many of his—" Coming to his senses, the president sits—almost slumps—in his chair. He studies his plate.

"We better eat," decides Dean Feng.

Chopsticks hang suspended over the cold dishes. Unspoken agreement has been reached on a point; being the first banqueter to tuck into the meal will have consequences. Someone at the English table pronounces the food "purty, but not *that* purty," and there is muffled laughter. No doubt about it: we are all grade-schoolers enduring a protracted punishment for our misdeeds.

Zhou Hong is equally paralysed. Her face is now expressionless and she pulls so hard on her hand I imagine it coming off with a sucking noise, like a cork from a wine bottle. Anger wells within me. Though I have no plan, except to end the humiliation, I stand up. A few gazes shift my way, including a startled and clearly disapproving Hong. Words are about to leave my mouth—I'm not sure in which language—when the blind vice-president, Wu Tong, re-enters the discussion.

"What's going on around here?" he asks. This time, he allows Dean Feng to help him to his feet. "That's what I want to know. Everyone unhappy, everyone leaving. No discipline. No authority. When I was young . . . when I was young. . . ."

So great is my relief at this intervention that I miss most of what the old man says. When I finally tune in, he is repeating the question, his free hand—the other grips a cane—extended in entreaty.

"Is it really so bad?" he asks.

No reply is forthcoming. Still, a quality of the silence, and of the squirming among the Chinese, appears to provide him an answer. I would ponder this more—after all, he can't see anyone squirm—were his next comment not so astounding.

"Because of *that*?" he asks. "It was nothing. The army taking care of a few hooligans. The state restoring order. Had to be done. We should all be grateful for—"

I lose him yet again. Frustrated, I scan the faces of non-fossil local faculty to fill in the blanks. None show overt anger or disagreement. What is evident, however, is a neutrality that borders on indifference, possibly scorn. Wu Tong sags back in his chair. Ancients around him touch his arm in approval of his thoughts.

Feng tries again. "Banquet finished," he says in English. "Everyone very busy. Goodbye!"

Zhou Hong gently corrects him.

"Okay, okay," he amends. "Banquet starts. Everyone eat. Welcome!"

Hong crosses to the head table. Her strides are mechanical, as if she is relearning the procedure. The meal lasts ten minutes. I try not to watch, not to be astonished as she makes smiling conversation with the fossils and laughs at a presidential witticism and even swallows a few bites of food, all while her cheeks continue to glow and her thoughts scatter everywhere. How could I possibly know the direction, or nature, of her thoughts? Because at this moment, the pulse throbbing in my neck, I intuit them. Not the particulars, I readily grant, but their force and passion. I intuit Zhou Hong's thoughts just as clearly as I observe her composure. Feng Ziyang, I notice, also keeps glancing over at her. Such grace is mesmerizing.

And I silently rage. Rage a little as I did back in Montreal, but more as I did the time in February when Clive from London lent me an insta-book on the Tiananmen Square massacre. Included with the text were a dozen photos of crushed bicycles and burnt-out buses, bloodied corpses and mutilated remains, plus the famous Changan Avenue confrontation between a tank and a young man carrying a shoulder bag. I read it in one sitting, then lay bug-eyed in bed that night. Had a Chinese general been in my apartment, I would have gone at him with a cleaver; had paramount leader Deng Xiaoping turned up, I'd have heaved him over the balcony. The rage had that sense of purpose. No less savage, I hasten to add: simply channelled rather than flailing, a dark outgrowth of circumstance rather than my nature. An outgrowth, too, of a new, yet nascent kind of politicization. Attitude and concern born of injustices perpetrated upon people I knew a little, in a time and place I could—in a small way—claim a stake in. A shadow of Adele's old mind-set, I supposed, stripped clean of the layers of cross-purposes and self-pity that eventually muddied her thinking. Clive encouraged me to show the book to Chinese friends. Zhou Hong merely covered her eyes at certain photographs; Wang Hua tossed it aside with a claim that he'd "wait for the movie." Later, he admitted he had seen plenty of articles and books already. Later still, he confessed that he had helped an American journalist compile a body count by sneaking into hospitals in the days following the massacre to add up the corpses.

Elaine Mueller, two seats away at the table, keeps trying to catch my eye. Finally, I acknowledge her.

"This will be bad for us all," she says.

"What, the Australian?"

"Bad for us all," she repeats.

"It's not about 'us all,'" I fire back.

"How we each act individually affects everyone," she says, her awkward words clearly intended as a threat.

I almost tell her to fuck off. "Nonsense," I reply instead. Rather than pretend to chat with Professor Moussa beside me, I show an interest in the calligraphy next to the exit. The scroll is huge and the ideograms that run the length of it look to have emerged from swarms of black ink splashed onto the paper. Lines are thick and rough; in one ideogram, made up of a dozen strokes, several characters have been blurred. The calligraphy is raw, almost angry, but the result is refined and serene. I recognize the two ideograms for the sun, and another picture that represents, quite literally, a flower. I also recognize, for perhaps the first time, the obvious artistry of the work. Zuo Chang, I realize, is owed an apology.

Dean Feng declares the banquet over. Locals and foreigners alike storm the exit. As usual, Hong plants herself beside the door to offer goodbyes. I wait until the last fossil has shuffled out. I also pause as Feng Ziyang stops for a word with her. Whatever he says, it works: she brightens, looping her hair with a laugh at one of his comments.

I approach, my eyes swivelling to admire the scroll from up close.

"Mao Zedong," says Zhou Hong.

"Sorry?"

"This calligraphy. His work. A famous poem."

The information, for some reason, is dismaying. I want to re-examine the thing. But she is already through the doorway, crossing the main cafeteria to the lobby.

"Hong," I say, catching up. "I'm sorry."

She turns to me. "I am not a child," she offers, both her fists clenched. "Not to be treated such a way."

I nod.

"The president does not understand what—" She bites her lip. To my dismay, her eyes empty out. "Ying's lunch," she says, indicating her purse.

Stealing banquet food is a college tradition. Guests leave with bulging handkerchiefs and folded jackets. The more brazen simply promise to return their plates to the front desk before dinner. Zhou Hong's purse is fragrant. "She loves the fish balls," she admits.

I display my handkerchief. "Wang will eat anything," I carelessly say.

Near the door to the lobby I fall back, in order that she can be seen leaving the building alone. But then Hong stops. I stand in some discomfort as she looks me over, like I am a job applicant whose appearance is under scrutiny.

"I like your tie," she says, thinking something else.

"Thanks."

I wait for her to speak the other thought. My intuition is not as strong now, but I am still hopeful that her words will be the ones I need to—

"Answer your phone this afternoon," she advises.


Three letters await me atop the radiator in the lobby. I am so pleased to get mail that I walk right past Deng Chen and sink into one of the armchairs by the door. Two of the letters have been slit along the seam; the third, posted a week after the others, appears intact.

The first is a huge relief.

*March 16, 1990*
*David,*

*Sorry for not writing sooner. I'm feeling pretty detached from the world these days. Informants assure me the winter has been hard, but from your/our bedroom window, it looks beautiful—soft and silent, pure. I am a happy prisoner in this apartment. Me and the sill pigeons. Me and the sad woman downstairs and the horny couple upstairs. Me and the phone that rings often but that I don't answer, allowing friends to leave messages of concern. Me and my mother, who drops off containers of dumplings and soup on the condition that I deny she has even visited. (Gregor has excised me from his will. The old fuck still doesn't get it!)*

*And Chantal, of course. She loves Titania's cooking, and has gained some much needed weight. She loves me, too, and is my nurse and sister, my lover in all but the flesh. But, then, the flesh is so deceiving as a measure of love. It tells the heart lies; it does not know itself. You'd probably rather not hear this, but it's the truth. Or a truth, I should say.*

*You love me as well, don't you? I'm grateful. It's good that you are away from Mile End, David. It's good that you aren't looking at me right now. I can't explain, but I can tell you a story. (I know: that is your thing. See how close we still are?)*

*Once upon a time there was an old man who was dying. He lived in a room with a woman who was young and healthy. She looked after him. He looked upon her with gratitude and awe, but also guilt. Finally, he said, You should leave me soon. Why? she asked. Because I am almost finished and you are just beginning. The two positions are irreconcilable. They're nearly at odds. Instead, continued the man, this room should be crammed with other dying people. We should keep each other company.*

*The woman laughed at his words. The space is ours to do
as we wish, she said. One to one is the only concise configuration. A room is the only concentrated setting. There are
no opposites because there are no exact matches. Nothing is
irreconcilable because nothing can ever be resolved.*

*Gay, eh? Fucking-A!*

*Ivan*

*PS: Carole called and promised that she and Lise would
visit. Adele, of all people, has been dropping by once a
week. I made a joke about her finally spending time in
your apartment, now that you're not in it. She grunted
and shouldered open the door to the balcony. Needs her
nicotine fix bad!*

*PPS: Your credit card arrived a while back. Should I for-
ward it?*

I pause before the absence of any actual information about
Ivan's health. I also recall the January afternoon in Remys
when he wept, and the window slats subdivided his face into
shadow and light, light and shadow. That image—along with
the letter—threatens to open my tear ducts. I vow to try calling him on the weekend.

The second letter contains a child's thoughts in an adult's
hand. It is in French.

*Papa,*

*I love you. We're going to France for the summer.
Mamma is going to marry Jean-François, who smells*

*nice. I made a papier-mâché mask at school. He's the
princess. I wanted green paint, but they had only pink.
Jean-François said there are lots of pink frogs. He and I
play in the basement, but only when you're not there. It
snowed last night. I smoked a crayon on the porch until I
got cold. My hands turned pink, too. I sneezed—haacho!*

*Kisses,
Natalie*

*PS: David: Natalie is spreading rumours. Nothing is cer-
tain about Jean-François or summer plans. She's actually
telling you the saga of her Ken and Barbie dolls. Lise was
right: I should never have bought her those terrible things.
(Lise says hello, by the way.) And what's this about you
living downstairs? What* did *you tell the girl??*

I smile indulgently at the basement business. Better to savour
that small victory, and trace the *x*'s and *o*'s on the envelope
with my finger, than to linger over the news—I believe my
daughter, not her mother—about Jean-François and France.
I feel, in fact, oddly calm about my life back in Montreal. I
don't think it has to do with distance or helplessness. Nor is
it the result of how uncalm matters are here. As proof, when
I look up from Natalie's letter and see the security guard fixing me his most menacing glare, I am momentarily puzzled.
Why is Deng Chen so hostile? Why is my phone always ringing? Why is everyone so anxious to visit my apartment?

The final letter is also in French. It is, moreover, typed,
possibly onto a computer.

*March 22*
*Dear David,*

*Luc and Julie Beauchemin, the perfect young couple
who've made me their good deed for the year, insisted I
learn computers, and spent dreary afternoons teaching a
technological retard about hard discs and printers. Luc is
convinced that a computer will "free" me to write my
book. They assume I am a genius, a brilliant academic
who has suffered for her ideals (and her gender, Julie
would add). The age is right for me to be fully discovered.
With the help of technology, with the help of these sweet,
bright-eyed fascists, my masterwork will be written.*

*A sprawling, bloated opus, I'm sure: not like my slim vol-
ume on trade unions, not like my terse articles. Eight hundred pages, plus footnotes, of revolutionary political science.
Luc and Julie take it for granted that I am lonely and
abandoned. They're confident I'd have wanted them for my
children. They regret your break up with Carole (yes, they
even understand you); what a stunning academic couple
you'd have made. Tenure by thirty-five, department heads
by forty. Instead, poor Adele endures an ineffectual lover
(Pierre has accepted an early retirement package, and
drinks more than I do), a hapless son and distanced grand-
child, a levelled career. And she smokes! Sweet Julie wrin-
kles her nose. Bright-eyed Luc asks if I'd like to join him on
the balcony, for some air.*

*Why do I bother with these people? They fascinate me,
I suppose. And they are the future, aren't they? And yes, I
am sometimes lonely. Ivan and his friend are far better
company. He is full of laughter and dignity. She is extra-
ordinary. A Grade Nine dropout—this province treats
education like a ten-week driving course—who can sit for*

*hours with one of your undergraduate texts. I am determined to get her into the university, once it is finished. I hope you will come home for the funeral.*

*I'm sorry to have to break the news, David, but you knew Jacob LeClair. Not for long, and you were very young, but your father was around the house almost until you started school. You've been denying this for years. Come to think of it, you began to deny you knew Jacob about the time you took up winter residence on the balcony. You'd ask all sorts of questions about him, which I'd answer. A week later, you would be accusing me of never telling you anything, of robbing you of a dad. Those outbursts would climax with you rushing off for an hour in your snowy coffin. Sometimes I had to push the door open and shout at you to come inside before you froze. Once, sweet boy, you fell asleep, and probably* would *have died had I not pulled you in. That mishap, plus your nightmares about the accident, compelled me to bring you to a psychiatrist. You were ten, maybe eleven. Believe it or not, he suggested we drop all mention of Jacob until you were more mature, more accustomed to "adult behaviour." (I remember the term clearly.) Such pearls of wisdom! Cost me money I could ill afford.*

*And now, all these years later, you really don't remember? Except for the brand of his aftershave—yes, Aqua Velva— and his preference for sports magazines, especially, as you rightly recall, boxing and hockey ones? Not even about what happened to your face? Next letter, a full biography of your glorious father.*

*Please spare me your critiques of China. I'm glad being there is helping clear your head and focus your attention. I'm glad the experience has been positive so far. But leave*

*socialism—or my socialism, at least—out of it. (You
know this already, don't you? Trying to egg me on, son?
Pick a fight? China is having a positive effect!) This wasn't
what we envisioned for the country in 1949, and you
know it. For China and Quebec alike, we sought only the
most concrete and humane improvements: jobs and a
decent medical program, equal opportunities for women,
fair treatment of minorities and immigrants. We believed
in collective government, not authoritarianism. We were
looking for a key to understand perplexities, not to incar-
cerate citizens. We sought one key only, I admit: perhaps
our greatest mistake. How do you protect worthy ideas
from the folly of their application? Too easy to blame the
ideas themselves. Too easy to dismiss the dominant para-
digm of successive generations of intellectuals as fodder
for state terror. There must be more balance, more probing. These were our passions. These were our lives.*

*Adele*

*PS: How long this letter is. Already I embrace the excesses
I once critiqued.*

I remain in the chair for so long that Deng Chen emerges
from behind the desk and stands over me. Though I notice
him, notice the letter about to slide from my hand, notice
even some activity at the front door to the residence, I am elsewhere. It isn't a seizure. Simply, my mind is so filled with
memory fragments—what accident is Adele referring to?—
that my brain sends no signals. I can't piece anything together.
I can't muster a response. Nor do I want to: the condition is

nicely indeterminate and gently sensual. I do scratch my itchy cheeks, though; I do run a finger along the crooked bridge of my nose.

"Okay?" Deng is saying.

"Mmm?"

"You sick?"

"No."

In his hand is a book the size of a department store catalogue. "Question, please," he says, bending over the chair.

I snap out of it. "Wang Hua isn't in the register," I announce, "and so can't be in my apartment. The curtains don't need fixing, and so Madame Chai can't come by. All right?"

Dean Chen's simian brow furrows. From so close, his skin is chalky and his eyes are less dead than run through with fatigue. It is the face of a sick man, I realize with a shock.

"This word," says the guard. "How to say it?"

He holds open the book. It is an entry-level English grammar, complete with drawings of apples and oranges, cats and dogs.

"*You're* learning English?" I ask.

"Little," answers Deng Chen. For the first time in nine weeks, he puts forth a smile instead of a smirk. The expression is pained, and reveals a mouth of crooked, yellowing teeth.

"Why?" I wonder.

"Sorry?"

"Why learn English?"

"To leave," he answers.

"This job?"

"China."

"You want to leave China?"

"For my—" Deng pronounces "family" in Mandarin.

It never occurred to me that Deng Chen would have a family. It certainly never crossed my mind that he, too, would want out. Aren't people like him living on the sunny side of totalitarianism?

"Children?" I ask.

"One only," he answers. Then, in his native language: "It is the law."

"Boy?"

"Girl," he corrects.

I am now contrite. But Deng Chen, perhaps sensing an opening, withdraws to his full height. All at once he is back in part.

"You are in room this afternoon?" he asks.

"No."

"Then Chai cleans."

"I mean yes," I correct. "I'm home all day. No cleaning, please. I won't even answer my door."

"Phone calls?"

I have to smile.

"You answer your phone this afternoon?" he presses.

"I'll try."

"Okay."

"Okay what?"

But Deng doesn't understand. Or else, more likely, it is me who doesn't. And who won't understand, in all probability, until long after the fact.

Wang Hua devours the banquet booty cold and drinks two bottles of Qingdao. He belches. He snaps his chopsticks. Now pallid and oily, Wang continues to refuse to shower or borrow clothes. On his third pack of Marlboros since the morning, he lies on the couch beneath a cloud, chugging beer, staring at the TV screen. "Waiting for the handsome Americans to come on," he explains. I sit with him for periods, then retreat into my bedroom, where I read and mark papers. Though I have smoked only two cigarettes, my spit is nicotine flavoured. Though I haven't touched the beer, I smell hops on my shirt. Despite a day of clean living, in fact, I am ready for an early bed and a dreamless sleep.

Phone calls provide a distraction. I answer each and every summons. To Deng Chen and Madame Chai, I politely decline offers of cleaning and curtain repairs. To Madame Shen in the English department, who speaks to me in Mandarin, I apologize for being unable to either drop by the office for a meeting—I have never been invited to a departmental get-together before—or welcome into my home a graduate student who, though he rejected my previous offers of assistance, is now desperate for Professor David's help. When Zhou Hong calls, she first tells me that she will be home later that evening, in case I want to visit. My heart leaps at the invitation, despite one constraining—if also pleasing— fact: her daughter will be home as well. Then she asks to speak with the other person in the room.

"This is my business, Hong," I say. "Why get mixed up in it?"

"Please put him on."

I pass the phone to Wang Hua. He listens for a moment, then produces a drawling "yes, ma'am" that bears a remarkable resemblance to the voice of an older Texan on staff. I can hear her speaking English, and listen with astonishment as Wang comes up with simple, clear responses using the vernacular of that American state. When he signs off, it is with a "see ya" of near-perfect pitch.

"I'm impressed," I say.

"Hell, yeah!"

"Where did you—?"

"Jim Johnson visits my room once a week," answers Wang, referring to the Texan. "He wants me to find God."

"In your room?"

"In my heart. Also in the Bible. Jim gave me two Bibles, one for my heart, one for a Chinese friend I should share the good news with. So far, I have found no one to share the good news with," he adds with a grin. "And now I have five books in my room. Two from him, two from Americans who left the campus during the Turmoil and one from a Mormon. His was sent by an angel."

"What did you do with them?"

"At first I hid the books, like you hide me. The Americans said I should. They said the truth was danger-ous—as I was once dangerous—and I shouldn't tell any officials about our conversations."

He cues me.

"My lips are sealed," I promise.

"But the Bibles are so thick and strong," he resumes. "Perfect for certain jobs."

I wait.

"Keep the window up," says Wang, counting with his fin-gers. "Stop the door from clicking open at night. Put the teapot on. Oh yes, and make my bed level."

"That's only four."

He flops back on the couch. "The last copy I donated to the library on our floor."

"You have a library—?"

"The door beside the stairwell," he adds. "You can smell it from my room."

Pleased by the banter, I finally ask what Zhou Hong said on the phone.

"She told me to borrow a toothbrush from you," he answers, cupping his hands behind his head.

The final call is fateful. The caller speaks French, and I momentarily stumble. A month ago I agreed to give a lecture to the French department on life in Quebec. The lecture is for seven o'clock tonight, and everyone in the department, including the new dean, is anxious to hear the Québécois accent. Could Professor LeClair please be at the auditorium in an hour?

"*Merde*," I say, hanging up. "I forgot about this."

"You teach tonight?"

"A lecture to the French department."

"In English?"

"French, Wang. My second language. Or maybe my first. It's a toss up, I guess."

Wang frowns. "Who do you belong to?" he asks.

"Sorry?"

"Your race—English or French?"

"Why does everyone keep asking me this?"

He shrugs.

"Besides, those are languages, not races."

He shrugs again.

"In Montreal, Zuo Chang told me to use only English in China. He said my stature would be higher as an English speaker. Dominate or be dominated, I guess."

"Eat or be eaten," says Wang.

"A nod is as good as a wink to a blind horse."

"Is it?"

"I don't really know," I confess.

"This is a Canadian proverb?"

"English, more likely."

"I must find a translation."

"It doesn't really mean anything."

"Perfect for Chinese language."

Suddenly tired, I sit. "I got a letter from my friend Ivan today," I say.

"The one who is dying?"

"He's doing okay, actually."

"Not dying?"

"No, just doing okay."

"I understand."

"All my friends are dying, aren't they?" I ask, the words astonishing even to me.

But Wang Hua is once more on his back, a forearm across his eyes. Within a minute, he is asleep again.

## 16

THE AUDITORIUM HOLDS TWO HUNDRED, BUT IS BARELY A quarter full, the fate of a foreign language ranked well down the list of desirable credentials. Though completed just two years ago, the building already boasts strips of peeled paint on the walls, bulbless fixtures dangling from the ceiling and enough missing panes of window glass to make the hanging-by-a-thread curtains necessary. Most of the seats are cracked, unwilling to either fold or unfold, and the podium ceases to list dangerously only once a book is jammed under it. There is a chalkboard, uncleaned in months, and a floor swimming in newspapers and handouts. As a rule, I've learned it is better to lecture during the day, when natural light can compensate; in many halls, it is better still to lecture in the morning, when odours from nearby toilets have yet to waft down corridors.

Dusk has settled over the auditorium, and the air is stained. As I greet the head of the French department, still unsure of what I will say, I realize I haven't switched my mental processes from English. Preliminary sentences of dodgy grammar and half-swallowed anglicisms take my host by surprise. I am no less startled. Before I know it, however, I am standing before an audience that is expectant, demanding and—if past experiences hold true—fickle. The crowd is also strangely dim; finally, it occurs to me to take off my mirror glasses.

"Two Canadian writers were once asked to collaborate on a story about their country," I begin, not bothering to pretend to read from a text. "One was from the prairies, where the land is flat and people speak English, and the other was from Quebec, where there are rivers and valleys and people speak French. The writers refused to even consider the project. 'How can I collaborate with someone who writes in French?' asked the writer from the prairies. 'How can I work with an English speaker?' said the one from Quebec. 'And besides,' added the westerner, 'I am Canadian, and proud of it.' 'And I am Québécois, and proud of it, too,' said the Quebecer."

I can feel the French returning. The long pause is not to seek out vocabulary or a verb tense, but simply to place my mind at least one sentence ahead of my mouth.

"So they decided to go home and write a story each, and then arrange them side by side in a book. They demanded that the book be half in French, half in English, with different-coloured pages and different typesettings. The writer from the prairies came up with a story of a lonely farm wife who betrays her husband with a neighbour, and ends up causing his death. The Québécois writer produced a tale of a lonely wife in a village who has an affair with a doctor, and together they plot to get rid of her unloving husband. The editor of the book asked the writers to provide an introduction, and offered to send each the other's story. Both handed in introductions without bothering to read what their colleague had written. In the introductions they explained why their world was unique and their language indelible and their sense of cultural identity so urgent, and fragile, that it demanded absolute fidelity. They said they were warriors in a long battle, and it was a win-or-lose, all-or-nothing situation. They said they were misunderstood and marginalized, and spoke for all people in that position, wherever they happened to live."

I smile at my own cleverness, allow the parable to sink in and then ask my audience the obvious question. "Do any of you know a single person whose behaviour *doesn't* get in the way of his beliefs? Whose humanity isn't complex? And yet who, again and again, champions beliefs over behaviour, principles over experiences?"

Maybe the question isn't so obvious. For sure, the new dean of the French department, a youngish man with the usual mop of hair, bespectacled eyes and cigarette-free hands, appears unstirred by my musings. At least he is still in his seat, and attentive. Already I am hearing the telltale murmurings from the students. If not dealt with at once, using a joke or idiomatic expression or, better still, a flattering comparison between China and the West, within five minutes the lecture hall will be cleared and I will have lost, as they say, face.

Which Professor David would not want. And doesn't want, kind of. Still, he—I—knowingly makes things bad to worse. "Let me change direction a little," I say, content that a proper French expression—"*passons à autre chose*"—popped into my head, rather than an anglicism. "I come from Montreal, a city of almost three million people. I could talk about it, but most of what I'd say would be very general. What I can speak about is the neighbourhood I live in. It's called Mile End, and is full of people and languages from all over the world. My grocer, Firoz Velji, uses an Indian language at home, but English and French in his store. At the café where I hang out, the owner is Italian. He curses his waitresses in Neapolitan. He's also learned enough Spanish to talk with the Guatemalan guys who hang around the poolroom. The woman downstairs of me, Lena Buber, was born in a part of Romania that was eventually annexed by the Soviet Union. Her first language is Yiddish, her second is probably Romanian. The thing is, she can't quite remember! Then there are the Hasidim in the neighbourhood. They're a Jewish sect who don't. . . ."

I am happy enough to keep going, but it is pointless. Students not chattering with their mates are packing their books and filing down the aisles to the doors on either side of the podium. They avoid my gaze. Professors, at least, nod as they flee. The hall is now so dark I might as well be wearing mirrored glasses. When a curtain billowing from a window flutters to the floor, signalling an invasion of phantom parachuters, not to mention a dust storm, the auditorium clears out. Even the dean, pointing to his watch, takes his leave.

At the building entrance stands a janitor with a silver chain in his hand. No, I am not going to be whipped for my performance; the man is impatient to lock himself in for the night. I listen to the links bumping between the handles while zipping my jacket on the sidewalk. Towards the end of the lecture I resumed thinking in French, the thoughts becoming words without mediation. Different words, obviously, but also different thoughts, innocent of the fevered mullings of recent weeks. So pleasant is the respite that I cling to the language for as long as I can. Halfway back across campus, though, my mind is already anticipating the confrontation with Deng Chen—he was still on duty when I left, long after the normal end to his shift—and another desultory chat with Wang Hua and, on a brighter note, the prospect of an hour with Hong and Ying. All English business; all anxious, troubling stuff. Before the French dissipates, I savour the moment during the allegory when my fluency peaked, the result, I realized, of speaking the words to a melody that was suddenly in my head. That music, in effect, was the cadence of Québécois French, and on hearing it again after so long, I found the melody haunting and beautiful—the language of my city, the song of my name.

A car idles outside the building, a tinted window cracked to expel cigarette smoke. The lobby is undefended. As I climb my stairwell, voices filter down from above. On the third-floor landing I curse and take two steps at a time. The first thing I glimpse on the landing is the upper torso of Elaine Mueller, extended out her half-open door. In her haste to withdraw, Mueller catches her sweater in the frame. A red tongue of wool stays exposed. The sight is so comedic I almost laugh. But my own DO NOT DISTURB door is also open, and the voices are coming from within the apartment.

Deng Chen is the only intruder not in a uniform. He leans against the wall outside the bathroom, arms crossed, sneer in bloom. Two campus cops in sagging khaki clothes keep a few feet back out of respect—or fear—of him. Seeing me, they grin in embarrassment.

"Another question about English grammar?" I ask.

"Tell him to come out," he answers in Mandarin.

"What?"

Deng Chen indicates the door.

"Are you public security?" I say in Chinese.

"None of your business."

"You're in my apartment."

"You're in China."

"I'll call someone," I threaten.

"Who?"

"I know people."

"I know the people you know."

"Get out," I say, stepping up to him. "Up" is the right word, for, though not Ivan's height, Deng Chen still towers over me. To my own surprise, I throw back my shoulders, plant my hands on my hips, and more or less challenge him to make my day. This is no bluff: my rage-switch has been turned on; I am primed for violence. Deng tries to act unfazed, but his arms drop to his sides. His sneer, though, widens.

"You get out," he answers.

"I live here."

"So do—"

"Crazy!" calls a voice.

Both our gazes shift.

"Wang?" I call.

"Come into my office, please."

"Do you really think—?"

"Bring beer and cigarettes."

I turn to Deng Chen.

"He must leave with me," he shrugs.

A cigarette, perched at table's edge in the living room, is seasoning the carpet with ash. I grab it and a bottle of beer. Though I glance at the phone, Deng Chen is right: he *knows* the people I know. Back in the dining area, the security guard and Wang Hua are exchanging insults through the wood. Several of the curses are familiar to me, thanks to Wang's teachings.

"Stand back," I order in both languages. "If you rush the door I'll—" Stuck for a threat, I wave the bottle, spilling beer on my shirtsleeve. Even the campus cops snicker at this.

The bathroom is the size of a small elevator. It is windowless and, instead of fresh air, the ventilation shaft pipes intimate sounds in from apartments below. The fluorescent tube above the mirror hums; the radiator clangs at night. Wang sits on the uncovered toilet seat. Before passing him the bottle, I take a swig; before handing over the cigarette, I steal a drag.

"How did they get in the apartment?" I ask.

"I let them," replies Wang. He runs a hand over his skull, a goose-bump-inducing scrape. "Someone knocked, I answered.

Only as I pulled the door back and saw Deng Chen's face did I think: Wang, you are stupid! Stupid and crazy! Too late."

I slide from the edge of the tub to the floor, propping my elbows on my knees and clasping my hands. Though I have—obviously—spent some time in this room, a quality of its decoration only now makes itself apparent. The revelation is quietly devastating. Reading my mind, or perhaps recalling my tale of wrongful arrest, Wang pronounces the attribute out loud.

"Very pink room," he observes.

"Amen," I say, running a finger over the wall. "If I had a penknife, we could carve our initials and the date in the tile."

"Hooligan," says Wang.

"China made me."

He smiles. I struggle to.

"What did you do, Wang?" I finally ask.

"Do?"

"Why are they arresting you?"

"Buying tomato soup."

"I'm serious. . . ."

"Right," he says, glancing around the cubicle. "Serious answer for David. Betrayal. I am being arrested for betraying—"

"I mean last year," I interrupt, guessing the direction of his thoughts. "Before June 4th. The night of June 4th. The days following. . . ."

But he will not be deterred. "My father spent a year in a cell like this. He was a professor at the college in our town. My mother, a Tibetan, was also a teacher. In 1966 he was locked in a shed behind our building. First, though, he was beaten and made to march through the streets with insults pinned to his clothes. Usually, he was alone with only a student guard outside. Sometimes they put chickens in with him."

"What did *he* do?" I ask with more weariness than intended.

"I could see the shed from my bedroom," answers Wang. He stares blankly at the tiles. "Every night, before going to bed, I would lean over the balcony and look down at the roof. Every day, instead of going to school, my sister and I stood outside the chicken prison listening to criticisms of my father. For eight hours, including a break for lunch and *shoeshui*, students, colleagues and old friends would call him names and accuse him of crimes against the people."

"That must have—"

"They cut a hole in the door to observe the criminal during his re-education. He had to stand all day with his head bowed and his hands behind his back. When people spoke, he nodded. When they didn't speak, he kept silent. . . . Father had to shit and piss in the shed. The smell was bad. On warm days, people used handkerchiefs. But with their mouths covered, their criticisms weren't clear." Wang covers his mouth and shouts: "*Waabushaa, shhrr buh shhrr, Jongwua!*"

Hearing the garbled Mandarin, Deng Chen calls out. In unison, we tell him to wait.

"But I thought you were a revolutionary hero," I say, "given a Mao button for denouncing Liu Shaoqi."

"I was."

"As the son of a counter-revolutionary?"

Using the words, even mockingly and in translation, makes me squirm. The language is grotesque, but that is not the reason for my discomfort. Of more concern is the ease with which I now deliver such epithets. It is as if the mutually agreed inappropriateness, even kitsch, of the vocabulary in no way detracts from its resilience or import. One can spout vicious nonsense in China and everyone will agree it is vicious nonsense and yet still, in some strange way, take the accusation seriously. Like when you step on the crack and really *do* break your back. Or when Jack's crown is split wide open, and Jill's tumble leaves her paralysed from the neck down.

Wang drains his beer. "When the school reopened a year later, I was a child of Mao Zedong. . . ." He runs his hand over his head again. "One month before my father was arrested he took me to a village in the Shaluli Mountains, near the border with Tibet. He was an anthropologist, researching a minority group. For hours we walked along the slopes of hills. The sky was always huge, with no walls or ceilings, huge and pure, white and blue, grey and white. Never, as in a city, any smears of red or yellow. Never any smokestacks or buildings. Only a pure sky and my father and me, alone with all this space. All this silence. All this. . . ."

He extends his arms wide, as if the vista is being projected from his memory onto the wall.

"Security?" I ask, also studying the surface. An insect, emerging from behind the baseboard, starts up the tile. It has a claret-coloured shell and multiple legs. Despite the appendages, however, the insect isn't moving very fast.

"What?"

"How you felt being out there with your dad—protected. Safe, somehow. The world as it should be, but almost never is," I add sheepishly.

"Maybe," says Wang. For no reason, he reaches out and squeezes my shoulder. For absolutely no reason, I blush. Our physical proximity is extreme: our knees brush when we shift, the glaring light magnifies the pores in our skin, and neither of us smell baby-powder fresh. All at once, I want out of the room, bad.

"One afternoon my father and I set off from a tiny mountain village," he resumes. "The earth was hard and without trees. The wind was loud and the sky kept moving: cloud, sunlight, cloud. Where there was no path, prayer flags pointed the way. All we did was climb and descend, climb and descend for hours, until it was night. I remember how scared I got, being so far away from the village, so close to sheer drops and wild animals. My father became angry with me. 'There are no people out here,' he said. 'What is there to be afraid of?'"

A hard rap on the door, and we both jump. Deng Chen issues another command. Only then do I notice that the bolt is not drawn, and stand up to do so. Next I step into the bathtub and squat on my haunches, like the men outside the college gates.

"No books were allowed in the shed," says Wang, "except *The Collected Works of Mao Zedong*, which he'd already read. He was let outside only for public struggle sessions, in the town stadium. Those were not relaxing for father. *He* was being struggled against, you see. I went into the prison once. . . ."

His eyes are now glistening. I stare ahead at the drain and faucet, the dove-grey porcelain sides. A watercolour of Goofy would fit nicely on one wall, Donald on the other. As for Mickey Mouse, an appropriate likeness would take up the entire floor of the tub. With that grin, those ears.

"How to become a revolutionary hero?" asks Wang in a dead voice. "Denounce a class enemy! They gave me a speech to memorize. I opened the door to the cell and accused my father of Liu Shaoqi revisionism and of working with the enemies of socialism. I stayed with the criminal for a minute only. Twice I forgot—"

"Wang," I say.

"Twice I forgot the words. Both times my father, who had listened to me memorize the speech before, provided the missing sentence. 'Go on, son,' he said, his head down. 'Do what is right for China.'"

Wang Hua wipes his nose with his sleeve. He also stretches across to the tile and crushes the insect, unwisely frozen at eye level, with the palm of his hand. Only an ink smear remains. "It is good to put someone like me in prison," he summarizes.

"You were a kid."

"We are all Mao's children."

He stands abruptly. Fearing he is about to surrender, I scramble to my feet. Thoughts flood my brain. I want to knock him out with a punch, switch our clothes, and fool Deng Chen into arresting me. I want to kiss him on both cheeks and tell him not to worry, that everything will be okay. At the very least, I want to look at him. As I tried to do with Ivan; as I suspect I'll soon try to do with Zhou Hong. And see this frail man with the narrow shoulders and stick arms of an adolescent, the skin and cheekbones of a beautiful woman, the too-clear eyes of an adult who believes himself fated, and—of course—the smooth skull of a resident of the Chinese gulag.

My friend, Wang Hua.

"Can I borrow this?" he asks, pointing to my toothbrush on the basin rim.

"It's yours."

Blowing air from his cheeks, he pulls back the bolt.

"Wait!" I say. "I found a proverb in a book the other day." I recite it: "The sky is a coffin lid and the earth is a coffin bottom. You may run three thousand miles and still be inside a coffin."

"A nod is as good as a wink to a blind horse," he answers without missing a beat.

He swings open the door and marches straight into the clutches of the two cops.

"Good haircut," Deng tells him.

From the balcony, I watch the men shove Wang Hua into the back seat of the car, one guiding his head under the door frame. Deng Chen also climbs in. Along the railing are a half-dozen empty beer bottles from last night. As the car reverses up the path to the main campus road, I hurl the bottles down at it. The first three land with crisp explosions, gunfire pops. Only with the fourth do I properly calculate the motion of the vehicle. It clunks hard on the front hood, not breaking. Breaks squeal, but I lose sight of the car in the darkness and the churned dust. When the driver shifts into first gear, and jerks back towards the entrance, I draw a startled breath. At once furious and frightened, I grab the last projectile and storm the stairwell. Elaine Mueller is lucky not to be on the landing this time around.

The night porter, Li Duan, stands in the doorway in his undershirt and boxer shorts. He glances at the bottle inverted in my hand, for use—I suppose—as a club, shifts his gaze to the clusters of glass along the path, then retreats a step. I ask about the vanished car. The old man points towards the north gate.

"Where are they taking him?" I ask.

"Taking who?"

"You know."

"I'm just the night porter," he replies.

Back in the apartment, I dial Dean Feng. Someone picks up, but the line dissolves into static. Zhou Hong's phone is busy. Five times I try her. At my desk I tape together four sheets of typing paper while counselling myself to keep calm, consider my actions. On the sheets I write, first in English and then in French: "WANG HUA HAS BEEN ARRESTED, 9:45p.m., April 3, 1990." I think about using a dictionary to piece together a crude Mandarin version, but decide to trust the translation to others. Because I have only a black pen, I retrace the words over and over. With each layer, the new lines straying inevitably, almost wilfully, from their original form, the letters grow more bold and idiosyncratic; more personalized, I guess. I make up another two bilingual posters, then spread them out on the coffee table. It takes a minute to realize what is missing. "DAVID LECLAIR" I print at the bottom of each one. The "professor" nonsense is dropped.

Li Duan is locking the building for the night when I reappear in the corridor. Seeing the demented foreigner approach, the porter slips the chain back off and holds the door open for me. The college is pale beneath a thin, cloud-obscured moon. Only the clicks of locks and clanging of chains disturb the silence. Rooms are uniformly dark; stereos that normally blast until midnight have fallen mute. News of trouble travels over campus wires with the speed of fax transmissions. The abrupt cessation of activity, the descent of a hush so pure it amplifies accidental noises, indicates a "call" has gone out. As I walk the paths, I begin to understand that my information about Wang will not constitute news—everyone already knows, apparently—but rather serve as the initial act of witness, not to mention the first, and possibly only, signed gesture of protest.

And I need to lie down. I did not sleep well last night; the day has been long; I barely ate any lunch or dinner. I sense the telltale deadening in the arms and legs. I feel the dizziness trying to take root in my system, like a kid struggling to get a top spinning on a driveway. I should close my eyes and slow my heart. I should be in bed, thinking of nothing, emptying out.

At the bulletin board beside the main student cafeteria I locate an open space, remove four tacks from my pocket and put up a poster. I repeat the operation at the board near the west gate, then again on the main door to the Arts Building.

While pinning the final missive, a swell of voices sends me scurrying for cover behind a lilac bush. A security patrol passes, young male faces cast in the moonlight. The men saunter, caps pushed back and hands in baggy pockets, laughing. Unless I am mistaken, one of the guards was in my apartment an hour ago. His nonchalance is mystifying.

I run into two more patrols en route to the Chinese staff compound. Both times, I sidestep them; both instances, my inner eye summons the tilting earth and looming precipice. Building No. 12 lies ahead, and my aim now is simply to make it there, maybe curl up in a cool corner of her stairwell, outside her door. That will be enough, I decide: for tonight. As I near, I hear the cicadas and smell the desert but also scent, for the first time, spring bloom—the earth unthawing, plants and flowers about to blossom. Strains of music colour the air. By the time I reach the door, I am certain: she is listening to a cassette—Schubert, I think—and is wide awake, waiting.

But the stairwell is locked from the inside. A padlock is visible through a crack between the door and the frame. Staff residences are never barred. The buildings have no porters; as far as I know, residents have no keys to any padlocks. Which means that people are either locked out for the night or—more ominously—locked in. By whom? And why? Tossing a rock at her window would involve going off campus, and alerting the guards at the gate. Returning to my apartment to call her, and then exiting again, would mean two more encounters with the night porter. Even a cooling down period in her corridor, amid the bicycles and trash, the dirt and smells, is now impossible.

Defeated, I slump to the ground with my back to the wall. My need to speak with her is dire. In silence, I begin: *Let's leave tonight. Before something else happens. Before they come for you as well. To Hong Kong. To Japan. A husband and wife, with their daughter. What could be more natural?* Don't tell me about skin pigment and immutable racial distinctions, I would add. Don't tell me about locks on buildings and security guards at gates; don't bother to explain passports and visas issued to keep citizens within a country, not facilitate their travel outside it. Don't tell me about a national border that scrolls barbed wire and mounts surveillance cameras on the *inside* of the fence. And please don't tell me about the Schubert or Dvořák that you are playing to be consoled; how the music is trickling down the stairs to the bottom landing, then under the bolted door to where I squat, letting it wash over me, too, dissolve the grime and dust, block out the noises: to be a vessel that we can drink from together, the liquid cool and sweet. Let me tell you instead about the fire in my groin and the rage in my soul and the woeful state of my brain. Let me tell you what is going to happen here, wisdom or folly, tragedy or farce. How I am terrified and exhilarated, triumphant and ashamed. Sorry, Hong, but it is going to be a doozy. Going to give us both second thoughts. Make us both look away.

# 17

AT SIX THE NEXT MORNING, I SHOWER AND DRESS. ONE HOUR later I dial her number. She is up, I'm sure: Ying's flight leaves at noon. For that reason alone, I recradle the receiver. The phone gurgles almost immediately. Convinced it is not Hong, I count the rings while boiling water in the kitchen: five, six, seven chirps. On the balcony I drink coffee and smoke cigarettes. The rings recommence at fifteen-minute intervals, always stopping after seven tries. Finally, at exactly eight o'clock, I throw on the tight-fitting leather jacket I discovered, with only mild surprise, at the back of my closet late last night, and descend the stairs. Reflected in the corridor mirror is the outline of the night porter, Li Duan, still on duty an hour into the shift of his successor, Deng Chen. The old man sits back in the chair, hands cupped, chin on his chest. At the glass door I pause, hear a snore snap the air, and exit.

People stare. On the pathways, as I cross the field to the Arts Building. Their shy looks are never for long and never show malice or anger. I smile back at the faces I recognize, nod to others. The main door to the building, normally hooked open for the day, remains closed, as if to better display my poster. Someone has added ideograms below the words. I hesitate for a second.

"Translation," says a student, not breaking his stride, "into standard Mandarin."

A dozen colleagues crowd the English department office. My

appearance swallows sentences and freezes gestures. The crowd parts as I cross to Dean Feng. Eyes lock on the jacket, a pleasure that partially offsets the apprehension stiffening my spine. Feng is dialling a number at his desk. Seeing me, he hangs up, orders everyone out. Teachers file past obediently, many turning for a final look. Secretary Shen shoos the last straggler.

"Bad, huh?" I ask.

The dean chortles.

"Do you know where Wang Hua is?"

"Arrested."

"Yes, but where did they take him?"

"Arrested!" repeats Feng, outlining with his hands a place—possibly a space—beyond the door. "That is enough to know."

"I want to—"

"Why are you wearing his jacket?"

"It fits."

"Wang Hua is crazy," decides the dean. "And you are crazy, too."

Feng Ziyang, who is presumably sober, tries to pop a cigarette straight from a pack to between his lips. As they did with me, the contents fly out, mostly onto his desk. Frowning, the dean raises a hand to cover, it seems, his twitching mouth. That the man may actually be aware of his own tics—and possibly even of his terminal disarray—is a stunning thought, and I sit down at AWOL vice-dean Li's desk, erecting a steeple with my fingers.

"Look at this office," he continues. "Look at me. Look at you, visiting Canadian professor. Hiding a Chinese in your apartment. Putting up posters. Crazy!"

I shrug.

"Boy Scout?"

"Friend," I correct.

He shakes his head.

"Feng Ziyang," says Secretary Shen in Mandarin. "You are shaming yourself."

"How?" he shoots back, hurt.

I ask for a cigarette. He tosses one over the paper skyscrapers, along with a box of matches.

"But he doesn't smoke?" Shen asks her boss.

"Intellectuals rarely do," I agree in Chinese. I strike a match, whiff the magnesium stench.

"It's bad for your health, you know," the secretary tells me in her own language. She gives me what amounts to a look of motherly concern.

"I feel terrible," says the dean. "Can't sleep at night. Headaches every day. And a pounding, right here, at the sides of my—" He taps on both his temples, showering a cheek with ash.

"Make him take off the jacket," says Secretary Shen. "We are all being shamed. Doesn't he understand?"

"I understand this," I answer in Mandarin. "One of your own faculty members has been. . . ." I switch to English. "What's the word for 'arrested'?"

"Stay in English," sighs the dean. "She can follow just fine."

"She can?"

"Shen has been teaching herself the language for forty years. But in secret. Not for use. Crazy, eh?"

The secretary glares at Feng, her expression less excoriating than she probably hoped. When she turns her glower on me, her eyeballs rising up over her spectacle rims like hot-air balloons, her attempt at wrath is undermined by the hurt, almost grief, in her pupils. "Wang Hua was arrested," she blusters, "and good riddance to him. He was a troublemaker. He didn't belong here."

"Do I?" I ask.

Her face all but collapses. Secretary Shen drops her gaze to the papers on her desk. "I have a son in America," she says quietly. Then, in slow, clear English: "University of Indiana, at Bloomington. He has been gone for nine years."

"Nine years?"

"A doctorate takes time."

I look to Dean Feng to speak. He looks to me.

"His English is perfect now," she continues. "I made him talk on phone with his uncle. His speaks excellent, right not right, Feng Ziyang?"

"Good, good," says the dean.

I flit from one face to the other. "You must miss your son," I say to Shen in Chinese.

"I am secretary," she answers in English. "But my boy will be doctor or lawyer."

"Or teacher?"

There is a pause. The desks are positioned beneath a huge wood-ribbed window that angles more and more light into the office as the morning lengthens. Though it is still early, and the sky is overcast, visible above our heads is a beam from the upper squares of window. Within the ray are filaments of smoke and motes of dust, churning in a frenzy. Cast in gloom are the office's beige walls, which look as if they've been sprayed with gunfire, and the wood chairs stacked in a corner. Atop a small table is a battered thermos and a tea set, along with a vase of flowers, its contents changed daily by Shen.

"Maybe I'll drive a taxi," says Dean Feng. "Taxi drivers earn two thousand yuan a month in Beijing. Keep their own hours. Don't get into trouble."

"What did Wang actually do?" I ask, for what feels like the thousandth time.

He glances at the closed door. "Made movies," he answers in a hush. "Of demonstrations and martial law. Of the massacre . . . er, the Turmoil. He and his friends borrowed video cameras from American TV crew, and filmed things."

"Things?"

"Students putting up statue of goddess on Tiananmen Square. Army marching along Changan. Shooting into crowds. Making arrests in alleys. . . . How should I know?"

"You haven't seen the videos?"

"I am English professor!" says Feng. His laugh threatens to devolve into a cry.

"We were told," provides Shen.

I drag on the local cigarette, which smells similar to burning garbage but actually tastes okay. "How did the police find out?" I ask, pinching tobacco from my tongue.

"This," answers the dean. He stretches across the desk and tugs on Wang's jacket. "Spies everywhere take photos and make videos of demonstrators and troublemakers. Many contain man wearing this jacket, with English words across back."

He motions for me to shift around.

"'Under a Blood-Red Sky,'" reads Feng Ziyang with another shake of his head. "What does it mean?"

"Nothing," I answer.

"Okay."

I think before asking my next question. "Did the German teacher inform on me last night?" I ask.

"What?"

"Elaine Mueller," I say. "Did she tip campus security off about Wang being in my apartment?"

"I am English professor!"

"Are you going to be arrested as well?"

This is going too far. Feng confirms the transgression.

"The Turmoil was made by hoodlums and criminals," he announces. "Not intellectuals. Wang Hua was never acceptable faculty member. His actions do not represent department or college."

"Right," I say, also standing.

Secretary Shen touches my arm. "Bad time," she says in a gentle voice.

"And I shouldn't make it worse?"

"Zhou Hong," says the woman.

"What's your son's name?" I ask.

She provides it.

"If I see him in America, I'll say hello from you and his uncle."

In the hallway I request a word more with the dean. Nothing is beyond me now, and I cross to the supply closet, ostensibly for privacy. Feng hesitates, then follows me into the room like an errant pupil into the principal's office. I shut the door.

He adjusts his glasses, his eyes making circles as they fly over the shelves of exams and undergraduate texts, the boxes of photocopying paper that partially block the one narrow window. We both clear our throats. I wind up hacking into a handkerchief, not from the cigarette but the air itself, which is, I decide, a kind of dust palimpsest.

"Was there a window then?" I inquire.

"Covered by newspaper. Once, I ripped the paper away. For this, I was beaten."

By forming a cross with my arms, I can use both walls for support. "How long were you imprisoned?"

"Re-educated."

"A month? A year?"

Dean Feng sits on a box.

"Where did they take Wang?"

"I am English—"

I ask again.

Sighing, he removes a pen from his pocket and scribbles something onto the corner of an old exam. He rips the page off. "Give this to taxi driver," he says. "Maybe he will bring you, maybe he won't."

"I'm sorry."

"Okay, okay."

I want to end on a more gracious note. "I appreciate what you did for Zhou Hong at the banquet yesterday," I say.

"I did not do it for you."

"Of course not. I mean—"

"There is never need to humiliate a person," interrupts Dean Feng. "Wu Tong and the college president do not understand this. Their generation does not understand humiliation as we do."

"Do you really think Wang Hua is guilty of a crime?"

"He is on video tape. I can do nothing for him."

"But do *you* think he did anything wrong?"

He asks me to please leave. I do, but linger at the top of the stairs, waiting for Feng to emerge from the supply closet. After five minutes the door has still not reopened, and I depart.


The closest taxi stand is outside a hotel near the zoo, a kilometre south of the college. The walk, my longest off campus in a while, is unsettling. Sidewalks are crowded subway platforms, roads are jammed parking lots. Bicycle lanes offer moving tangles of wheels and spokes, elbows and legs. Dust whips off the road and the grassless embankments; dust is swept up and flung into the wind by street cleaners in baker hats and surgical masks; dust chokes the newly planted saplings and powders the already gnarled bushes. At the stand, the first taxi driver glances at the address and then rolls up his window without comment. The second man studies the paper closely, as if committing it to memory. When he hands it back to me, I am ready.

"Take me near it," I say.

"You speak Chinese?"

"Take me close, and I can walk."

"No way."

"Is it far?"

"Pretty far," he answers.

"Leave me a kilometre away. Indicate the building, or even just the street."

"The what?"

"My Mandarin is so poor," I say.

"No, no," he insists. "It is excellent, for a foreigner."

"I have to work harder at it."

"You're doing well."

"Just show me the building, okay? From a distance. No one will know how I got there."

The taxi heads first northwest, then due north in the direction of the Great Wall at Badaling. Only once I'm settled in the back seat do I remember what is in the pocket of Wang's jacket: Dean Feng's hologram Mao button, stolen off his desk this morning. I have no idea why I took it. What, if anything, I intend to do with the button is an even greater mystery.

The landscape dissolves quickly into the semi-rural countryside that rings the capital, a blur of work units and factories, planted fields and greenhouses, along with the ubiquitous red-brick apartment blocks siding the main roads. The anonymity of all but Beijing's inner city elicits a stock response in me. I switch off, allowing the department stores and construction sites, the soda stands and roadside markets, the traffic jams and bicycle pile-ups, and the people, all drably dressed, all small and black-haired, all either hurried or being hurried along; I allow this harsh, alien world to drift by, unconfronted, almost unobserved. Twice the taxi is diverted onto a bumpy shoulder by road repairs and comes to a halt. Then I become a caged animal on display. Open-mouthed, dead-grinned locals surround the vehicle for a gawk. They smile and point fingers. They call me a foreign devil, not meant as an insult, and laugh at my grotesque features. For them, my world is not harsh but alien, and their curiosity about it, at best, is middling.

My thoughts drift to Hong and Ying at the airport on the far side of the city. Queuing for an hour at the check-in. Queuing for another half-hour at customs. Being grilled by an officer, documents frowned upon, declared inadequate. Zhou Hong asking to be admitted to the restricted zone—her daughter is only five, after all—and of course being refused, and of course demanding to use a telephone to call a high-ranking airport official, and of course being waved through by the officer with a resentful shrug. Ying wide-eyed and tremulous, squeezing her mother's hand. Hong finding out who will be seated next to the girl, befriending the person, and explaining in bright tones that she is being delayed by work, but will be joining Ying and her father in Canada before the summer—fall at the latest. Telling the lie loud enough for the child to hear and possibly believe, and for passengers in the waiting lounge to hear and not for a second believe, to look at Zhou Hong differently: less inquisitive, more unpitying. Hong retying strands of hair and licking her lower lip. Ying retying invisible strands of hair and studying the movement of her tongue over her own lips, going cross-eyed in the process. Fear battling excitement in the daughter as the first boarding call comes. Despair battling determination in the mother as people storm the door to the tunnel. Ying refusing to leave. Hong insisting. Ying in tears. Hong dry-eyed. Her reconnecting with the traveller in the next seat and silently begging the man—a woman, with any luck—to take the girl's hand, once she has unpried it, finger by finger, from her own. Saying, Everything will be fine, Ying. Your father will be waiting at the other end, and strangers will be kind along the way. Insisting they depart, saying, Go on, be brave, and then standing at the tunnel mouth observing the child descend a short set of stairs, one, two, three, four, suddenly gone. On her tiptoes for a final look. Turning to see who is watching, asking a flight attendant if the plane can be observed from a window, told it cannot, and so recharting a lengthy corridor to the main terminal with the thought: *I am abandoning my baby in a tunnel! I am leaving her to die!* The smile making her jaw ache. The vomit climbing her throat. One step at a time. Breathe in, breathe out. Easy.

I should be there with her. With them. I should be saying goodbye to my daughter.

The taxi has stopped. It is idling, in fact, the driver craning his neck to rouse me. The Mao button on the seat catches his eye. His face already wears a frown; on seeing the grinning Chairman, fear narrows his features. We are parked on the shoulder of a road flanked by columns of willow trees. Four hundred metres further north is a large compound that sprouts foliage high above its brick walls. The road appears to end at the compound gate. Pointing to it, the driver names his sum—a month's wage for a Chinese professor—and implores me to hurry. The taxi is into a three-point turn before I've even closed the door.

If I am seeking publicity for Wang Hua's case, a warning call to a Western television crew would have been wise. If I am looking to prove myself to Zhou Hong, informing her about the plan beforehand might have been prudent. If, however, I long subconsciously to either be arrested for my sins—

the collective guilt business I wanted to tell Ivan about after the arrest in Montreal—or else simply to return to Canada nine months sooner than planned, then storming a Chinese prison is probably a superior scheme.

Heads pop out of doors as I stroll up the road beneath flat clouds and a gauzy sun. Based on my one weekend outside Beijing in March, I am expecting to be followed, Pied Piper-like, to the gate. But in this neighbourhood, innocent curiosity is obviously not treated as such, and I reach the compound minus stragglers. The brick walls are five metres tall and the gate is twice the height of those at the college. Instead of a barrier to screen vehicles, a steel fence opens and closes electronically, with two armed guards positioned before it. In a small booth sits a third guard, reading a newspaper. The quiet is uncanny and the menace is as palpable as night soil over fields. I count cameras: one mounted on either side of the gate, another atop the guard room.

The guard with the newspaper saunters over to me. "Are you with—?" he asks.

I don't catch the word.

"Newspaper? Television?"

"I want to see a friend," I explain.

A stocky man who is still a size too small for his uniform and cap, the guard is perturbed. "You're not with the media?"

"I'm a teacher."

He absorbs the information. "Get lost," he orders.

"Pardon?"

"This is a restricted area. No Westerners allowed. No Chinese, either. Get lost, or else—"

Again, I can't keep up with his accent. I do, however, get the gist of his next utterance: he issues instructions to the other men, who approach.

I hold my smile. "I want to see a friend," I say. "Can I please speak with someone?"

"You have no friend here," he replies less whimsically. "Go back to your hotel."

"I'm a teacher," I repeat, naming the school. "My friend is a teacher also. He came here last night. I want to see him."

On command, the other guards advance. Both are adults, unlike most security police around the city, with locked jaws and practised glares. One of them draws so close I smell the grease stench of the automatic weapon he holds across his chest. Anger at the intimidation mingles in me with a new experience of fear. I think about pushing the guy. My bowels loosen.

"His name is Wang Hua," I manage, "and he has done nothing. I want to talk to him."

All traces of false geniality vanish from the senior guard. He repeats his command, adding the threat—presumably—of arrest. I use the strange word to taunt the men. From their expressions, I gather that I make no sense. But I also lack options, and need time to think.

Suddenly the road begins to quake. Pivoting, I watch as an army truck roars up the street towards the gate. The barrel of a rifle is abruptly against my stomach, and I am being shoved backwards. In his haste, the guard knocks me onto my ass, where I stay, a body length away from the vehicle's path. A khaki troop carrier shudders to a halt almost at my feet.

Opening my eyes, I study the back flap. The canvas is drawn but not sealed, and is easily parted by a breeze or a motion from within. I stare at the bar of black between the fabric and listen for voices. All I hear is the idling engine. Most likely, the cabin is either empty or else full of more guards. But suppose it holds prisoners? Suppose one of those prisoners is—

Up on my feet, I wipe my palms against my thighs. One

flap balloons, begging someone to pull it back. I walk right up to the rear and—

The truck lurches forward. Ahead, the sentries have moved aside; the gate is opening.

Clearly possessed by demons, I follow the vehicle to a line scratched into the asphalt by a sliding gate pole. The line, of course, is *the* line: cross it and everything changes. For the first time I blink, content—I tell myself—to survey the prison before making a move. Along one shoulder of the road is a mesh fence; along the other side are ordinary apartment blocks. There is a playing field and a paved courtyard. There are trees and benches. Thirty metres further in stands a small watchtower, no higher than the outer walls, and beyond it is another building. I notice plenty of fences that subdivide areas and force pedestrians down certain paths. I also distinguish lots of wood poles, atop of which sit swivelling cameras and drooptongued loudspeakers. No barbed wire, though, and no patrolling guards. No people, in fact: not a living soul crosses my vision. With some shock I realize that the compound could pass for a university campus. That would make me a Beijinger, lingering at a gate to gape at this exotic, perilous place.

Two sentries push me with their rifle barrels. Once more, I land on my ass. When the senior guard grins, so do his juniors. I grin back.

"I want to speak with someone," I say from the ground. "I won't leave until I do."

"I could arrest you."

"Good."

The guard tells me I am crazy. But he also returns to the booth and picks up a phone. I position myself so that all three cameras have a good view, and pocket my hands to hide the earthquake erupting within my nervous system. After five minutes a steel door next to the gate opens and an elderly man in a Mao suit emerges. He has the wizened look of many older Chinese, an expression often associated in the West with sagacity: eyes half buried by bushy brows, skin almost translucent, hair wiry and grey. His smile, though, reveals teeth so white and regular they must be capped. He speaks for a minute in what sounds like Mandarin. For reasons I cannot fathom, except that his accent is hard-core country, I understand virtually nothing.

"I speak a little French," says the man in that language. "Would that be acceptable?"

"You speak French?"

"An error of youth," he answers with a Gallic shrug.

"Your accent is good," I admit.

"Yours is strong."

"I'm from Canada."

"You mean Quebec?"

"Right," I say in amazement. "I mean Quebec."

He steps closer. "How can I be of help to you?" he asks, his tone at once civil and humouring.

"Are you the warden?"

"I am the—" He provides the French word for manager or director.

"The director?"

"Correct."

"Isn't this a prison?"

"Who told you that?"

"Isn't it?"

"It is a place where people stay."

"Are they forced to stay?"

"No one tries to leave," he answers.

"Could they, though?"

"I am puzzled," he lies.

"Could the people who stay here leave if they wanted to?"

"It is best to stay."

"Then it's a prison."

"If you say so," says the man, shrugging again.

Since greeting him, I have sensed only power and intimated only dread. I have also given up expecting results. My reasons for persisting are selfish: it has become a test.

"What have the people who are staying done wrong?" I ask, careful to use his vocabulary.

"Nothing, as far as I know. Do you have any information you'd like to share with us?"

"I want to see a friend who was brought here last night. His name is Wang Hua."

"It means nothing to me."

"He's a teacher at—" I name the college.

"I know the school," replies the man. "My oldest daughter studied Japanese there. Still, this teacher. . . ."

"He was arrested because of the massacre last June."

"What massacre?"

"The Turmoil," I quickly correct.

He nods.

"He's wearing this on the videotapes the police made of him," I say, modelling the jacket.

"I see. And did the teacher also wear that on the videotapes?" he asks, indicating the Mao button, which I pinned to the lapel.

"That was my idea."

"Not a very good one, either."

I can feel the blood in my cheeks. My audacity is a house of cards; one huff and puff, and it will blow down. The warden does not take his eyes off me.

"My friend's head is shaved."

"Oh?"

"And he's Tibetan," I add, playing my ace.

All the man does is shift from foot to foot. No scrunched eyes, no nervous cough. Am I flattering myself? I don't think so. I think he knows. "Sorry I can't be of assistance," he says, taking my arm. "This is not a place for you. I wonder how you even learned the address."

"Lucky guess."

"Should I call you a taxi?"

"I can walk."

"Fine, er. . . . What was your name again?"

I answer.

"I was in Montreal once," he says. "Three years ago, for a conference. Very beautiful city. Very quiet."

"Not too many people," I supply.

"And so much snow!" he smiles.

The intersection where the cabby let me off seems a hundred kilometres away. My pace is challenged by a wind so stiff I can lean into it. Normally, I would walk with my back to such a breeze. But glancing over my shoulder is out of the question. Even the terrifying rumble of a vehicle—another army truck—advancing up from behind me is insufficient inducement to turn around. Being turned into a pillar of salt is one thing; looking any longer at a prison that is not a prison, full of prisoners who are not prisoners, including a friend who is likely no longer a friend, is another. Houses and shops notwithstanding, the road is deserted; a city of ten million to the immediate south aside, the panorama is of trees and fields and a vast, endless sky. What sweeps through me is a sense not so much of desolation as randomness. I don't precisely mean Wang's arrest. I don't precisely mean my hurrying along this street. Nor am I exactly thinking of the arbitrariness implicit in my ever having met Wang Hua at all, or gotten to know Zhou Hong and Ying, or wound up in this particular place at this particular time. I am thinking of the "fact"—if you will—that above us are the sky and the stars and the sun and the moon, and below us are the trees and the plants and the earth and the oceans, and that these are the solid, ordered components of the universe. We, on the other hand, are perpetual accidents of fate and fortune, and the meanings we affix to our lives are personal, acts of imagination rather than nature. No less important, I hasten to add: simply conjured. Earthquakes truly occur. The earthquake that shook me fifteen minutes ago, like the one that will probably shake me again tonight, happens in my mind only—a more evanescent space would be difficult to conceive.

Wang would be pleased with these thoughts. He is, after all, a man who resides most happily in the country of his often besotted imagination. Twice he has told me about a dream. Though it is reoccurring, it is also unfinished, forever interrupted by a waking roommate or corridor clamour. To date, it has gotten this far: *He is walking along a path in a valley. He meets a beautiful Tibetan girl who asks him, without using words, to accompany her. She points up a slope to a ridge. Beyond the ridge is a snow-capped mountain. Beyond it are more mountains, more ridges. A line of stupas, each displaying a prayer flag stiff in the wind, marks the route. In silence they join hands and set off.*

He thinks the dream is about suicide. I don't see this, but then—at the end of the day—I don't really live here. Out of respect, I complete the dream for him. *Wang and the woman ascend a steep gravel slope. The wind rasps their cheeks and burns their skin but also fills their ears with music. Reeling birds make them dizzy. A moving sky causes the earth to slide underfoot. Always they hold hands; sometimes they stop to regulate their breathing, co-ordinate their heartbeats. Atop the ridge is a wooded area, which they pass through. At the far end, the air is thinner and the path is vertiginous. Up they climb, legs curiously light, vision blurring as clouds sag to embrace them. Thoughts, too, abate—as unnecessary as speech, as language. The sun sets below. The moon tangles their hair. Another ridge looms, and behind it another snow-capped mountain. They will soon reach the ridge, and it will soon be dark.*

I am barely inside the campus gate when I run into a student on her way to Professor David's three o'clock lecture in the Arts Building. The student is bright and chatty; I must sound stoned. We walk to the hall together. The poster still clings to the main door, and is now covered with messages, most in English, Japanese or German, with the elegant squiggles of Arabic visible in a bottom corner. I stop in an acrid bathroom to douse my face. Happily, the room has no mirror.

"Short class today," I announce, leaning so hard on the podium it nearly topples forward. "Simultaneous translation exercise. I'll tell you a story in English and you copy it down in Chinese. Tonight, you translate it back. Monday morning I—or someone—will collect your work, and put all the stories together to create one huge tale."

While students scramble for pen and paper, I examine my cupped hands and stubby fingers.

"A man and a woman live on a farm in northern China. His name is Lu, hers is Zhimei. One day, Lu has to leave to fight in a war. He's gone for many years. While he's away, Zhimei, whose heart is pure, assumes her husband is dead and remarries. A sick Lu returns from the war and walks in on Zhimei and her new husband late one night. It's winter and the snow is waist-high. He sees her in bed with someone else and rushes back out into a terrible storm. Villagers come upon him the next morning, half frozen to death. Only, because of his changed appearance—the long hair and caved-in cheeks—they don't recognize him. They also mistake him for a woman. The local inn agrees to take the sick stranger in. Zhimei, a kind person, plans to visit the poor woman as soon as the snow melts. But Lu dies and is put into a tomb in the mountains nearby."

I hear murmurs, rustlings.

"Too fast?" I ask.

As usual, no one answers. A sea of bowed heads and placid faces; a ringing non-endorsement. I resume the study of my hands.

"Moments before he died Lu confessed his true identity to the innkeeper. He made the old woman promise to keep it secret. But after a week of agonizing the innkeeper went to Zhimei's house. She travelled over the fields on a strange evening, the moon twice-ringed, the sky blood-red. Crying out at the news, Zhimei rushed to the mountain and begged the grave to open. The rock wouldn't move. Only when she sang for it, a sad, beautiful song, did the boulder slide away. Zhimei entered the tomb and leapt into the grave. Moments later, two butterflies emerged from the cave, wings interwoven, lovers beyond death."

Woven like my fingers are now twined. Like my thoughts feel all braided with her thoughts.

"Got it?" I ask.

There are further murmurings and rustlings, plus a few sullen early exits. No smiling faces. No Professor David fans today.

"Class dismissed," I say.

## 18

AFTER A SHORT REST, KEPT SLEEPLESS BY THE TELEPHONE'S remorseless gurgling, I take a cold shower, eat some jam and bread, and pack—as a precaution—my suitcases. At 5:45, wearing a jacket and tie, my face freshly shaved and my hair respectable, I descend the stairwell. Wang's jacket is thrown over my shoulder.

A man I have never seen before sits behind the security desk. He wears tinted glasses.

How can I be so sure that I love her? Because of the way my heart races at the bell of her voice; the bounce that guides my step at the mental image of her. Because of the smile on my face when she smiles; how I have to laugh when she does, even if the joke isn't funny. Because of the happiness I feel when she seems happy; the sorrow that weighs on me before even a narrow window onto her troubles. Because of the quickening of my thoughts to amuse her; the ebbing of my worries when we're together. Because of my astonishment at how the world looks to her, how she misses the gravity that brings most people down, the precautionary sadness that cripples lives. Because of the shimmer of her hair, the nutmeg of her skin; her owl eyes and peach-fuzz upper lip.

Most of all, because I have felt nothing like this since I first met Carole Lapointe a decade ago. Meaning, I think, that at long last Carole is finished. Which itself means that I am an organism capable of only the most basic life sequences: a death before a birth, an end before a beginning. A children's parable. A folk melody.

She is waiting outside her building. The concert isn't for ninety minutes, but the city centre is twelve kilometres—and two bus rides—away. Hong runs back up the stairwell with Wang's jacket. Oddly, she asks me to remain on the bottom landing. Traces of mascara fail to disguise the red rims of her eyes. Protracted silences cannot hide the impatience in her voice.

"Very foolish, David," she says at the bus stop.

"I thought it was worth trying."

"For who?"

"You?" I throw out.

"I don't think so."

"Me then," I correct.

"There will be consequences."

"I'm sorry," I say. My impulse is to muster no defences tonight, tell no lies. "It was selfish and pointless. Maybe even destructive."

She pauses, reties her hair. "People are amazed," she says with a nervous laugh.

"They shouldn't be."

"Some think you are crazy. Others say you are brave, and a good friend to Wang Hua."

"Wang has been arrested," I answer. "I couldn't do anything for him last night or this morning. I should have been at the airport with you and Ying. That would have been practical. That would have made me a good friend."

A bus pulls in.

"You could do nothing for us, either," says Hong.

Her tone does not bode well. Never mind for the evening as a whole: she needs her strength to deal with the accordian bus screeching to a rib-rattling halt before us. Options are limited: either we pile-drive our way through the throng swarming the rear doors and ride a wave up into the cabin, or else we wait behind the self-appointed shovers in the hope of squeezing onto the bottom step. The reality of the former tactic is suffocating physical contact; the fact of the latter is likely failure. Both options involve discomfort and self-abasement, but only one guarantees transportation. Experience has taught me to abandon hope of an empty bus miraculously pulling in two minutes later. A bus may indeed show up early, and be less sardined, but over the course of that interval dozens of new commuters will emerge from alleyways and apartment blocks and—it sometimes seems—the very air itself.

I lack the stomach for this, and routinely fail to board three or four times in a row before hiking it down to the zoo to hail a cab. Today is no exception, and I turn to Hong to suggest a new plan. I look first behind, then to either side and finally up ahead at the mob. Among the straining bodies and flailing limbs she stands, pushing with both hands on the back of an old man whose feet no longer touch the ground. Zhou Hong has opened a hole for us, as fleeting as the space a football guard creates for his running back. Noting her expression, I hustle into it. The bottom step is attainable. I climb gingerly. But then palms are applied to my back, as friendly assistance, and I lurch forward. For a moment the crest we are atop meets resistance, and the prospect of being spewed back out is real. That makes even me mean, and I use my—by local standards—sumo physique to spearhead a fresh surge. A heave-ho, and Hong and I are abruptly not only up the stairs but inside the rear cabin. Us and the old man. Us and a hundred other people.

The door slams shut, opens to expel a few half-ins, slams again, jerks part way back, then closes for good. It is not uncommon for Beijing buses to roar up streets with arms and legs pinned between the rubber mats of the doors. It is less common, but far from rare, for a human head to ride outside the cabin. Whatever is happening at the doors now, I don't see it. Bodies reduce my sight to mops of black hair atop oily faces. To those around me, I smile and say hello. Some return the greeting, others the grin. A few are too shocked at my presence and look away. Hong and I exchange words in English, which elicits giggles, and once touch hands. At least, I hope it is her hand that I grasp momentarily. Because she, too, is invisible. Only an arm—I recognize the blouse—protrudes from the tangle.

The ride is interminable. At each stop, a surreal demonstration of natural selection takes place. At each stop, the impossible happens: more people board than get off; the air tightens its choke-hold; an elbow already in my rib probes for my appendix. I close my eyes and hum a song. I count to a hundred in English and French, then in Mandarin. Finally, I hear the driver cut the engine, and sense the first shudders of the motion that will sweep us back out the door.

Hong is already on the sidewalk.

"That wasn't too bad," I say.

The next ride is. Several hundred people mill around the zoo terminus. Cattle pens, designed to funnel them into the front and rear doors, are effective until an actual vehicle appears, whereupon a mob attacks it, forcing the driver to either take lives or halt well short of the spot. I refuse to swarm, and restrain her from doing so. As a result, we are among the last to board, and never make it further than the bottom step. When the doors open at a stop, we come face to face with a mob whose intention is to get into the cabin at any cost. Hong responds with glares and sharp words. I hang on for dear life.

"That was bad," she says, back on the street.

The concert hall is a kilometre west of Tiananmen Square. With time to spare and muscles to relax, I suggest we stroll down to it along Changan Avenue. Though I've been off campus with Zhou Hong before, we've never walked such a highly visible, and politically sensitive, stretch of the city. I notice the stares and make sure our arms do not brush. If she acts unperturbed by the attention, she also clutches her purse with both hands and wears her smile tight. The sky is still ashen and the temperature, for early April, is warm. I sweat in my apparel. Hong is dressed more practically: thin black trousers that climb at her ankles, the pink blouse opened at the collar. A sweater is folded over her arm.

"I should know these places better," I say as we pass Zhongnanhai, the government leadership compound where armed soldiers keep watch over a row of marble lions.

"I should know them not so well," she answers.

What I should know about this part of Beijing is information readily available, I gather, so long as I don't ask for it, and amply evident, so long as I know where to look. Despite my crafted solipsism, some knowledge has insinuated itself, the way melodies settle into the memory without intent, an indication of how full the air must be with a kind of music. I should know, for example, to look at the vermilion walls of the Forbidden City and see the bullet marks in the bricks, and to study the asphalt of Changan Avenue like it was an archeological site and uncover the APC tread impressions, and to actually feel beneath my feet on Tiananmen Square the gouges left in the pavement—and in the collective memory of a quarter of the earth's citizenry, perhaps—by clumsy, murderous tanks. Maybe it is fair that I cannot know exactly what happened here, and in the streets around here, on June 4th of last year. That is not spoken of, or at least not in a voice loud enough for a person like me to hear. But I should know more of how the square, and the city, appeared during the weeks before. I should be able to recreate the scene. Tiananmen a half Woodstock, half bus terminal. The Goddess of Liberty gazing at the portrait of Chairman Mao. Officials gazing at protesters from inside the Great Hall of the People. Students rushing into the city to prolong the carnival. Hunger strikers being rushed to hospital along paths created using human chains. Families strolling the banner-festooned square to gawk, men to snap photos of insurgents. Popsicle sellers doing brisk business. Kentucky Fried Chicken boxes littering the ground. Blistering sunlight, brutal downpours. Eerie moons, starry heavens. And the downtown core: how it functioned during that period should also be in my mind's eye. No police or authority: seemingly, no one in charge. A village of overnight posters and street corner debating societies and newspapers temporarily reporting the news. A population suddenly outspoken and incautious and, by all accounts, in better humour than any could remember. Civic-minded. Friendly. A city briefly liberated. A city briefly gone mad.

What Zhou Hong knows about this part of Beijing, I gather, is acute and painful. But is it also private? I have never tried to find out. This, despite Zuo Chang's cryptic reference back in November to his wife's "foolishly brave" activities during the Turmoil, and to Wang Hua's comment not long ago that Hong was both his only true ally and someone whose fate would be so different they actually shared little in common.

We stop at the corner of Changan and the street that runs along the western flank of the square. To our left is the Gate of Heavenly Peace, Mao's portrait a button on its lapel, and the outer walls of the Forbidden City; to our right looms the

Great Hall of the People. Separating us from the expanse of Tiananmen—unlike most squares in the West, it is devoid of greenery, and could pass for a launch pad—are wide boulevards liquid with traffic. An underground walkway ferries pedestrians across the road to the designated centre of China—the point from which all distances are measured, all clocks are set. For a centre, it is curiously empty. For a pounding heart, it sounds no beat. A few dozen strollers scurry over the asphalt; given the dimensions, they are ants on the tarmac at Cape Canaveral. Halfway down the square, near Mao's mausoleum, a man flies a red kite. It soars high over the obelisk, high over the architecture, but keeps well below the curve of cloud. Hong shows no interest in descending the stairwell.

"I should not have come down here," she suddenly says, her eyes narrowed by the light. "Feng Ziyang knocked on my door very late, after midnight, to say he had found a driver who would bring us into the city. We were going to look for students and convince them to return to campus. Feng was so upset that I became concerned for his safety. That is why I agreed."

She clutches the purse more tightly. I make sure we are standing a solid metre apart. I also nod every few seconds, to pass for a tourist receiving a private tour of the splendours of both imperial China and the People's Republic.

"Feng is a good person," she adds. "He cares for his students, loves his family. Ying calls him 'old uncle.'"

This first mention of the girl silences us both. The moment is awkward.

"Did you rescue any students?" I ask.

She shakes her head. "We got separated almost immediately. Too much darkness and confusion. People running and shouting. The sound of gunfire and army vehicles."

"Here?"

"Back towards the concert hall," she answers. "I wound up in a *hutong* behind Xidan Street. Soldiers were chasing people off the main streets, and I hid inside a house." She pauses to retie her hair, made wild by the same gusts that are encouraging the kite skyward. "At first, I thought the house was empty. In the darkness I was blind, and the room was silent. Then a voice spoke to me, the voice of an old woman. I told her my name and apologized. She asked me what was happening outside. Then she served me tea. I stayed with her until morning, and so saw only burnt buses and army trucks. Also tanks and soldiers lined up back there"—she indicates an invisible barrier across Changan—"blocking anyone from seeing onto the square."

A few people have stopped to watch us. The look on her face, and perhaps on mine, is undermining the tour guide ruse. Without touching her, I turn us both around, away from Tiananmen, back along the boulevard.

"I did nothing brave," says Hong. "Rescued no students, helped no people. The woman's grandsons were out fighting the army. One worked in a factory and the other had been waiting two years for a job assignment. Her husband was killed by the Japanese."

"And her son?" I ask without purpose.

"He did not support the students. She thought he spent the night drinking with friends."

It occurs to me that Hong may want to go onto the square, as silent vigil. Though the concert starts in fifteen minutes, I ask her.

"Never again," she answers. "I would like to visit the woman some day, though. To see if her grandsons are okay."

Outside the hall I attempt to clarify a point. My posing of

the question is crude, not to mention presumptuous. Happily, Hong cuts me off with the desired answer.

"Feng Ziyang and I are being protected by the college," she replies. "Authorities asked the administration for a list of any faculty who passed through the campus gates on June 4th. Our names were left off."

"What about Wang Hua?"

"Not so lucky," says Hong, wetting her lower lip with her tongue.

"Which isn't your fault."

"Of course not," she replies.

The hall is nondescript. In design, the building is without cultural imprint: it could as easily be in Montreal or Bombay. Along corridor and stairwell walls are portraits of Western composers; in the upper mezzanine is a kiosk retailing warm Coke and cheap cassettes of Beethoven and Mozart. The auditorium itself is narrow and dim, with a sloping floor and a recessed balcony. Canopying the stage are hanging saucers to aid sound projection. Covering each and every seat, and most steps, are chattering people. To claim our places in the balcony Hong must usurp a couple who occupy the seats, despite having no tickets. An usher attempts to eject them from the hall, but gives up after a token tussle. The couple join the dozens of other gatecrashers in the aisles. Faces are animated and murmurs rise and fall in waves. Faces are also all Han; I am the only Westerner not hanging from a wall. I have never seen a group of Chinese—including, unfortunately, my own classes—this animated. Hong, too, speaks quickly and drums on her purse. Her eyes dart around the hall. Her cheeks show increasing colour.

I am happy for her. For us, too. Stranger still, sharing equal space in my thoughts is a desire to do anything to keep her happy this evening—as would a man in love—and to do what is necessary to have my way, as would what Ivan calls a "proper asshole." The coexistence of these impulses makes me wonder if I am demented.

The lights are still up when the conductor, a silver-haired man in a tuxedo that may have fit him five kilograms ago, appears from a side-door and hastens past his tuning orchestra to the podium. The scattered applause dies before he gets near the stand. As if noting the reception, he raises his baton while still climbing onto the perch and, without fanfare or warning, the concert begins. Zhou Hong, who guards the Mandarin-only program, whispers that the first selection is a Haydn symphony. The information is as useless as her hushed voice. Around us, music lovers shell peanuts and slurp sodas. Conversations go unmodulated; ushers settle ticket disputes using abusive language and scolding tones. The stage could still be empty, for all anyone cares; the conductor could still be in his change room, squeezing himself into his tux. Franz Joseph Haydn is not being ignored; he is being dismissed from the universe.

The clapping fades before the man can even swivel around, let alone take a bow. My own incessant applause—for at least five seconds—draws stares.

"Didn't exactly bowl the audience over," I comment.

Hong crooks her head.

"The music wasn't popular," I clarify.

"People have come for the other piece," she replies, taking a pen and notepad from her purse. She writes "bowl over" on one side of a page, then fills the opposite sheet with ideograms.

A thought I've been pondering for some time is delivered without consideration. "What's funny about that book," I say, "is that you rarely use idioms in conversation. Your English is excellent, but it's also clean and simple."

To my surprise, Hong nods in agreement, almost in relief. "They don't sound right when I speak them," she answers. "Not comfortable or natural."

"But you still take notes?"

"Maybe one day it will be different."

I ask her to tell me about the program. "Which are the words for butterfly?" I say, pointing to a cluster of typed characters.

"The concerto has a different name in Chinese. Its English title is actually more beautiful."

I am, for some reason, disappointed.

Hong jots down two ideograms in the margin of the page. Heads on either side of us turn in interest at the literary activity.

"These are for butterfly," she says. "First one is combination of leaf, generations, and worm. The wings of butterfly resemble a folded leaf. Also, like leaves, butterflies go through changes."

"What about the worm?"

"Sorry?"

"You said there was a worm?"

She examines the calligraphy again. I lean close enough to smell the shampoo in her hair. I also place my hand on the armrest. "This radical"—she points, though I don't even look—"is found in most words for insects and tiny creatures."

"And lovers?"

Hong sketches two more ideograms. The first is complex, the other simple, like a tepee. "Also just two characters," she says.

"One to one is the only concise configuration," I reply dreamily.

Blushing, she wonders aloud what I mean.

The musicians straggled back out while we were chatting and now the conductor reappears. He is accompanied by the soloist and is greeted with sustained applause. The smile is on his face, but the clapping is for the young man trailing behind him. No older than twenty-five, the violinist sports a tuxedo sculpted to his slender form. His shoulder-length hair is blown dry and he wears two rings on his bow hand that, reflecting off a saucer, fire daggers of light up onto the ceiling. Beside the podium he bows to the conductor, then positions his instrument under his chin. The bow is held aloft, like a sabre whose lowering will signal the start of a battle.

"Very famous musician," whispers Hong in Mandarin. "Studied in New York and Toyko."

Sensing no hope, my entreating hand closes up. Eventually I return it to where it belongs: cupped with its partner, locked between my thighs.

*Butterfly Lovers* opens with a flute over a plucked harp. The solo violin enters softly; the principal melody is announced. I recognize it at once, partially from Zhou Hong's humming, partially from the stairwell performances of Madame Chai with her mop, and partially, no doubt, because it resembles so many other traditional Chinese tunes. That I can hear the opening notes of the concerto is amazing. The hall has fallen quiet. Actually, the hall has ceased to breathe. No whispers, no shuffling feet, no coughs. Entire rows lean forward in their seats. Aisle squatters and scornful ushers, kids who drowned out Haydn with crinkling candy wrappers: all are suddenly still and alert. I study the faces. At first, the attentiveness reminds me of the rows of cadres panned by cameras during the nightly news footage of party meetings. Those on television, however, have hollow eyes. Most of the people around me, even if viewed just from an angle, and in dimness, blaze with occupation.

My knowledge of music is too meagre to expoujnd on how

the concerto works. *Butterfly Lovers* relates the story of the star-crossed youngsters, Hong once explained, their forced separation—both had been promised in arranged marriages—and eventual tragic reunion, but in still another language I have not learned. The structure is simple, and the plaintive, lovelorn melody appears so inviolable the score strays only briefly from it. Some sections are bright, others sombre. In the middle is a passage of orchestral thunder: hard-bowed strings, brass and percussion. Then comes more sweeping violin and cello, with the soloist, whose swagger vanished the moment the conductor raised his baton, rocking first back on his heels and then forward on his toes. Though *Butterfly Lovers* doesn't seem technically difficult—the dramatic shifts are in emotion, not tone—the young man is clearly challenged by some requirement of it. Despite the overcrowding, the audience in the Beijing Concert Hall is small. But my sense is that the violinist understands his duties to include playing for legions of people not actually present, perhaps not even alive, yet still somehow involved in, and integral to, the performance. My sense is that the concerto is as much resonance as sound, memory as music.

Nonetheless, I am still expecting it to end with a bang. The finale, though, proves even more hushed than the opening. The violin does not fade so much as recede: I—and everyone else in the hall, I suspect—keep on hearing the melody long after the air has emptied. That sound, or aftersound, causes goose bumps to rise on my arms. It is a ringing, eternal silence, like nothing I have heard before. I almost check my ears to make sure they are not plugged.

Around me are a thousand people who are inhabiting the silence with more confidence. I have no idea what, or even if, the crowd are thinking. Nor are my own thoughts entirely explicable. An image that was at the back of my mind throughout the performance is now front and centre. The image, simply, is of water. Trickling in a flower bed, flowing in a stream. Murmuring over pebbles, roaring through rocks. The rush of it. The relentlessness. The colours, too, depending on light and shade, wind.

And Zhou Hong's thoughts? Her face is relaxed. Her smile is serene. Though she gripped the armrests for much of the concert, her hands are presently in her lap, fingers intertwined. The moment is obviously special, and private. I do not intrude.

Eventually, there is applause. As it grows, and the violinist returns for a third bow, the now-confident conductor beaming at his side, I begin to take exception to the audience response. Reactions seem too wholesale, too programmed. *Butterfly Lovers*, I decide, is not only sad and bittersweet, but also sentimental. Clearly, emotional buttons are being pushed: clearly, cultural clichés are being evoked.

As we file out, basking in the trancelike calm of the crowd, I critique the music. All Hong does is ask if I enjoyed the concert, first in Chinese and then, catching herself, in English, and, ignoring the fact that her question is more polite than inquiring, all I stupidly do is answer.

"The music affects us deeply," she replies in a hurt voice. Though the "us" is a common verbal tic among students, I've never heard her use it.

"I'm sure it does," I say. "And I liked it enough. I just found parts a little—"

"Whether the concerto is excellent or good or just okay makes no difference to us—I mean, to me," she interrupts. "It makes us think of how sorrowful life is. How our own lives are this way, too. Also it. . . ."

We are back on the street. Night has fallen, and Hong puts on her sweater.

"Yes?" I ask.

"It connects us with things. Gives us feelings of passion, and of importance."

"Of course."

"If the music can do that, it must be great."

I concur.

"Should I care if it is not as famous as Haydn?" she asks. Clearly, she is incensed. And overwrought. And I am a moron. About to be sent home for the evening, for the duration of my stay.

"Haydn is irrelevant," I try.

"You don't believe this."

"But I do," I protest, forming an opinion on the spot. "Quality is important, but that's not the reason why people love a song or listen again and again to a tale."

She is silent.

"The legend of Romeo and Juliet wasn't less universal when it was known only in Italy," I continue. "Everything is local. Everything is about you and me and the next person."

My thought stops her in her tracks. She even smiles. "Like the story of Liang Shanbuo and Zhu Yingtai," she says.

I don't know these names, and simply say so. But that, too, is an error. A bad one, apparently. I catch up to her shortly before the bus stop.

"Weren't you thinking of Ying during *Butterfly Lovers*?" I ask.

"When I was crying?"

"You were crying?"

She surges ahead, and this time I hang back. The final bus of the night is pulling in. We will be the last to board, again, and will pay for our passivity. How could I have missed her weeping during the concerto? I don't miss the tears now, despite her efforts to block her face. The streetlamp is useless. The moon, however, is a floodlight. It pours silver light, as if from a jug, down onto the city, and us. And I don't miss the tears glistening on her cheeks.

Her vacancy during both bus rides back out to the campus doesn't escape me, either. The cabin is dim—public buses have no interior lights—and the noise, of rattling chairs and panels and a gearbox that sounds like it is being wrenched from the engine whenever it is shifted, precludes communication. All of which is fine, for Hong is not really beside me. She is off where *Butterfly Lovers* has taken her. Where she is transported by music. Away from here and now: from her troubles; away, perhaps, from me. My puppy-dog gaze and embarrassing avidity. The decision I am pressing upon her, at a moment when she needs such pressure least.

## 19

"WHAT DO YOU WANT FOR YOUR DAUGHTER?"

"Natalie?"

She nods.

"Safe passage into adulthood, I guess," I answer. I sit down to think. "For nothing terrible to happen to her. No strangers luring her into their cars. No teachers telling her she's stupid." I pause. "For her to not be permanently scarred by what's happened. To still believe in parents, in grown-ups. In me."

"Why wouldn't she believe in you?"

Her question causes water to well up in my eyes. "The usual reasons, I guess," I say, grateful for the weak light.

Hong is genuinely puzzled. "You feel you must earn her love?" she asks.

"Isn't that how it works?"

She makes no reply.

"I know I have to change to keep Natalie," I say. "Be someone else. Someone she can admire. But it's no different with adults. . . ." I stop, count to ten, clear my throat. "It's the judging I can't handle. People deciding if you're good enough now or will be in the future. I always come up short. Like I'm disabled. Like I can't even write down a name and phone number." Then, to myself: *Mr. J. Kapinsky. Area code 201. 374-1900.*

I don't look at her. Nor do I dare glance around the apartment. Her apartment, I should add: Hong's private space, which ought to be in shambles—clothes strewn, dishes unwashed—but is in fact tidy and clean. Even Ying's stuffed-animal family are on display: two pandas and a lion, a mouse propped atop the opened cot. The guard at the west gate clearly saw us stop at the path to her building, clearly saw her extend her hand—her hand!—to me, clearly saw us walk as a couple to the first stairwell. Now it is fifteen minutes to curfew; the residence, like the campus, is dead; the air smacks of night soil. I am getting us both into BIG trouble. I am making it worse.

She stands in the kitchen doorway. Officially, she is waiting for the kettle to boil. Unofficially, she is keeping as far away from the bed, and me, as possible. But Hong also ignored the light switch on entering and instead lit a candle centring her table, as if in preparation for a late dinner. The tape player stays under its veil. The silence, though different from at the concert hall, is equally astonishing. With the window closed and the cicadas too cold to sing, I hear virtually nothing. We are inside a sealed chamber, only the scraping of a chair and the whistle of a boiling kettle, plus our own heartbeats, as noise. In the dark, Zuo Chang's artwork looms. The severe brush strokes and austere characters: the uncompromising artistry and piti-less vision. I am reminded of the walls of a Qing tomb I visited outside Beijing. Faintly visible in the confessional light of the chamber were carved columns of ideograms relating Buddhist scriptures. Tonight, however, I am uncomfortable with Zuo's calligraphy. Besides shrinking the room by half, the writing has the threatening quality of graffiti. Worse, the words don't, I decide, make sense. All doggerel. All babble.

"And you," I ask. "What do you want for Ying?"

It is as if I've punched her in the stomach. Hong doubles over, using the doorway as support. "I want her to be with her mother!" she sobs.

I cross to her.

"I let her go away," she adds in Mandarin. "I let her go!"

My hands are in front of me, between us. Of course I should be her support. Of course I should—

She is in my arms.

"She should be with her mother," repeats Hong in a whisper.

Holding her tight—for dear life, really—I respond. First, not using words: from my mouth comes a sound amusingly close to the *coo coo* of the Mile End sill pigeons. I have barely recovered from this when a sentence slips out: "It's okay," I say in her ear. "We've only the loan of them, anyway."

We don't rip each other's clothes off. I probably couldn't; she clearly wouldn't. Instead, we undress beside the bed, fold our garments over a chair and slide under the comforter. I am hard from the start, and bump against her. Our kisses are too forced, then too timid. I touch her too quickly, she touches me not quickly enough. Her body is surprisingly boyish: wide shoulders and small breasts, narrow hips and skinny legs. My body is slimmer than it has been in years, but still must feel alien and unpleasant to Hong. Neither of us are firm muscle. Neither of us are seventeen. For the first minutes I worry that I will pass out, a diver in deep, warm water who cannot bring himself to resurface for air. My skin has a pulse. My eyes grow cataracts. As soon as it seems appropriate, I wander from her breasts down to her belly. It is all I had hoped for: soft and rolling, the hole delicious. Sooner than I would ever have thought likely, Hong takes me in her hand, then in her mouth. Images blur. Thoughts reel. For once, the dislocation is not a portent of illness. For once, it is simply an abandonment. Her neck is slender. Her rib cage is outlined. Her face, meanwhile, first in profile and then from above, is blameless. I study her—and us—in the lovers' light and am grateful. I also sweat and moan and, yes, murmur in French. She uses Mandarin. Happily, no names are mentioned.

We may doze afterwards. Time definitely passes. Not that the sound level changes, or the moonlight between the curtains diminishes, or the calligraphy on the walls fades away. It is all still there. We are still here, sealed off from the world, protected. But then, not exactly: from where I lie, my chin on her shoulder and my hand against her belly, the phone is visible on a cabinet shelf. Were I to sit up, light seeping under the door from the corridor would sting my eyes.

"Your seduction is complete," says Hong.

"My what?"

"Wang Hua told me of your plans."

"He did?"

She smiles. "He said you wish to be known as a merciful man who takes what he wants."

"Mercenary," I correct with reluctance.

"Sorry?"

I repeat the word and define it. The definition is a hit; Hong trembles with laughter.

"What's so funny?" I finally ask.

"This person is not you, David."

"Are you sure?"

I don't mean the question to be menacing. But she stiffens in my arms.

"You aren't?" she asks.

*I am, I'm not* would be the correct answer. An impossible one to give, of course. And Hong doesn't appear to require a reply. She wriggles until I release her, then sits up, pulling the comforter over her breasts. Hip to hip, we barely fit in the bed. The wall is a block of ice against my back.

"Zuo Chang would not be sure of the woman I am now,"

she says. "He would say I am far away from the girl he married. Maybe even from the wife who gave him a daughter."

"He doesn't know."

"He knows everything," she corrects. She gazes across the room at the cabinet and the scrolls on either side of it. "Zuo became my husband in Tibet. When I was seventeen, and he was twenty, being punished for painting in the traditional style. He was sent to my work unit. I was his boss."

She reties her hair. I, meanwhile, suppress a sudden feeling of agitation. My eyes also fall on the artwork.

"A strange place," she continues. "Two hundred kilometres from Lhasa, and another thousand metres above the earth. No village or roads: only yak shepherds and mountains. Beautiful mountains on all sides. Us in the valley."

I ask.

"To grow wheat!" she answers, her blitheness forced. "Chairman Mao wished to increase wheat production. Work brigades were sent to remote areas to become farmers. Cadres in Chengdu gave us a manual on how to operate a generator, and Mao's books. Nothing else. The soil was too shallow and the air was too thin. Little grew up there, except barley, which was not permitted. Two girls in my brigade died the first winter. Another ran away and was found in the spring. She tried to walk over a mountain."

"Was she beautiful?" I say, conjuring images that are not my own, but about which I feel proprietorial.

"Who?"

"I mean Tibet—was it beauitful?"

"Very beautiful," she replies with a sigh. "But I still could not wait to return home."

"Did you meet many Tibetans?"

"Almost none."

"Not even—?"

"I was lucky to be sent far away from towns and villages. Enough trouble to be in charge of a work unit and twenty other Red Guards. I did not want to involve innocent people. . . . Zuo Chang helped me. He made our survival possible."

Each mention of the name deepens my agitation. The calligraphy is now an insult. It is mocking her, and me.

"How did he help?" I hear myself ask.

"He was openly critical of the party, even of Mao Zedong. Very bold and careless. At first, I planned to report him. Then I began to understand that he was trying to impress me. He was flitting."

I leave the mispronunciation be.

"He was handsome and intelligent," says Hong, grasping the comforter with both hands. "Also a Beijinger. I was immature. What he said about China, and the party, seemed true—what I might have thought, had I known how to. I came under his influence."

"You fell in love with him?"

"Zuo and another bad element, a writer from Wuhan, were the only unit members with life experiences. They saved us from starvation or death by cold. He saved me."

"Were you in love?"

My question bothers her. "I respected him as a partner and a comrade," she answers stiffly. "He was strong and forceful, but also gentle and kind. With me, and later with Ying. He is a good father, David. A good man."

"Don't cry."

"His life was not his own for thirty-eight years. Now it can be. Now hers will be better also."

Fuck Zuo's strength, I think to myself. Fuck his kindness.

"Have I ever told you why my marriage ended?" I ask.

She shakes her head.

I make myself more comfortable. Our legs rub; our shoulders touch. "There were lots of reasons, naturally," I say. "All legitimate, mostly my fault. I wasn't a very—"

"Stop!" she nearly shouts.

"Stop what?"

"You don't know?"

I admit my confusion. She gives me a look that is at once sympathetic and pitying. I recognize the expression from arguments with Carole, and am duly unnerved. Hong gestures for me to proceed. Wisely, I let the earlier sentence drop.

"What finished it off was the death of our dog," I say. "Potemkin was a black Labrador, very friendly, pretty stupid. Carole—my wife—was already back at work and I was writing my thesis and looking after the baby. One afternoon I took her and the dog to a park. When Natalie fell asleep in her stroller, I decided to lie down on the grass. The dog bounded out into the road. A truck hit him. . . . She loved that animal madly," I add quietly.

"Was it on a—" She mimes a leash.

"I fell asleep, and he got away." I pause before a lie repeated so often I have to remind myself of what it is. "Except that I didn't exactly fall asleep. I lost consciousness for a brief time—sixty seconds, tops—and Potemkin wandered off."

"Lost consciousness?"

"I have a problem. A disease, I guess. I black out sometimes. It's nothing serious. Nothing I can't handle."

"Do you use medicine?"

I explain my medical history. "Carole maintained that I let the accident happen," I summarize. "She decided that my not taking the drug was an admission I didn't want to change or improve myself. That I was giving in to fate, and could only let things happen to me—not make things happen."

"Not a merciful man?"

"Not a merciful man," I concur.

She reties her hair. "Is that a good reason to break up a family?" she asks.

I should accept her condolences. I should simply agree. "There was more to it," I reply instead.

The phone rings. To my ears, the noise is no longer a twitter or gurgle: it is nails on a blackboard.

"Don't answer," I say.

She is on her feet.

"Let it—"

A naked Zhou Hong lifts the receiver. I curse and turn my face to the wall. The gesture grants her some privacy. It also puts me six inches from a framed sample of Zuo Chang's work.

The conversation is a non-conversation. Someone shouts at Hong; she absorbs the abuse. Aside from a few "okay"s and "I understand"s and one "your position is very difficult," she keeps silent. This goes on for five minutes. When the call is finished, it is because the shouter has hung up on her. She does not bother to offer a face-saving goodbye to the dial tone.

"The president of the college," she says. "He thinks that you should—"

Backing her into the kitchen, I storm around the room destroying her husband's calligraphy. The rice-paper sheets, held up with tape, are easiest: within a few seconds they are crumpled balls, flutterings of ribbon. The work is satisfying, but child's play. The scrolls prove more resilient, and having yanked them from the wall, I manage just to tear them into sections. Two framed pieces of calligraphy are protected by glass. I debate ramming my fist into their centres; cutting myself would feel good. Only that might prove too much for her.

Why then do I demand that Hong return to the main room and, taking her hand—her face is chalk, her eyes are empty—almost drag her over to Ying's cot? Why do I shout insanely about the inappropriateness of having the cot still open, and the girl's stuffed animals still on display? And why—my God, why?—do I pitch the pandas and bunny against those same walls, and fold up the cot with such haste that I catch my finger in the joint, cutting it open—yes, drawing blood?

Because I am having a seizure. Like no seizure I can remember. Like no seizure I could have imagined. Part way into my diatribe about the cot I experienced what doctors call an aura: a weird sensory trembling, like when the lights in a house flicker before an outage. The idea is to use the aura as one would use a jump in the electrical current—as warning. To turn off your computer; to stop whatever you are doing. To find candles and matches; to lie down and empty out. As far as I know, I've never really had an aura, or at least not one of such force. I am aware, in other words, that the fit is coming. I am aware, and do nothing to ward it off.

"Hong," I manage.

She guides me back to the bed.

"Are you—?" she asks.

"I'm not stopping it," I say. "Sorry."

When I come to, I am lying atop the coverlet in my underwear. She is perched at the edge of the mattress in a dressing gown. Her cheeks are dry; her hair has been combed. Up on my elbows, I survey the dark room: it has been tidied again, and the walls are now bare. Even the framed calligraphy, which I didn't touch, is gone. Ying's cot is open. But the stuffed animals, too, have been put away.

It is raining outside. I hear the drops against the windows and walls. The sound is non-invading. Nothing, I decide, can invade our space now. No one can touch us in this place. I sit up beside her. The fabric beneath my legs is kinetic; the smells in my nostrils are pungent; the faint light is alive with dust particles. Even my own skin feels alert, almost prickly. When Hong reaches for my hand, I nearly jump at the contact. When she leans over and kisses me on the cheek, as would a sister or mother, it is all I can do to keep from squirming, like a boy giddy after too much tickling. Her position below the window catches her in the beam that is splitting the curtains. I do not question the inconsistency: moonlight while it is raining? I study her face. What I see is a peasant woman with big bones and soft eyes and a smile that, like all adult smiles, acts as a measure of faith in the world. Hong's smile rejects pessimism; it affirms decency and openness. I see a thirty-six-year-old who, one year ago, had a husband and daughter, but who is now alone. And who will be alone—no, I am not forgetting about me—for some time to come.

"This is a nice moment," I say.

"I feel changed," she replies.

The knock on the door is hardly a surprise. I rise to answer it. Hong says I don't have to. She says I can let them knock. I gently pry my hand from hers. Another, more bullying knock greets me as I slip on my pants and shirt and cross the room. Still, I feel under control. I feel ready for what I am going to make happen. I feel ready for what is going to happen to me.

The stone is rolled away. The tomb opens.

Four uniforms huddle on the landing. Behind them stand Deng Chen and a nasty colleague of Hong's in the Foreign Affairs Office. Neighbours watch from the rear; an elderly couple, unable to fit onto the landing, bob up and down on the top step for a look. One policeman wields a video camera. Careful to block the doorway, I greet the visitors in Mandarin. Next, drawn to the glimmering red light, I shift my attention to the equipment. First I smile for the camera. Then I calmly take my best swing at the human being behind it.

## 20

Back in Montreal, Lena Buber tells me this:

In May 1946, we boarded a ruined old ship in a ruined old country to be taken to an even older country that was ruined thousands of years ago but was about to be made new. As a spring morning. As a swaddled baby. All this done to house people like us. To blight a May morning with a snowstorm. To offer a grandmother's tit to a child. Think I believed any of it? Yehiel did a little, and he forced me to go along, for Uri. Let the boy believe all the positive things, Lena, said Yehiel. The things we stopped believing in ages ago; the things we couldn't possibly start to believe in again.

We rode a train from Austria, where we had been waiting in a camp since the end of the war, down through Milan to an Italian port city. Secret cargo once more. Sealed boxcars. Boy Scouts—called Mossad—helped us with food and shelter, false papers. Boy Scouts dragged us across the dangerous street of Europe to the curb of the Mediterranean. Displaced persons looking to displace persons. An inn with No Vacancy out front. I had to laugh. Yehiel, though, told Uri all the stories and legends about our race and history and glorious destiny. Guff, if you'd asked me: fables for children.

The blockade was on, and few ships were making it through. Our route was circuitous and crafty and even the captain would not know where to land until the final hours. We steamed below the deck and baked atop it. We slept in rain and slid in our own vomit. People made jokes about shitting and pissing and finding a corner to be with their wife— or someone else's wife. I had no complaints about such talk: harmless banter to keep up the spirits. But certain fools also insisted on serious conversation. About their lives before. About the war. When does it cease to matter if the person who is shoving you around is friend or enemy? You are still being led. Your fate is still not your own. Passengers began to whisper and even to shout until they were silenced with hugs and tears and, in my case, glares. Ever been spared a kick in the gut by a phrase? Ever had your house or village saved by a speech?

Be careful on those stairs, Uri, we warned our son. Stay clear of the upper deck. Don't bother the crew, boy. Don't climb up there!

Four days out of Haifa, the child limps back to our spot, his heel punctured by a nail. Three days from Palestine, his muscles are torturing him and he can't hold down liquids. A doctor from Prague says he requires medicine to combat the infection. Forty-eight hours away—the captain can't change course for Cyprus; he is not a heartless man: we are welcome in no Mediterranean port—Uri lapses into a coma. Wake up, Uri! Wake up! Twenty-two hours short of the Promised Land, lockjaw kills the boy.

As we prepare to disembark up the coast, crew

members drape a banner against the side of the hull:
WE SURVIVED HITLER. DEATH IS NO STRANGER TO US.
Survived the Nazis, but not a rusty nail? Uri is eight.
I am thirty-nine. Romans evicted the Jews from
Jerusalem in 70 A.D. We showed up in 1946 to
claim the city back. With our nightmares and dis-
eases and dead children. He was eight. I was thirty-
nine.

The photo beside my bed was taken by a crew
member—a Parisian Jew who later emigrated to
New York—hours before the accident. I saw it only
in 1953. Here in this city, this apartment: I open a
letter from Tel Aviv, and it is attached with a paper-
clip. Until that moment, Yehiel and I had only
sweet images to remember him by; suddenly we
possessed imcriminating evidence; suddenly, our
guilt was inescapable. (What crime? Only a Boy
Scout would ask such a question.) They had been
looking for us, you see: other survivors of the exo-
dus, now good Israeli citizens with a fondness for
reunions, for recalling selected periods of their past.
They thought Yehiel and Lena were lost. Which we
were. They thought we had given up. Which we
had. In Montreal, Canada. On Esplanade Street in
the neighbourhood called Mile End.

Seated at the edge of the bed in my apartment, in her lap Max
the cat—returned a few weeks before by a sheepish, Toronto-
bound Denis—and holding her hand an avuncular Ivan
Fodorov, stylish in powder-blue pyjamas and pink slippers,
his head clean shaven and his grin plastered to skull and

bone: in a soft voice and to the music of Québécois French, Chantal Mitsotakis tells me this:

I went to see him the other day. First time in three years. Ivan forced me to go. No, he just persuaded me; the decision was mine. (Don't squeeze so hard, Ivan!) He still lives in Park Ex. *They* still live in that squalid place: she has never left him. Never challenged his lie. I used to get so angry with her. You betray us, Mother, I once told her on the phone. She thought I meant me and my sisters. That was enough to reduce her to tears, though her sobbing was more a keen, as if she lay draped over the body of a child. But I meant that she betrayed all women! God, I was foolish. . . . I blame the apartment in part. Four rooms for two adults and three kids. Neighbours below us arguing through the floor. Neighbours above us making the ceiling tremble. On either side, too: people watching TV too loud, listening to music too late. And my parents' room, a box within a box, barely wide enough for their bed. Shouting at each other in Greek. Him slapping, her weeping. Mostly at night, long after we were supposed to be asleep. Lying together in my—as oldest—bed. Please, Daddy, we whimpered. Please, Mummy.

Should I forgive him because he's had a hard time? Because life in Greece stunk and life in Quebec proved no better? Because even though he gave his first daughter a French name—my younger sisters are Anna and Angela—and quickly learned both official languages, and took night courses at UQAM instead of Concordia, and dangled the fleur-de-lis over our balcony on Jean-Baptiste Day; despite all this, he still wound up a janitor. A dozen jobs in a dozen years. Silly uniforms and graveyard shifts. Mother claimed he had bad luck. He said this country lied about wanting newcomers. Could it be that Nick Mitsotakis was difficult to work with: unhappy with himself, sour with others? Could it be that people didn't really want the guy around?

I know what happened that night. Coming in late, I absorbed the meat and cigarette smell that hung across the hallway like a drape, and tiptoed past their room. Anna and Angela were still up, terrified in a way I'd never seen before. Anna explained: Angie, only eleven, buried her face in a pillow. I stuffed our schoolbags with clothes and, because she was hysterical, Angie's ancient teddy bear, which she still slept with. I even snuck into the hall closet and emptied his wallet. Somehow, we slipped out without them waking. The air tried to choke us. The cold made us dizzy. You know how January nights can be here: brilliant, almost glittering, but also pitiless and inhuman. I ended up carrying Angela the two blocks down to Jean Talon Street. Where to, kids? asked the cabbie. A cheap motel, I answered between gasps.

The girls went to a family in Dorval. I lived in a halfway house in NDG until I turned eighteen. Quitting school was a mistake, but I wanted money. The guys, the drugs, the jobs in places like Remys: all mistakes. One counsellor—a man, naturally— pushed for a reconciliation. Even though my father refused to admit he'd done anything wrong. Even though she chose to believe him, a violent, twisted person, and not us—her own children. (The scar over my eye? I fell down some stairs when I was five.) Why would we have lied? How *could* we even have lied about such a thing?

Being back there was depressing. The Sally Ann couches and chairs, the threadbare carpet, the quilt my grandma in Greece knitted for us: everything looked worn and sad. I could smell his cigarettes and her dinner—grilled egglant and potatoes, my favourite meal: I cook it for Ivan, though he barely eats—and couldn't believe how small, and cramped, the apartment was. Memories flooded in. Some were okay: Mamma wiping her brow with her apron in the kitchen; us girls *shhh*ing each other as we tried on lipstick in the bathroom; me sitting by the bedroom window watching the snow fall around a streetlamp and thinking how each flake represented a child gazing out a window in a house somewhere in the world. But I also recalled being locked in that room for entire afternoons. Not allowed out even to pee. And I remembered the three of us being too scared to *leave* the bedroom when they were going at each other. Feeling our own hearts pounding. Staring at the door in fear that it would swing open. And those weekend mornings when she sat us before the TV, the sound turned so low we couldn't hear, and begged us not to make noise. Don't wake him up, girls, she'd plead.

What should I have said? Mother—Sophie—you don't have to keep doing this. It's not the Old Country: marriage isn't a prison sentence here. You can get money to live on your own and learn more French and English, and even study at school, acquire a skill. Or you can come stay with me. I'll take care of you. I'll make you well again. . . . Those would have been strong, helpful words. They might have made a difference. But instead I just hugged her, and whispered for her ear only that Anna, Angie and Chantal STILL LOVE YOU. That's it. That's all. I had to hold her up. Shh, Mamma, it's okay. As if we were a couple waltzing in their hallway. As if she was my child. Why couldn't I say anymore? Shh, Mamma, I kept repeating, my vision blurred. It's okay. Anna, Angie and Chantal WILL ALWAYS LOVE YOU.

Really, Ivan, I'll be fine. I'm smiling, aren't I?

After running her hands over my cheeks, her touch feathery as a buyer inspecting fabric, her eyes cognac-glazed despite claims of sobriety, and then inviting me to sit while she made sure the answering machine was on, though the conversation will still freeze when the phone rings, in order that she can assess each message, disparage each caller; after much uncharacteristic fussing and two prematurely stubbed Gitanes, my mother tells me this:

Those letters from China about your father make sense now. Minus the beard and weight, you look like him again. The wide face and flat chin. The lopsided grin. Even your lovely brown eyes, always his colour but somehow murkier, glow with Jacob's sensuality. Your father was a lover of food and sunlight, sleep and skin. Touching and hugging. Screwing, too, though who had time for that. Does this look like Greece? I would tease him. Do you mistake me for Aphrodite? Three decades after his departure, a quarter-century since your features rejected their inheritance, he's come back. Home to age with dignity. In you, my boy.

How you adored the man. Being tucked in by him, a silly blanket game he devised to get you to bundle up on winter nights. Listening to his stories of secret doorways in closets and holes in the earth that opened onto underground kingdoms. One tale I still remember. A boy who is ice-skating ploughs into a snowbank. The bank is suddenly a tunnel. At the other end of the passage is a glass room filled with trees and plants, birds and monkeys. The room is a magical place, and at first the child is thrilled. Then he starts to feel lonely; he wants to go home. He tries to find the tunnel, but it has closed back up. He tries to find a door in the room, but it is all glass, with only blue sky beyond. . . . Don't scare the boy, Jacob, I would beg him. He'll be awake later on with nightmares. Which you were, regularly. Guess who sat with you? Fathers didn't concern themselves with such parenting chores back then. *Your* father sure didn't. No man I've known since slept the way he did. Dead to the world. Alive to his own intense—I assume—dreamscape. Sawing, meanwhile, a cord of wood.

I didn't adore his snoring or his womanizing or his temper. I didn't enjoy living with someone who forgave himself his trespasses so easily. Who decided that the strong were merely stubborn and that disappointment permitted weakness. A man who raised his hand to me once and got a fist in the throat as reply, and who became violent with you a single time as well, but with far graver consequences. You honestly don't remember your stay in the Royal Vic? All those tests? All those bandages? Yes, you were only five. Yes, it was devastating. Jacob blubbered, but I still threw him out. This time he stayed away. Wrote a letter in his odd, childlike scrawl saying that he wasn't good enough for me. That I—we—deserved better than he could ever be. After that, there were only phone calls, and eventually just at Christmas and Easter. He used a different name, as we had agreed, though not one I approved of. Do you recall taking down messages from a Mr. Kapinsky? I worried that you recognized the voice. Each time Jacob rang, you held the receiver like it was made of crystal. Your shoulders hunched; your voice got tiny. I almost asked you the question. It perched on my lips. But how could I? What else would I have had to inquire about? So I just sat there in the chair, jabbing my cigarette in the ashtray, wishing my glass was not empty. My glass, and my life: all those wrong decisions, all those foolish words.

You didn't know it was him? Just as well.

By the mid-fifties, the party had been reduced by state paranoia and police harassment and—no question—internal squabbling and stupidity to small core factions, the entire French side able to fit into Lily and Gilles Houle's East-end flat for Friday night spaghetti dinners. Nonetheless, we were still devout. We always assumed Fred Rose had been framed. We always assumed the Rosenbergs were innocent. As for the reports out of the Soviet Union, they were easily dismissed: Cold War distortions, capitalist propaganda. Remember that it *was* a war, and we were foot soldiers. Obeying orders and doing our duty, then enjoying the sleep of the untroubled. (I lie: of course we woke up in a sweat some nights. Of course we knew that Stalin had been a vile man.) Must I explain again that most of us were motivated not by conditions halfway around the globe but by the injustices evident right here? If you knew the half of what went on in this city before the war. Our own brand of anti-Semitism. Our own state fascism. And then Drapeau, and Duplessis, and the neighbourhood thugs in their collars and cassocks. Besides, politics is almost never about ideas. Always personalities. Always power. We said so ourselves: to change the world, we first had to change our own skins. Long ago, I came to realize that personalities were immutable. What hope, then, for the world?

Take Jacob. His devotion to the party was wholesale, even though such commitment clashed with his nature, which was not at all narrow and focused, like mine. He was a Jew who rejected Jewishness, including his own name—Bernard Kapinsky was your grandfather, Denise LeClair your grandmother, though you never met either of them—and a half-francophone who dismissed the concerns of French Quebecers. Who dismissed *my* concerns, even though he proposed marriage and insisted that we stay with the French faction and work in that language. But he also demanded that you be raised an anglophone. Only English spoken on Clark Street. Only English for his boy. What a mind he had: mercurial and scattered, equal parts astonishing and dismaying. None of these qualities added up to a functioning adult, however. None made him strong or resolute. When it all fell apart, he simply could not pick up the pieces and start again. He could only bail out.

How he raged. The dementia had to be chemical—neurological, even. During the worst tantrums, Jacob had little control over his thoughts or actions. In a way, it's a miracle he only swung at me once. That terrible night served to padlock the door to a room best sealed off. A necessary disaster, I think. I'm only sorry you woke up into it. He was destroying the apartment. Not drunkenly, nor drugged. Sober and dead-eyed—when he was angry, Jacob's irises drained of feeling—your father was taking a baseball bat to every piece of second-hand furniture that we owned, every chipped plate and cracked glass in our cupboards. All those things bore the imprint of his—our—failure. All were useless junk, destined for some basement. You emerged from your room, still half-asleep, at the worst possible moment. Get the boy out of here, Adele, he thundered. Again, I remember his eyes: they were vacant: he was capable of anything. I tried moving you from harm's way. I really did. But you got it into your head that I was banishing you to a dungeon. I won't go back, you shouted. Don't send me back there!

Let the phone ring. And turn down the volume on the machine. Right down, so we can't hear it. Honestly: I don't care who's calling.

No, it won't be him. In 1972, a car accident in Newark, New Jersey, where he had been living for a decade. Remarried, apparently—we were never legally divorced—with two small kids. All under his father's name; he would never have gotten into the States otherwise. Jake Kapinsky worked in a factory

and voted in his union. He coached his son's softball team and brought his daughter to the "Y" for swimming lessons. Both were carrot-haired, he told me once: I bet the boy—a young man now, I suppose—looks like you. No way I could go down to the funeral. Those blacklists from the fifties still exist: I'm on them, I know. Also, I had just moved here from Clark Street, and met Pierre.

It was that foolish psychiatrist who persuaded me to keep you in the dark. Later, you stopped asking questions and I stopped telling lies. Errors of judgement, I admit. What I ought to have done was invent a story, and then stuck to it. Your father off fighting imperialism in Vietnam or organizing the revolution in Chile. A lecturer in Moscow. A military adviser in Africa. You've always had faith in stories. A true believer. I notice it with Natalie as well: nothing stops the girl from squirming like the prospect of being read—or better, told—a good yarn.

My mind does not work this way, though. I do not believe in stories. I do not believe in people. I certainly no longer have faith in revolution or transformation. Adele Guy the chameleon, a secret stick-in-the-mud. All I believe in are ideas. The ones that reside inside my head. The ones that are my only friends.

Let it ring! Don't pick up. Please.

When Carole told me about your epilepsy, I called a doctor acquaintance. The first thing he asked was had you suffered a blow as a child: a tumble from a bicycle, an accident on some stairs. He explained that in many cases, especially with psychomotor, the disease is thought to be triggered by an early jolt to the brain. I called Carole with the information. She said that your own doctor had asked the same question, but that you denied the existence of any such incident. Sweet David. Maybe that was what you were doing all those hours in your balcony grave. Silently communing with Jacob. Absolving him of his sins.

Now that you have his face, please return him his blame. We are all responsible for our lives.

Seated in Remys the day after the funeral in July, the people around me mostly strangers, my own skin feeling strange and loose, like a coat a size too large; seated there, able to see from the window where the Velji *dépanneur* used to be, a twenty-four-hour chain store now in its place, a beer truck partially blocking Bernard and a line for lottery tickets snaking out the door, I silently tally the disappearances. First, the domestic ones: Ivan and Firoz, Zuo Chang and his daughter Ying, whom Suzanne-the-prof tersely dismissed as having "emigrated" to Toronto, and Carole and our daughter Natalie, residents since late last month of a Paris suburb. Next, I move on to the international vanishings, information both murky and unreliable, surmised over hissing trans-Pacific phone lines and muddied at the other end by hostility and idiomatic

Mandarin: Dean Feng Ziyang "on long-term leave" from the English department, Foreign Affairs Officer Zhou Hong, no longer employed at the school but believed to be working at a college in Shanghai (I contacted a dozen Shanghai schools: none had heard of her), and of course the teacher Wang Hua, an individual whom several administrative officials, plus Deng Chen at the Foreign Experts Building, plus even the born-again Jim from Texas, who declared my calling him in his apartment a malicious attempt to compromise his "work" in China, all agreed with fundamental certainty and absolute conviction had *never been employed at the college.* Seated in Remys the day after the funeral in July, the pavement outside buckling in the heat, my body pleasantly detached from my mind, as if I am weightless in water, adrift in a steady current, I tell my friend and saviour of these last three months, a woman who approves of my shaven face and groomed hair, going so far as to call me distinguished looking, who appears to see me candidly but still contentedly, and most important, whose judgements I am slowly learning not to automatically equate with personal failure—I tell Lise Lapointe this:

> The night before Natalie left for Paris, helping build an outer wall to her bed using bears, cats and a rabbit, and working both to calm her excitement and quell her fears, I explained what happened to her mother and me.
>
> Once upon a time there was man who slept constantly. His name was David. He was married to a woman called Carole, and they lived with the dog Potemkin in a small room that had drawings on the walls and a window looking out onto a strange street in a strange city. They were pretty happy

together. Except that David slept most days and every night, and didn't really want to be woken up, even by his wife. He figured sleeping was the best way to deal with things. He figured he—and Carole—were better off that way. He even decided it was the age they were living in.

One day there was a knock on the door. Carole asked David to open it, and he surprised her by immediately crossing the room. (David had not been outside in ages: not since some bad stuff happened to him.) But at the door, his hand on the knob, he hesitated. Who is it? he called. A story-teller, answered a voice. Here to shake you awake with a tale that is funny and scary and speaks the truth. Carole encouraged him to let the visitor in. We'd better think about it first, David countered, releasing his hold. How will being woken up by a story improve our lives? She had an answer. It will mean we can leave this room together, she said. It will change us forever. Won't it? she asked the story-teller.

Maybe, replied the voice. Maybe not.

David had doubts. Suppose I do stop sleeping, he said. Will I like the new me? Will you? And suppose we do leave this room. Isn't the world cold and menacing? Doesn't it make you mean?

Have more confidence, advised the story-teller. Be more bold. Mostly, trust yourself. And me, added Carole. And even—a little—the world.

Or trust the tale I will tell you, offered the voice. After all, it will be your own. The story-teller asked them to hurry up and decide. There are lots of other people waiting for me to call on them, it said.

Carole was convinced. She was also sad; her beloved David, she sensed, was still not ready. So, kissing him on both cheeks, she turned the knob and walked through the doorway. Potemkin trailed after her. The corridor was now empty—David scoured it for the face behind the voice—but she descended the staircase anyway. He remained in the frame. For a long time David just stood there, fairly sure of what he needed to do, not yet able to manage it. Story-teller, he whispered. Are you still there? Is anyone still there?

Carole knew exactly what to do. She went off and had a baby. A beautiful baby girl. Her hair was wheaten. Her skin was honey. And her name? Her name was candy in her parents' mouths. Her name, Natalie, was you.

# 《梁山伯與祝英台》

何占豪　陳鋼
關聖佑　編鋼琴